24 HOURS
TO DOOMSDAY

Colin M Barron

OTHER BOOKS BY COLIN M BARRON

NON-FICTION

Running Your Own Private Residential or Nursing Home

The Craft of Public Speaking

Planes on Film: 10 Favourite Aviation Films

Dying Harder: Action Movies of the 1980s

A Life By Misadventure

Battles on Screen: WW2 Action Movies

Practical Hypnotherapy

Victories at Sea: In Films and TV

Travels in Time: The Story of Time Travel Cinema

FICTION

Operation Archer

Codename Enigma

To my wife Vivien

CONTENTS

CHAPTER 1

A SECOND CHANCE

The River Thames, by Westminster Bridge, London

Tuesday 21 June 2022, 13:17 hours

This is the happiest day of my life, thought Rick as he leaned on the railing of the 70 foot, white cruise boat and enjoyed the view of Central London. It was the longest day of the year, warm and sunny, and he had just married the woman he loved. Two years before, things had been different. His first wife, Helen, lay dying in hospital with brain cancer, an astrocytoma as it was called. The neurosurgeons had operated twice and then proclaimed that nothing more could be done. As Helen slipped in and out of consciousness, drowsy from the morphine infusion, sweat-soaked bandages round her now hairless head, she squeezed Rick's right hand and spoke her last words:

'Don't be sad because I'm leaving. Find someone else. Be happy, Rick.'

Two minutes later her heart stopped. The cardiac monitor by her bed emitted a constant tone and red lights flashed, but no crash team arrived. In her case-notes, the consultant had written DNR – do not resuscitate. Rick was now alone.

Yet, just twenty-seven months later, all that was behind him. He had just married another beautiful woman. He had no idea how it had all happened but was really glad that it had. He had always believed that no woman could ever compare with Helen – but then he met Laura, all blue eyes and blonde hair with an outgoing personality and a wicked laugh. It had started as a close friendship but had quickly developed into a passionate romance. Laura had held him in her arms as he relived the trauma of Helen's death. The tears had run down his cheeks and then dried. Slowly, he had learned to love again, to smile once more, to see the funny side of things. He'd been given a *second chance* at happiness and had grabbed it with both hands.

Now, two years after that awful night when Helen died, he stood on the aft deck of a small pleasure craft – aptly named *Deuxième Chance* – watching it pull away from Westminster Pier, its Perkins six-cylinder marine diesel engine chugging as it ploughed through the calm waters of the Thames. Normally a casual dress kind of person, Rick had opted for a traditional grey morning suit, which suited his muscular frame, square jaw, six-foot height, and dark shiny hair with just a hint of grey at the temples. It was a scorching hot day. Central London was packed with tourists in their brightly coloured summer clothes. Shorts and T-shirts. Flip flops and sandals. Most people wore sunglasses and some kind of hat. Rick smelled fresh sweat and sun-cream. The hot sun beat down relentlessly from a cloudless sky.

Rick and Laura had participated in a brief wedding ceremony at Westminster Registry Office with another couple as witnesses and were now proceeding to Richmond to enjoy a late champagne lunch on the patio of a small hotel. Even now Rick could imagine what it would be like, the smell of freshly cut grass and flowers, the scent of Laura's sweet perfume and the gentle touch of her soft, perfectly manicured right hand on his.

As the boat sailed under Westminster Bridge, with Big Ben and the House of Commons to the right, Laura walked to the bow of the vessel and leaned against the angled flagpole at its prow. Rick followed, stood behind her, and put his arms around her slim waist. Her long white wedding dress flapped around in the breeze. In the distance, Rick could see a rusty orange tugboat pulling three barges. He also spotted a black Zodiac inflatable with an outboard motor. Four men were on board. Rick noticed that two of them wore scuba gear with their masks pushed up on their foreheads, while the others had yellow high-viz jackets.

Rick sniffed Laura's immaculately coiffured blonde hair. It smelled of apple shampoo.

'Wow Rick, we're just like Jack and Rose in that film *Titanic*.'

'Sure we are darling. I'm King of the World. It's a moment I will remember forever. I never knew I could be so happy!'

Laura turned round to face Rick and kissed him on the lips. Rick tasted champagne. At that moment while his eyes were still closed, he heard a strange buzzing sound above him. He pushed Laura away gently as his facial muscles tightened and he looked up. Something was wrong. His well-honed senses and years of SAS training had just kicked in.

High in the sky, just south of the boat, an object was approaching, sunlight sparkling off its highly polished skin. It was making a noise like a petrol lawnmower combined with the *whumph, whumph, whumph* of rotor blades and a high-pitched whine.

'What's wrong Rick? You're frightening me! Is something the matter?'

'Wait here darling, I'm going to the wheelhouse to see if they have any binoculars. I'll only be a minute.'

A moment later Rick had acquired a pair of powerful Leica binoculars and stood on the aft deck as he studied the mystery craft through powerful lenses. There were actually *two* objects in the sky, not one, but they were flying close together. One was a blue and white civilian Bell Ranger helicopter, the other was what looked like a large, silver military drone. It resembled an American Predator, with its narrow long-span wings, bulbous nose and rear-mounted propeller. Rick estimated the craft were flying at 2000 feet. But what were they doing over Central London? Rick was sure that such activity had been banned by the government in view of the recent spate of terror attacks.

As Rick watched, the two mystery aircraft flew closer until they were almost directly overhead. Then the Bell broke off and headed due north at high speed. A moment later there was a loud bang to the west and a smoke trail appeared in the sky behind a fast-moving glowing ball of light. It was a surface-to-air missile, though faster than any Rick had ever seen in all his years in the military. A second later, a large orange fireball bloomed in the sky as the rocket scored a direct hit on the drone. Large black blobs of metal radiated from the explosion. The debris was falling to earth…heading straight for them!

Rick screamed a warning to Laura:

'Get below decks, now!'

But it was too late. Seconds later, a huge chunk of metal – which Rick thought was probably the drone's fuel tank – landed on the foredeck, spilling burning petrol everywhere. Laura's white lace wedding dress caught fire, her exposed skin burning.

Laura screamed in agony as her alabaster skin blistered and then turned red raw. Her entire body – apart from her right arm – was ablaze, her golden hair frizzling in seconds. There was a disgusting smell like roast pork which Rick remembered from many battles.

'Rick, help me! I love you!' screamed Laura through the flames.

Before Rick could react, another chunk of drone wreckage hit the rear deck, smashing into his ribs and striking his left elbow with such force that he was knocked overboard into the filthy Thames water. Rick sank to the riverbed, weighed down by his waterlogged morning suit and handicapped by a fractured left arm and smashed ribs. He was surrounded by darkness. Even in summer the river water was freezing cold. Looking through the gloom, he could just make out the bottom of the boat's hull above him through the murky water, its bronze propeller still rotating. All around him bits of drone wreckage were sinking to the riverbed. He couldn't swim back to the surface because of his injuries and he wouldn't survive without air for long. *He was about to drown!*

CHAPTER 2

AIRFIELD RAID

Forty years earlier

The waters north of the Falkland Islands

15 May 1982, 02:05 hours

Trooper Jack Fernscale of D Squadron, 22 Special Air Service squatted uncomfortably on the cold metal floor of the Westland Sea King HC4 helicopter of 864 Naval Air Squadron as it headed towards its destination: Pebble Island, north of West Falkland. The cabin reeked of sweat, bad breath, gun oil and the almond-like aroma of plastic explosive. Rivulets of condensation ran down the green painted metal walls of the troop compartment. The deafening racket of twin Rolls-Royce Gnome turboshaft engines, a whining gearbox and whirling rotor blades above his head made it hard to hold a conversation. Every cubic inch of the helicopter's passenger cabin was crammed with soldiers in green camo battledress and black woollen hats, weapons and equipment.

It had all kicked off two months earlier when scrap merchants tasked with dismantling an old whaling station had landed on the British island territory of South Georgia and hoisted the Argentine flag. Things had escalated since then. On 2 April· the Argentine armed forces had invaded Port Stanley, capital of the Falkland

Islands. The small garrison of Royal Marines put up stiff resistance and inflicted heavy casualties on the enemy – even sinking a landing craft and knocking out an AMTRAK amphibious, armoured personnel carrier – but they had been forced to surrender to avoid further bloodshed. Another Royal Marine detachment on South Georgia had also fought well, downing an Argentine Puma helicopter and damaging a corvette with anti-tank missiles and small-arms fire, but it had also been forced to capitulate.

Britain had been humiliated on the world stage and an emergency session of Parliament was held on Saturday 3 April. But there was cross-party support for military action. Even the Labour leader Michael Foot – a lifelong pacifist – had condemned Argentina's 'naked aggression.' The then Prime Minister Margaret Thatcher sent a naval task force to recapture the overseas territory, led by the aircraft carriers HMS *Invincible* and HMS *Hermes*. By early May, things had escalated into a shooting war.

The Royal Navy hunter-killer submarine HMS *Conqueror* had sunk the cruiser *General Belgrano* while the Argentines had destroyed the Royal Navy's Type 42 Destroyer HMS *Sheffield* with an AM 39 Exocet sea-skimming missile fired by a Dassault Super-Etendard aircraft. Both sides had suffered aircraft losses and an Argentine submarine, the ARA *Santa Fe*, had been severely damaged at South Georgia. Now a strong force of SAS troops (forty-five men carried in two helicopters) was on its way to Pebble Island to destroy the Argentine aircraft which were based on the small grass airstrip there as they were considered a threat to the amphibious landings due to take place on 21 May.

Jack wiped condensation off one of the scratched, square, Perspex cabin windows and caught a glimpse of the second Sea King flying through the gloom beside them, while maintaining a reasonable distance to reduce the risk of collision. He consulted his luminous Rolex military watch. Just nine minutes till touchdown.

Like all the troopers in the two helicopters, Jack was carrying a lot of kit: a heavy rucksack (or 'Bergen' as it was known in the SAS) containing plastic explosive charges, detonators and timers. Some men carried 81 mm mortar tubes, others had baseplates, while some had a few mortar bombs. Most soldiers had American M16 5.56 mm assault rifles, some of which had underslung M203 40 mm grenade launchers, and as many spare magazines as they could stuff in their ammunition pouches. A few troopers had L1A1 66 mm LAW light anti-tank rocket launchers slung round their necks, while others had a few grenades. The assault force also had a couple of general-purpose machine guns (GPMGs, also known as 'Gimpys') plus plenty of spare 7.62 mm ammunition belts. Every man also carried a combat knife, a canteen of water, chocolate, energy bars and boiled sweets in their belt kits.

Jack felt a wave of nausea sweep over him as the Sea King wobbled in a strong gust of South Atlantic wind. He thought he was going to throw up but then the helicopter entered stiller air and his feeling of sickness passed.

Ahead of him, the pilot spoke a few words into his microphone as he peered through his bulky night vision goggles. Miller, the SAS troop sergeant, heard every word through his headset which was plugged into the helicopter's intercom system:

'Two minutes to infil point. Prepare to exit. Good luck!'

A crew member wearing an olive green flying suit and white bone-dome helmet slid the main cabin door open, letting in a blast of freezing South Atlantic air. Then the helicopter touched down on the long wet grass of Pebble Island and kept its twin Rolls-Royce Ghost turboshaft engines running, and its rotor blades turning, as the SAS soldiers leapt out with their heads well down. Despite their heavy backpacks, they were all out in thirty seconds. Immediately, the two helicopters lifted off in a nose-down attitude, turned round and headed east towards the aircraft carrier HMS *Hermes* where mugs of steaming hot coffee and 'egg banjos' (fried egg sandwiches) awaited their crews. Jack smelled the burnt paraffin odour of gas turbine engine exhausts as the two Sea Kings disappeared into the gloom.

They were six kilometres ('klicks') from the airfield but that had always been the plan. Any nearer and the helicopters might be heard or seen by alert sentries. Even with their heavy loads, six klicks would be just a ninety minute 'tab' (march) for the fit SAS troops.

*

Ejercito privado Miguel Garcia stamped his booted feet on the damp ground to keep them from going numb. The temperature was just above freezing point but it felt much colder due to wind chill. He wore thick gloves, a parka, US army style battledress and a Polish-manufactured helmet but he still shivered. He was a conscript rather than a professional soldier and couldn't understand why that fat oaf Galtieri had wanted to invade the *Malvinas* in the first place. A few islands inhabited by a couple of thousand kelpers and lots of sheep. The wind blew almost constantly, so much so that few trees grew anywhere. It always felt cold, even in summer, and there was no natural shelter.

Along with another 149 troops, he had been tasked with guarding the airfield which was nothing more than a grass strip. The runway was too short and too sodden to handle heavy A-4 Skyhawks, Mirages or Super Etendards but a few light, propeller-driven aircraft were now based there.

The previous afternoon he had counted six Argentine-made, twin-engine Pucara counter- insurgency aircraft, plus two Beech T-34

Turbo-Mentors and a boxy Short Skyvan light transport. The Pucaras and Turbo-Mentors would be dead meat if they came up against Sea Harriers but they could still be effective against ground troops. The Pucaras in particular were armed with four nose-mounted 7.62 mm FN machine guns and two 20 mm Hispano cannon. They could also carry rocket pods, high explosive bombs or napalm.

There was also a small radar installation, and ammo and fuel dumps. Did the British even know about them? Hopefully they wouldn't bother about Pebble Island. At the start of the month, Port Stanley airfield had been bombed by an RAF Avro Vulcan flying from Ascension Island. The delta-winged bomber had dropped twenty-one 1,000 pound bombs but only one had struck the runway. There had been follow-up attacks by Sea Harriers, and then raids against Goose Green airfield by more Harriers using cluster bombs. So far though, Pebble Island had been left alone. *Well let's hope that continues,* thought Garcia.

As he ruminated about the military situation, Garcia wished he was back in Buenos Aires with his wife, tucking into a large bowl of *Carbonada Criolla,* that especially delicious Argentine beef stew. Galtieri had claimed that Argentine beef was the best in the world and he was right. Garcia could imagine the smell and taste right now and felt his mouth filling with saliva. And there would be a plate of warm, freshly-baked crusty bread to mop up the gravy. Perhaps he could wash it down with a bottle or two of *Araucana Rojiza Fuerte,* his favourite beer. So cold that condensation ran down the glass. No, the British weren't coming tonight. He was sure of that. Instead of freezing his balls off he would go into one of the huts to stay warm. Maybe he could get a mug of hot cocoa and something to eat. There might even be a couple of dirty magazines he could look at. Garcia shouldered his Belgian-made 7.62 mm FN- FAL rifle and headed towards one of the nearby huts.

*

Just two hundred yards away, at the edge of the airfield, hidden in bushes and long grass, lay the forty-five men of D Squadron. In the pitch black of a South Atlantic night, they were invisible, particularly as their pale faces had been covered with dark camo cream. Troop Sergeant Miller scanned the area through his binoculars and couldn't believe his luck. His men had slipped past the only sentry on duty. Now there wasn't a single Argentine soldier to be seen and there were no sentries posted by the aircraft. They must all be in the huts and tents which were dotted round the airfield. Sleeping or just trying to keep warm. Their negligence would soon cost them dear.

As planned, fourteen SAS soldiers crept out from the undergrowth, each carrying a plastic explosive charge, a timer and a detonator. The other thirty-one soldiers aimed their M16 rifles and GPMGs at the tents and huts, ready to strike down any Argentines who dared to interfere.

The bomb carriers ran towards the aircraft and placed charges on each one. They were following a protocol first devised by the legendary SAS officer Major Paddy Mayne in 1942, when he was given the task of blowing up Italian and German aircraft on North African airfields. Mayne realised that the best way of destroying a plane was to place an explosive charge inside it rather than on it. Also, to cause maximum inconvenience to the enemy, it was best to lay the charge on the same part of each aircraft to prevent an easy repair of the plane by cannibalising other planes. If that was not possible, then the second-best option was to lay an incendiary bomb on top of the wing directly above a fuel tank, resulting in a catastrophic fire. One of his colleagues, 'Jock' Lewes, had devised a special munition, the 'Lewes bomb,' which was specifically designed to destroy parked aircraft.

Within minutes, the bomb carriers had affixed explosive charges to every aircraft. The remaining charges were laid in the fuel and ammunition dumps and the base of the whirling radar scanner.

Jack consulted his watch. It was just three minutes since the bomb carriers had departed the bushes and some were already on their way back. Four minutes later all had returned. And still the Argentine soldiers were none the wiser.

Three minutes later the nearest Pucara exploded in an orange fireball which lit up the whole field. Its shiny Perspex canopy flew 50 feet into the air and landed in the centre of the airfield. Then, one after another, Pucaras and Turbo Mentors burst into flames. One Pucara collapsed on the ground, its undercarriage buckled by the blast and its propeller blades twisted to a crazy angle. Soon, the airfield was brightly illuminated by the flames of burning aircraft. Jack counted nine blazing hulks. But there were supposed to be eleven planes on the strip, including the Skyvan. *Two of the bombs had failed to go off.*

By now the Argentine garrison had woken up to what was happening. Doors of huts flew open and soldiers, some wearing pyjamas, spilled out onto the darkened airfield, swearing in Spanish.

'*Lo que esta pasanda! Es el jodico Britanico!*' ('What is happening? It's the fucking British!') screamed one Argentine private as he put on his helmet and slapped a magazine into his FN-FAL rifle.

A klaxon sounded. Lights came on. The English pirates were attacking! But where were they? Were they being bombed by Sea Harriers? Or had they been hit by a Vulcan strike? Why had Galtieri not provided them with anti-aircraft guns? In a state of panic, the Argentines fired their FN-FAL automatic rifles into the air without aiming. All they did was waste ammunition and risk casualties from falling ordnance.

CHAPTER 3

LIFE OR DEATH?

Forty years later

Tuesday 21 June 2022, 13:47 hours

St Thomas's Hospital, South Bank, London

The white and fluorescent yellow Mercedes ambulance screeched to a halt outside the red-canopied entrance to the Accident and Emergency Department with a squeal of brakes. Its siren shrieked and its blue light flashed. The smell of a London summer hung in the air, along with the odour of burnt tyre rubber and diesel fumes. Two uniformed porters raced out of the entrance to help four sodden paramedics in hi-viz yellow jackets unload two stretchers from the back.

One of the A&E Consultants, Dr Roberts, came out to meet them, Littman stethoscope swinging round his neck. He smoothed back his blonde hair from his forehead as he listened to the paramedics' report:

'Two casualties from a suspected drone attack. One female, age thirty-one. Extensive burns. The other male, forty-three. Suffered a near-drowning episode. Fortunately, we were nearby in a Zodiac at the time, on a training exercise. Two of us were already wearing scuba gear so we dived in and brought the man back to the surface and carried out immediate resuscitation. All the same, I guess it was a close call. Another minute underwater and he would have drowned. We reckon he must have been very fit.'

The porters rolled the trolleys through the automatic sliding doors of the A&E Department, where they were placed in adjacent curtained-off bays for urgent assessment and stabilisation.

'I'm not too worried about the man,' said Dr Roberts. 'But the female is a different story. Apart from her right arm and hand, her entire body has burns and much of it looks like full thickness. Get a drip in the right arm and give her saline. Plus 10 milligrams of diamorphine... the pain must be horrendous... page the on-call anaesthetist... we may need to intubate her or perform an emergency tracheostomy. We'll get her stabilised and then have her transferred to the burns unit... if she survives that long!'

In the bay next to Laura, Rick gradually regained consciousness. *Where was he?* There were pale green curtains round his trolley and he felt an oxygen mask on his face. His throat and nasal cavity felt red raw and his rib cage and left elbow hurt. There was a drip in his right arm. A nurse in blue scrubs was standing at the foot of the trolley, filling in a chart with a biro.

'Where am I?' said Rick. 'What's happened? Where's my wife, Laura?'

'You are in the A&E Department of St Thomas's Hospital. Your wife is in the next bay. We're doing everything we can for her. You just need to lie still for the moment. We think you've broken some ribs and your left elbow. We'll get X-rays to confirm this. In the meantime, you must not move.'

Rick was aware of a flurry of activity in the next bay. He could see vague shapes moving behind the translucent pale green curtains.

A junior doctor had inserted a green Venflon cannula into a superficial vein in Laura's right forearm and a saline drip had been attached. Disc-shaped electrodes had been placed on her chest and were connected to a heart monitor by wires.

Dr Roberts took the pulse from the radial artery on Laura's unburnt right wrist.

'Better take off blood for Us and Es and full blood count. We'll need blood gases as well.'

Apart from Roberts, there were four people round Laura's trolley. Two A & E nurses and two junior doctors. A plastic airway had been inserted into Laura's mouth.

A steady bleep from the monitor showed that Laura's heart was in a normal, healthy sinus rhythm.

'How long till the anaesthetist arrives?' asked Dr Roberts as he studied Laura's observation chart which was affixed to a red clipboard.

'Any minute now. He's just intubating another patient in one of the side rooms and then he'll be here,' said one of the nurses.

Just then the noise from the monitor changed from an intermittent bleeping to a constant tone. The display monitor showed a straight line instead of a wave and red lights flashed. Roberts reacted:

'She's gone into asystole! Page the crash team. Everyone else stand back. I'm going to have to shock her. Give me the paddles!'

Dr Roberts placed two electro-shock paddles on either side of Laura's chest.

'Charge to 200. Stand clear.'

Dr Roberts pulled the trigger to fire an electric current through Laura's heart. Her entire body convulsed with the powerful charge. But still the monitor showed a straight line.

'Charging again to 360. Everyone stand clear!'

Bang! Another electric shock coursed through Laura's body. The display remained unchanged while the audio tone was constant.

Dr Roberts shocked Laura with the paddles four more times, gradually increasing the voltage. Then he put both hands flat on her burnt chest and carried out cardiac massage. Bits of burnt skin fell off her chest as his hands pummelled her raw, blackened, fire-ravaged body.

The A&E Department charge nurse shone a pen torch in Laura's eyes.

'Fixed dilated pupils. And her heart stopped five minutes ago! She's gone Dr Roberts. You did your best!'

Roberts wiped the tears from his eyes and regained his composure. He glanced at the electric Smiths wall clock and turned to his colleagues.

'OK, time of death 1.57 p.m. Thank you everyone.'

Dr Roberts pulled up the white sheet that lay over Laura's legs and covered her head.

In the next bay, Rick had heard enough to know something serious had happened. Summoning the last of his strength, he ripped the drip out his right arm, stood up and pulled back the two curtains which separated him from Laura's body as blood dripped from his right forearm onto the spotless blue hospital floor.

A vaguely human shape was lying on the trolley covered by a white sheet. Rick pulled it back and witnessed a sight that would live on in his flashbacks and nightmares.

Rick had seen many dead and mutilated bodies during his years in the army. Men who'd been decapitated. Soldiers who had lost limbs or been cut in half by an improvised explosive device. But this was the most gruesome sight he had ever seen. The only part of Laura was that was still recognisably human was her right arm, complete with beautifully manicured and painted long fingernails. The rest of her body was blackened and charred with weeping, red, raw areas. She was lying in a large puddle of tissue fluid which was oozing from raw areas on her torso. Her wedding dress had burned away to nothing and her right tibia was sticking out from her shin like a candle. Her grotesquely swollen head resembled a black turnip lantern. All her beautiful blonde hair had burned off and her nose and ears were just charred stumps. Where her nose used to be were two oval holes lined with glistening pink tissue. She lacked eyebrows, eyelids or lips and her beautiful blue eyes stared at the ceiling with huge dilated pupils. Her white teeth remained immaculate and grinned at Rick. And the smell of burned flesh – like pork sausages that had been left too long under the grill – would be in Rick's nostrils forever.

Rick felt his stomach contents rising up his oesophagus. He leaned forward and vomited copiously on the spotless blue hospital floor. His sick smelled of stale champagne. Then everything went grey as he fainted and banged his head on the metal trolley as he fell towards the floor.

CHAPTER 4

RECOVERY

Ward A1, St Thomas's Hospital

22 June 2022, 09:47 hours

Rick rested in his uncomfortable, white metal hospital bed – too short even for someone of average height – and read the only newspaper left on the Royal Voluntary Service trolley that had stopped outside his room. It was that day's copy of *The Sun* which had re-used a headline from one of its most famous editions from 1982.

Underneath a huge banner headline which read GOTCHA! (originally used in 1982 when the Royal Navy submarine HMS *Conqueror* had sunk the Argentine cruiser ARA *General Belgrano*) was a story titled ARMY BLAST TERROR DRONE!, featuring a photo of three grinning soldiers in camo battledress and berets standing beside a high-tech, lorry-mounted missile battery which had recently been deployed in Hyde Park. The article revealed that the new system, Sky Sabre, had been deployed in the Falkland Islands since 2020 but had also been set up in Central London recently, after a tip-off that a drone attack was imminent.

During his army career, Rick had encountered a number of surface-to-air missile (SAM) systems such as the old Rapiers and Blowpipes that had first seen action in the Falklands in 1982. He knew that the Blowpipe had been replaced by the more advanced Javelin, and then Starstreak, and that Rapier was now being phased out as well. However, he had never heard of Sky Sabre. Once he got home he would check it out on Wikipedia.

He had slept little the night before, and when he did drop off, he had dreamt about Laura going up in flames. Even now, when he closed his eyes, he could see her charred, mutilated body, smell her burnt flesh and hear her screaming in agony. Would these horrible memories haunt him for the rest of his life?

His left arm was in a collar-and-cuff and there was a dressing on the right side of his forehead. The left side of his rib cage ached with every breath he took but he knew he had got off lightly – well, physically at least.

As Rick ruminated about his situation, the door creaked open and Dr Roberts walked in. He was wearing a dark blue suit and an open-necked white shirt. A laminated NHS identity badge hung round his neck on a lanyard.

'How are you feeling?' he said. 'You've been through quite an ordeal. You've suffered an undisplaced fracture of the head of your left radius – that's a small bone in your elbow joint – and two broken ribs, plus that head wound. There's no skull fracture, so you should be ready for home tomorrow. You can start to wean yourself off the collar and cuff after a week and then begin gradual mobilisation of the arm. I expect it to heal completely in about six weeks. The ribs will mend slowly as well, though you may need to take painkillers for some time.'

'I'll be fine,' said Rick. 'I suffered far worse injuries when I was in the army. I'm more bothered by what happened to my wife. We'd only been married forty minutes when she died, you know.'

'My sincere condolences for your loss, Rick. Laura suffered full-thickness burns to much of her body as she was splashed with petrol, which burns at a temperature of more than a thousand degrees centigrade. Most people who are burned that badly don't live long. They can die from fluid loss, shock, septicaemia and kidney failure, among other things. It's remarkable she lived as long as she did. Even if she had survived, she would have needed years of painful skin graft surgery and rehabilitation and would have been left severely scarred, disabled and disfigured, and possibly blind as well. Believe me Rick, we did everything we could.'

'I know you did, doctor. I don't blame you or the NHS. Neither do I blame the soldier who fired the missile that brought down the drone. He was only doing his duty. I would have done the same thing if I was in his position. No, the person who is really responsible for this tragedy is whoever ordered the drone attack in the first place. What about the other people on the boat? Were they injured? Two of them were our friends. A married couple who attended the ceremony.'

'There were no other serious casualties. The Captain was in the wheelhouse at the time so he only sustained a few minor lacerations from broken glass. There were just two other passengers on board plus an engineer and they were all below decks so were unharmed. One last thing I wanted to ask you, though. How did you survive a near-drowning incident? The paramedics were amazed.'

'Well, that's quite simple,' answered Rick. 'I spent some years in the SAS but was then seconded to the SBS – the Special Boat Service. I received training in diving and learned how to hold my breath for a few minutes. At medical school you were probably taught that people can't survive without oxygen for more than three minutes. Most people can't even hold their breath for just two minutes. That's true, but trained divers can hold their breath for longer than this. There's a Serbian lady called Branko Petrovic who trained hard as a diver and eventually held her breath for almost twelve minutes. She's in the Guinness Book of Records. The secret is to fill your lungs with air before you go under the surface. If you breathe pure oxygen for a moment or two you can hold your breath for even longer. Because of my past diving training, I instinctively filled my lungs with air as I fell into the river and that made all the difference.'

'Fascinating. I didn't know all this. You learn something every day.'

There was a firm knock on the door, which then swung open on creaky hinges. Dr Roberts turned round to be greeted by two men. One was about five foot six inches tall with greying, receding dark hair, looked about fifty-eight, and was dressed in a rumpled two-piece grey suit which was in need of a good press. His gaudy red tie had a toothpaste stain on it and hung over his beer belly. His scuffed, unpolished brown shoes matched his worn brown leather belt and he spoke with a Glasgow accent.

'I'm DCI McAllister and this is my colleague DS Brown.'

Brown was six foot two inches tall and wore a trendy black Italian suit, open-necked white silk shirt and highly polished black Gucci shoes. His short black hair was slicked back with gel and he was wiry. He looked the sort of guy who liked to jog and eat healthy food.

One short and fat, the other tall and wiry. Rick thought they looked like a modern-day Laurel and Hardy.

'We're sorry to bother you, Mr Fernscale,' said McAllister. 'I've read your statement and I reckon there isn't much more you can tell us, but we're obliged to interview all witnesses to the drone attack. Is there anything else you can remember?'

'There's something else I just recalled. The civil aviation registration painted on the Bell Jet Ranger was G-APEL. I saw it through the binoculars. When I was in the SAS, we were taught how to remember the tiniest detail.'

McAllister scribbled in his notebook with a pencil and then spoke:

'Well, that's very interesting. We'll check that out. Of course, the terrorists could have applied a fake registration. We found the helicopter in a field in Essex two hours after the attack. It was completely burned out. We think the terrorists torched it before abandoning it. Our forensic teams are sifting through the wreckage. We're also looking for eye witnesses and checking CCTV and smartphone footage. If you do remember anything else that might help, give me a call. I'll leave my card. For the moment, I'll leave you in peace. Oh, and sorry to hear of your loss.'

'Thank you.'

*

After interviewing Rick, McAllister and Brown enjoyed a late breakfast at the Blue Dolphin café on the South Bank, just a stone's throw from St Thomas's Hospital.

McAllister opted for the Blue Dolphin's speciality, the 'belly buster' all-day breakfast: bacon, sausages, black pudding, two fried eggs, mushroom, tomato, hash brown, baked beans and two slices of fried bread. Two rounds of toast with marmalade. All washed down with a half-pint of fresh orange juice and a large mug of tea with two sugars.

'I can't imagine what your coronary arteries must be like,' said Brown as he enjoyed his free- range scrambled eggs on brown toast accompanied by green tea, while he perused *The Guardian*.

'Cooked breakfasts never did my dad any harm,' said Mc Allister as he inverted a bottle of HP brown sauce and deposited a big splodge of his favourite condiment over his sausages. 'He had bacon and egg every morning for breakfast you know, and he lived to the age of eighty-three. Mmm… these sausages taste better with a bit of brown sauce. This place does them the way I like … extremely well done. Pity you can't get Scottish square Lorne sausage down here.

Food of the gods!'

'I hear it has an even higher fat content than round sausages,' said Brown with a look of disapproval on his face. 'According to an article in *The Guardian* today, we should all be eating muesli and preferably the variety made with oats. It lowers your cholesterol you know.'

'Muesli is for rabbits,' said McAllister as he wiped some brown sauce from round his mouth with a paper napkin. 'If I had my way, I would get a weekly food parcel from Scotland containing Tunnocks caramel logs, Tunnock's teacakes, tinned haggis, Scottish Pride white bread and full sugar Irn-Bru.'

Mc Allister put up his right hand and caught the waitress's eye. 'Could I have another couple of slices of fried bread please, hen? I'm famished.'

He turned to face Brown.

'I could do with a fag as well. What muppet dreamed up the smoking ban! It's a load of shite! By the way, what did you think of Fernscale?'

'Clearly a tough guy with an impressive service record. Both his father and his grandfather were in the army. His dad was with the SAS in the Falklands War and his grandfather fought in North Africa alongside the legendary Paddy Mayne. He seems to be taking the death of his wife very well…at least so far.'

'I picked that up as well. But then maybe it's the people who appear to be taking things well that we need to worry about. He doesn't strike me as the kind of man who will forgive and forget. No, I think we will need to keep our eye on Mr Fernscale.'

CHAPTER 5

POST-MORTEM

Cabinet Office Briefing Room A (COBRA)

Whitehall, London

22 June 2022, 09:30 hours

The British Prime Minister brushed back his mop of thick, untidy blonde hair as he studied the documents in front of him. A bold terror attack in Central London had nearly succeeded…and the target might well have been him!

Members of the Cabinet and top civil servants, including the heads of MI5 and MI6, sat round the polished mahogany conference table. As they sipped teas and coffees, they looked at the morning papers with some satisfaction. As always happened during a crisis, the British public had rallied round their Prime Minister and their government and there was a new mood of patriotism sweeping the nation. The same thing had happened two years earlier during the virus pandemic.

Most of the papers supported the government and the Armed Forces in their fight against the new terror threat and even the more left-wing publications had grudgingly accepted that the government had done the right thing in setting up a missile battery in Hyde Park. An opinion poll by You Gov showed the Prime Minister's approval rating was at an all-time high.

'Thank you all for coming here today,' said the Prime Minister. 'I know you all have a lot to do so perhaps we can cut to the chase. You've all seen the news on TV and read the papers so you know what happened yesterday. A drone controlled by terrorists was shot down over Central London. There were just two casualties, a woman of 31 who died of severe burns and a 43-year-old man who suffered minor injuries.'

The Prime Minister turned to his Defence Secretary, David Marshall, who was sitting to his left. 'David, do we know anything about the drone that was shot down?'

'Yes, I have some news about that. The drone was blown to bits but police divers have recovered enough pieces of debris from the riverbed to achieve a partial reconstruction. We now know that it was an Iranian Shahed 20, a small unmanned aircraft similar to the American Predator. It is powered by a Rotax 914 four-cylinder petrol engine driving a rear-mounted propeller and armed with four Sadid 345 guided missiles. They have similar capabilities to the American Hellfires which the Predator uses.'

'So it was made in Iran. Does that mean that Iran was *behind the attack*?'

'No, Prime Minister. We're not exactly bosom pals with the Iranians but even in their maddest moments we don't believe they would ever have attacked the UK directly. No, as a result of intelligence supplied by the CIA in Langley we believe the drone was one of three captured in Syria by ISIS fighters.'

'So is ISIS behind the attack, then?'

'We don't think so. Our intelligence indicates that the drones were passed on to another terrorist group in exchange for a large cash payment.'

'I see. You mentioned that these drones carry guided missiles. Was it about to launch one?'

'Yes, Prime Minister. We believe the drone was about to release one of its four missiles when it was destroyed.'

'Four missiles! Do we have any idea what the targets were going to be?'

'It's impossible to say Prime Minister. Central London is a target-rich environment. They could have been attempting to attack 10 Downing Street, the House of Commons, MI5 HQ at Thames House, the MI6 building at Vauxhall or the MoD in Whitehall. Maybe even Buckingham Palace. Considering what actually happened, we had a very narrow escape.

'Also, we were fortunate that Sky Sabre brought the craft down over the Thames. If it had landed on the streets of Central London the death toll would have been much higher,' said Marshall.

'I understand we have the Israelis to thank for that,' said the Prime Minister.

'That's correct, Prime Minister. The Sky Sabre system employs a very effective surface-to-air missile, the Land Ceptor, but it owes a lot of its efficacy to the fact that both the missile and the launch vehicle's Giraffe air defence radar are integrated with elements of the Iron Dome system which we purchased from Israel. The fire control computer in Iron Dome is made by Rafael and is the most sophisticated of its kind in the world and was originally developed by Israel to defend its territories against missile attack. In the engagement yesterday, the computer chose the precise moment to fire so that the debris fell into the Thames where it would cause less casualties. Two years ago, we installed the system in the Falkland Islands to defend the main RAF airbase at Mount Pleasant. It is far more capable than the old Rapier units.'

'So Israel has been helping Britain! I can think of a few back bench MPs who won't be happy about that! One other question I have for you. Why was the drone accompanied by a civilian helicopter?'

'A good question, Prime Minister,' answered the Defence Minister. 'We think it was a tactic to confuse the defences. A drone accompanied by a civilian helicopter would look like a filming sortie. At the very least, it would make missile aimers hesitate. No one wants to be accused of shooting down a civil aircraft. In addition, it is known that missile fire computers can become confused when two targets are flying very close together. That happened on two separate occasions during the Falklands War. On 12 May 1982, HMS *Brilliant* shot down two Skyhawks using her Sea Wolf missiles. A third crashed into the sea while trying to evade a Sea Wolf. However, a second wave of two Skyhawks arrived shortly afterwards. This time they were flying so close together that the computer couldn't decide which to shoot at first and turned the system off.

'The same thing happened to HMS *Broadsword* on 25 May 1982 when it was unable to down any of the first wave of Skyhawks which attacked her and HMS *Coventry*. So we think these were the two reasons behind this strategy.'

'Fascinating,' said the Prime Minister. 'You've obviously done your homework. Of course, they are unlikely to use that tactic again. All the same, from now on I want any unidentified and unauthorised aircraft, helicopter or drone flying over London to be shot down. We're going to have to adopt a policy of 'shoot first and ask questions later'. Is that understood? We'll also have to ensure this new policy is explained to the media.'

Everyone round the table nodded in agreement. The Prime Minister continued:

'The big question though is this – are they going to try again?

They still have two drones and maybe other high-tech weapons as well. Is there anything else we can do to beef up our defences?'

'There are some things I can suggest, Prime Minister,' said the Junior Defence Minister, Tony West, who had previously served in the Royal Navy aboard Type 23 frigates and Type 42 destroyers. 'We could deploy one of our new Type 45 Daring class air-defence destroyers in the Thames Estuary. They have Samson 3-D radar and the Sea Viper missile system which can engage multiple targets, even if they are as small as a cricket ball and travelling at supersonic speed. They are far more effective than the old Sea Wolf and Sea Dart systems. As the saying goes, 'if it flies it dies!"

David Marshall glared at West.

'I can't agree with that move. We only have six of these vessels and we may need them elsewhere. However, I do suggest we redeploy one of our RAF Typhoon squadrons to a base in South East England. Missile defences can be highly effective but a manned fighter is better if you want to go up and take a look. For example, we might be faced with a 9/11 type scenario in which terrorists attempt to fly a hijacked airliner into a building. Manned fighters would be more useful for dealing with this. I also suggest we put some troops and light armour on the streets of Central London as a visible deterrent, plus armed police at stations and airports. And I'll put 22 Regiment SAS in Hereford on standby to move to the capital at short notice. We'll need to raise our level of alert to red.'

'Very well. I give my authority. And I also agree with Tony's suggestion to move a Type 45 to the Thames Estuary. We have to be seen to be doing everything we can to deter another terror threat. Are we sure we have no idea who is behind the attack?'

'We're largely in the dark,' said George Keen, the head of MI5. 'All we know is that a new terrorist group has appeared. They call themselves *The Seven* and are comprised of hardliners from various terrorist organisations including HAMAS, ISIS and dissident Irish Republican groups. One thing they have in common is a loathing of capitalism and all it stands for. The country they hate most is the USA, who they perceive as the 'Great Satan'. But in their view we are almost as bad – the 'Little Satan', as they put it – being perceived as the American President's lapdog.'

'So, do we have any leads at all?' asked the Prime Minister.

'One eyewitness spotted a civil registration G-APEL on the side of the helicopter. Unfortunately it appears to be phoney. G-APEL was the civil registration applied to an old Vickers Vanguard airliner when it entered service in 1961. The aircraft was later converted to a Merchantman freighter and crashed without loss of life in France in 1988,' said George Keen, consulting his notes.

'On top of that, the agent who gave us the tip-off about the drone attack has been murdered in Paris. So we are completely in the dark. And this group known as *The Seven* could strike anywhere without warning. Until we get any further leads, we are completely in the dark!'

'I understand,' said the Prime Minister. 'And somehow I don't think *The Seven* are going to twiddle their thumbs for long. They're going to hit us hard...and soon!'

CHAPTER 6

INVASION

Forty years earlier

21 May 1982, 09:22 hours

Sussex Mountains, East Falkland

SAS Trooper Jack Fernscale felt the straps of his heavy Bergen dig into his shoulders as he negotiated the wet, slippy ground on the downhill slopes of the Sussex Mountains in his heavy mountain boots. His face was numbed by the South Atlantic chill as a weak winter sun appeared above the hilltop to his east. It was a crisp, clear day. As well as carrying fifty pounds of equipment in his Bergen, he had a full belt kit plus his principal weapon – the new American General Dynamics FIM-92 Stinger portable surface-to-air missile. The Yanks, with their love of acronyms, had designated it a MANPAD (Man Portable Air Defence) system. With its five-foot-long launch tube, the Stinger resembled a WW2 bazooka, but with a box of electronic gizmos added near the front end. Yet, it was considerably more complicated than that simple weapon. The bazooka was just a metal tube that fired a small rocket with a hollow-charge warhead. The Stinger though was cutting-edge technology and had only been issued to US forces the previous year. Originally designed as an improved version of the Redeye missile, which had entered service in 1969, the Stinger had a more sensitive infra-red seeker head in its nose which would home the missile onto the hot tailpipe of an enemy jet and destroy it with a 6.6-pound warhead.

The equivalent British weapon was the Short Blowpipe, which was larger and heavier. It was also less technically advanced as it required the operator to acquire the target visually through an optical sight and then steer the missile to a 'kill' using a thumb-operated joystick. The SAS had looked at the Blowpipe but felt it was too cumbersome for their requirements and put in a request for the new American missile. Unlike the regular army (which the SAS referred to as 'the Green Army'), the SAS often used foreign weapons such as the American M16 rifle and the Heckler and Koch MP5 submachine gun. D Squadron had acquired six Stingers and had brought them to the Falklands. But would they get a chance to use them in action?

Just two days earlier, the SAS Stinger expert had died in a night-time accident when a Sea King helicopter had ditched while transferring troops between ships. It was thought that a large seabird, possibly an albatross, had got sucked into the engine intakes. Jack had received only a cursory training on the Stinger and had not read the full manual. But would that be enough and would he get a chance to use his weapon?

Earlier that morning, thirty men of D Squadron had made a diversionary night-time attack on Argentine positions at Goose Green. They had detonated flashbangs, thrown a few grenades, and sprayed rounds from their M16s at any targets of opportunity. The aim of the exercise was to cause as much noise as possible and distract the Argentines from the main amphibious landings at San Carlos.

Now, as the thirty SAS troopers descended the slopes of Mount Sussex, they could see an armada of British ships congregated in San Carlos Water. Much to his surprise, Jack saw the huge P&O liner S.S. *Canberra* sitting in the middle of the flotilla of ships. It was a very distinctive looking vessel with its enormous white hull, now streaked with rust after its 8,000-mile voyage south, and twin yellow funnels mounted near the stern. It was no wonder that troops called it the 'Great White Whale.' Its swimming pools had been planked over to create helipads for Sea King and Wessex helicopters. GPMGs had been strapped to its handrails to provide rudimentary air defence while several Royal Marines stood on the upper decks with chunky Blowpipe launchers perched on their shoulders. A steady stream of soldiers in green and brown camo battledress exited from hatches on the side of the vessel and boarded numerous landing craft, which sported black camouflage stripes over their navy grey paint, while Mexeflote rafts carried supplies to the shore. Also crawling ashore from the requisitioned North Sea ferry M.V. *Norland* were eight Scimitar and Scorpion light tanks.

Several warships patrolled San Carlos Water while others, including the two Type 22 frigates HMS *Brilliant* and HMS *Broadsword*, lay further out in Falkland Sound. There was a single County Class destroyer which Jack knew was HMS *Antrim*, sister ship to the *Glamorgan* which had provided naval gunfire support during the Pebble Island raid. There was also a huge Royal Fleet Auxiliary RFA *Fort Austin* plus the two assault ships HMS *Fearless* and HMS *Intrepid* which contained floodable docks at the rear with four landing craft.

The most common air defence weapon in use on the first day of the landings was the navy's Short Seacat SAM which had first entered service in 1962. But would this elderly first-generation missile which (like Blowpipe) needed to be steered manually to its target by a joystick, be effective against fast, low-flying jets? San Carlos Bay had been chosen for the landings because the surrounding steep mountains offered some protection from air attack. But they also made the job of anti-aircraft gunners and missile operators more difficult as they would only have seconds to acquire a target visually and then open fire. The Seacats were backed up by WW2-vintage, 40 mm Bofors and 20 mm Oerlikon cannon which were mounted on the bridge wings of many ships.

As Jack watched, an endless procession of Sea King and Wessex helicopters lifted underslung loads from the ships to the shore. Jack knew the first items to be put ashore would be lightweight 105 mm howitzers and twelve Rapier surface-to-air missile batteries. Each Rapier unit had three components connected by thick cables – a launcher, a tracker and a petrol-fuelled electric generator. The Rapiers would be needed soon – but how long would it take to set them up? Surely it would only be a matter of time before the Argentines realised what was happening and sent in airstrikes?

As if on cue, Jack heard a new sound to the east. It was the characteristic high-pitched whistling noise of a prop jet engine. *No, it was actually two engines*, thought Jack. A moment later, an odd- looking aircraft with small twin turboprop engines, an elongated canopy like that on a jet fighter and a tailplane mounted high on the fin flew over the crest of the mountains, heading directly towards San Carlos Water. It was an Argentine Pucara. It could have attacked D Squadron with its guns and rocket pods but the pilot was apparently more interested in the ships that were gathered in San Carlos Water.

Jack knew he could down the Pucara if he acted quickly. If he hesitated for even a moment the opportunity would be gone. As the Pucara flew directly towards him, Jack slapped the Battery Control Unit (BCU) – about the size and shape of a large baked beans can – into the cylindrical aperture under the launch tube. As well as providing electrical power, the BCU contained liquid argon to cool the infrared seeker head. Jack remembered that the missile had to be fired within 45 seconds of inserting the BCU. Otherwise, the BCU would have to be removed and a new one inserted.

Jack checked his watch. The Pucara was now directly overhead. Just twenty seconds had elapsed since the BCU had been installed. Two seconds later the Pucara was ahead of him, travelling west towards the ships. Jack turned off the uncaging switch at the front of the launcher to make the infra-red seeker 'live', looked through the optical sight and pointed the weapon initially at clear blue sky to the left of the Pucara before shifting his aim to the aircraft's port engine exhaust. An electronic buzzing noise told him the infra-red seeker head had acquired the target. Jack pulled the firing trigger. A small charge exploded and projected the missile out of the tube at high speed. Then the main rocket motor ignited and propelled the missile forward at a rapidly increasing speed. The projectile streaked through the sky towards the enemy aircraft, leaving a white smoke trail behind it.

Two seconds later, the missile's annular blast warhead exploded close to the rear of the Pucara's port engine nacelle. Bits of metal flew off the aircraft and black smoke poured out of the rear of the engine. The men on the ground cheered loudly. The Pucara had been hit but would it still make it back to base on one engine? For another thirty seconds the soldiers tracked its progress as it flew lower and lower. Then there was a loud bang, the canopy flew off and the pilot ejected. His seat fell away as a white parachute canopy bloomed and the pilot floated down to earth. A moment later, the stricken Pucara belly-landed on soft mossy ground, bending its propeller blades in the process.

All thirty SAS men whooped loudly and waved their hands in the air.

'Well done, Jack!' said one.

In the distance there was applause and whistles from men on the decks of the ships. The first Stinger kill in the world had been made by a trooper from D Squadron who hadn't even received a full training in the weapon. Jack received a few claps on his back and some of his mates promised to buy him a pint when everyone got back to the SAS base at Stirling Lines in Hereford.

*

Jack stood in the wet, hastily-dug slit trench at San Carlos, sipping coffee from a Thermos flask. The landings had gone well, although the defending Royal Navy ships had taken a pounding. HMS *Argonaut* had been attacked by a Macchi MB.339, using rockets and cannon fire. Despite being a relatively slow aircraft, the Macchi had successfully evaded a Sea Cat missile and escaped by hugging the ground. The crucial Rapier missile batteries were still not ready for action and the Blowpipes had proved ineffective.

As Jack reflected on the military situation, he opened his Bergen to reveal his loot – a Browning 9 mm pistol which he had captured at Goose Green, along with plenty of ammunition.

'What have you got there?' asked Trooper Oates.

'Just a little souvenir. There's a tradition in the British Army that soldiers collect bits of enemy kit to take home. I've already got a folding-stock Argentine FN-FAL rifle that I picked up at Pebble Island. And I'm hoping to get a captured helmet before this war is over.'

'No-one is going to be bothered about a helmet or two. But we're not supposed to take captured weapons home. It's against the gun laws in the UK. And you could be on a charge if the MPs find out,' said Oates.

'Well, they won't find out will they, unless someone tells them? By the way I've also got this.'

Jack produced an old dagger which a long, double-edged blade.

'I've seen one of these before. Is that not the type of dagger which appears on the back cover of *Commando* comics?'

'That's right. It's known as a Fairbairn-Sykes commando knife. Double-edged. Ideal for slitting a sentry's throat. This one is believed to have been used by my late father when he served with the LRDG in 1942. It was found in a Chevrolet truck which was abandoned in the Western Desert. I regard it as a good luck charm. One day I intend to pass it on to my son. You never know when one of these things will come in handy!'

CHAPTER 7

THE WOLF'S LAIR

Near the Maginot Line forts at Merlaux, Eastern France

9 August 2022, 09:59 hours

Pierre Dupont loved his red 1973 Renault 4 *Fourgonnette* van. He had first seen it two years before, rusting and neglected in a farmer's barn, red paintwork faded and oxidised from years of standing in the French sun. Its ashtray was filled with Gauloises cigarette stubs and empty fag packets were strewn everywhere. The headlining was stained brown with nicotine. It was covered in dust and hay with four flat tyres and a missing nearside front wing. The farmer didn't want to sell it. It was of great sentimental value as his late wife Anne-Marie had bought it for him as a thirtieth birthday present four decades earlier. In 2021, he had died, his body riddled with incurable lung cancer, and Pierre purchased the dilapidated vehicle from the deceased man's estate. The lawyers were amazed that anyone wanted it as they expected they would have to sell it for scrap.

Pierre's son, Jacques, owned an auto repair shop in Amiens and restored the vehicle to its original condition in just six months, sourcing many missing and replacement parts from eBay, and other internet sites. He polished the repaired and resprayed bodywork with carnauba wax till the red paint gleamed like glass. Now it was just like a new vehicle, as fresh as when it had rolled off the production lines at Renault's huge factory at Billancourt, Paris, in 1973. Pierre had received a few offers from collectors who wanted to show off the pristine van at classic car shows, but he turned them all down because he intended to use his *Fourgonnette* as a working vehicle for his *boulangerie* business, taking fresh bread, croissants and rolls to local shops, cafés and restaurants.

Pierre loved the simplicity of the *Fourgonnette,* with its reliable 845 cc four-cylinder engine delivering just twenty-eight brake horsepower, drum brakes all round, and a fascia-mounted gearchange. The soft torsion bar suspension gave a comfortable ride over rural potholed roads. It even had a rear-view mirror which was mounted on the dashboard (no Health and Safety in 1973), sliding windows and no airbags. The only luxury feature (an 'optional extra' at the time) was an original 1973 Philips AM radio with a mechanical push-button tuner. But, thought Pierre, who needs sat nav, rear parking sensors and anti-lock brakes when you are only delivering bread to local businesses? No, the old Renault 4 van with its practical boxy shape and unique 'giraffe hatch' at the rear met his needs perfectly, he thought, as he took a short cut to a café down a narrow, potholed country lane. It was a hot morning. The sun was high in a cloudless sky and even at 10:00 a.m. there was a heat haze over the nearby ploughed fields. Pierre opened both sliding front windows and the vent below the windscreen to let in fresh air, which had the smell of a French summer. He also flicked the dashboard-mounted rocker switch to turn on the single-speed fan.

The lane passed close to some old Maginot line forts which had been built in the 1930s to deter a German invasion. Ah, the Maginot line, thought Pierre. *A great example of French technology and bad planning.* It might have prevented the German onslaught in May 1940 if it had run the full length of France's eastern land border. Instead, it stopped at Belgium. The French Government didn't want to extend the line along its border with Belgium as it regarded that country as an ally. The Belgians, in turn, were reluctant to build fortifications along its own boundary with Germany in case it was seen as a provocative move.

It was obvious to military experts that the whole concept of the line was flawed as it was incomplete and it was no surprise when the Germans simply went round the northern edge of the Maginot line in May 1940. Yet, some decades later, many of the fortifications remained, as it was almost impossible to demolish reinforced concrete. Some forts and tunnels were dilapidated and overgrown with weeds and moss while others had been turned into popular tourist attractions.

The Merlaux forts had been left to rot until three years before when there had been a flurry of activity. Almost overnight, a number of construction vehicles had appeared. Tipper trucks, cement mixers and excavators. Portaloo toilets. Electric generators and air compressors. A temporary site office. Plus, scores of men wearing white safety helmets and high-viz yellow jackets, wielding picks, shovels and pneumatic drills. The rumour going round the village was that the old forts were being converted into a retreat for a famous rock star, complete with an underground recording studio, swimming pool, gym and sauna.

Then – as suddenly as they appeared – all the vehicles and construction workers vanished overnight. If any work had been done, it must have been underground because the external appearance of the forts was unchanged. The area was fenced off. Gates were padlocked and signs warned people to stay away from this *bâtiment dangereux* (dangerous building). It seemed that the rock star had changed his mind – or maybe just run out of money. By now it was

2022 and the world was suffering from the severe economic depression which had followed the virus pandemic. People had been sacked. Businesses had been closed and construction projects had been cancelled. So it was no wonder that the bunker restoration project had been scrapped, thought Pierre, as he drove slowly past several cars which were parked on rough ground near the bunker. Probably people going for a walk in the woods, he thought. After all, it was rather pleasant weather.

Pierre didn't know it at the time, but just 100 metres from his van was a concealed entrance to the bunker which led to an eight-person lift installed by construction crews. It, in turn, allowed access to an extensive underground complex of meeting rooms and dormitories. There was a power plant, kitchen, dining room, food stores, freezers, toilets, showers, a laundry and multiple computers. Even an armoury and a shooting gallery. The whole complex had been modelled on the series of secret bunkers which had been built all over the UK during the Cold War, some of which were now tourist attractions.

Another thing that Pierre didn't know at the time was that he had passed within 200 metres of the most wanted terrorist on the planet and had lived to tell the tale. Known to most people as just Khalid, he had been Number One on the FBI's 'most wanted' list for twenty years and had been implicated in a number of terrorist atrocities across the Western world, including hijackings, kidnappings, murders and suicide bombings. He had survived a number of assassination attempts which included an attack by an American Predator drone armed with Hellfire missiles, and two separate bombings by the Mossad which had nearly succeeded. He had proved hard to track as he didn't have a mobile phone or a credit or debit card, never slept two nights in the same location and had three surgically-created doubles.

As Pierre's Renault van disappeared into the woods, bumping up and down on its soft torsion bar suspension and tracked by a concealed CCTV camera, Khalid sat at the heavy wood conference table and looked at the faces of the six terrorist leaders, who were all studying laptop screens. Khalid was a big man, heavily built, and six foot four inches tall with long, dark greasy hair. The right half of his face drooped and the eye on that side did not move because it was artificial, the legacy of a failed Mossad bomb attack on his Mercedes in Damascus twelve years earlier. His bodyguard, Sercan, had spotted the Honda motor scooter coming towards them and had pulled his boss out the car just before the Zionist agent stuck the magnetic mine on the car's body. They were just two metres from the car when the bomb exploded, sending glass and metal fragments everywhere. Sercan had taken the full force of the blast and had died from a torn aorta but Khalid had survived with facial injuries and a smashed right forearm and hand. The surgeons in the military hospital in Damascus had patched him up and applied a skin graft to the right side of his face but were unable to save the right eye. They also had to amputate his right arm below the elbow. This incident had magnified his hatred of the State of Israel and increased his desire for revenge.

'I thank you all for coming here today,' said Khalid in perfect Oxford-educated English as he attempted to work his laptop mouse with his myoelectric right hand, which made whirring sounds from its inbuilt electric motors. His artificial hand was powered by a battery which had to be recharged every night and had an outer vinyl covering which gave it a near normal appearance. Although it gave him some function in his right limb, it could never provide sensation or proprioception, so he often preferred to use his left hand for most tasks.

Around the table were six other men in their forties, all senior officials in various terrorist organisations with one thing in common

– a hatred of Western capitalism and all it stood for.

Khalid continued. 'As you all know, our activities over the last few years have been very successful. The Covid 19 virus attack, which we planned and executed, caused economic devastation in the West. As expected, most countries responded to this outbreak by introducing lockdowns. The economic damage caused by these measures has been incalculable, far worse than what happened after the attack on the Twin Towers. Our dear departed brother Osama Bin Laden would be proud of what we achieved without firing a shot or detonating a bomb. A death toll far higher than 9/11 plus worldwide economic devastation. And to think that all we had to do to start the process was persuade a Chinaman to eat a raw bat. He agreed to do it for a hundred American dollars! The greatest recession for over three hundred years and it only cost us $100.'

'A raw bat! I hope he put plenty of soy sauce on it first,' said Maurice L'Arconne, the French terrorist leader, as he stroked his short, blonde curly hair and then polished his spectacles. Everyone laughed.

Khalid chuckled. He enjoyed hearing about the suffering of others. Then he continued:

'The success of the Covid 19 operation exceeded our expectations. And it augurs well for our next major project, *Operation Armageddon*. In the meantime, our bombings, kidnappings and missile attacks will continue. As you know, our recent attempt to assassinate the British Prime Minister was unsuccessful. We have never carried out such an operation against the American President because the White House is so well protected by anti-missile defences. Downing Street has had no such defensive weaponry fitted until just a few weeks ago when a system called Sky Sabre was installed in Hyde Park. Some of you may be unfamiliar with London, but Hyde Park is a huge green space in the centre of the city. As such, it has a clear view of the skyline for miles around and was used as a site for anti-aircraft guns during the Second World War for that very reason.

'The new British Sky Sabre uses the fire control computer from the Israeli Iron Dome system which was developed to engage rockets fired against the Zionist state by our brothers in Palestine. Proof, if any were needed, that while the USA is the Great Satan, Britain is the Little Satan. The United Kingdom is nothing more than a puppet of the Americans and the British Prime Minister is the American President's lapdog. But when we implement our great plan, the USA, Britain and Israel will be brought to their knees. America and Britain will be forced to withdraw from the Middle East and cease their support for the Zionists. The days of Israel will be numbered and we will dictate our terms to the West. No longer will the Americans bully the ordinary people of the world with their missiles, tanks, nuclear submarines and aircraft carriers. International Marxism will reign supreme. The State of Israel will be dismantled and re-occupied by its rightful owners. The will of *The Seven* will prevail and there will be a New World Order!'

The dissident Irish terrorist Patrick Devlin listened to Khalid's rant with interest. As a hard-line Republican who wanted the British kicked out of Northern Ireland, and an Independent Marxist Irish Free State established, he was quite happy to go along with Khalid's plan. Since the signing of the Good Friday agreement, and then 9/11, support for Irish Republicanism in the USA had ceased and funding had dried up. Even former IRA leaders now believed in a peaceful solution to the Irish problem and that angered Devlin, who felt he had a score to settle with the British.

'It was a pity the drone attack failed,' he said in a broad Derry accent. 'But we might have succeeded with a more low-tech approach. In the 1990s some of my fellow freedom fighters nearly killed the British Prime Minister using homemade mortar tubes mounted on the back of a lorry. It was all very low-tech but also very effective.'

'Yes I know,' answered Khalid as he mopped saliva from the drooling right side of his mouth with a handkerchief. The plastic surgeons had never managed to correct that problem.

'The British Prime Minister remains a priority target,' continued Khalid. 'And our brother Mahmoud Rashid has a plan to eliminate him. Have you not my friend?'

Khalid's myo-electric hand whirred as he pointed at his Palestinian colleague.

'Yes indeed, Khalid. Tomorrow I will be taking the Eurostar to Britain where I will start preparations for an attack on the British Prime Minister. I will die as a result but the sacrifice will be worthwhile. Hopefully there will be many civilian casualties, which will be a bonus. But success is not possible without martyrdom and it will be an honour to give up my life for such a worthy cause.'

'I admire your dedication,' said Khalid. 'And rest assured someone else will rise up and take your place when you have travelled to Paradise where seventy-two virgins await you. The rest of us will meet again in one month's time and details will be sent to you by encrypted email. I have been assured that our encryption system cannot be broken by the Western Intelligence Services. And when we do meet, we will finalize our arrangements for the implementation of *Operation Armageddon*. The world is going to be in for quite a shock. They won't know what's hit them!'

CHAPTER 8

REHABILITATION

11 August 2022, 07:37 hours

Rick glanced at his bedside digital clock. It was 7:37 a.m. Bright sunlight peeked round the edges of his dark blue blackout curtains in the bedroom of his Islington flat. After nearly eight weeks of insomnia, he had finally cracked it – a full seven hours sleep. He still had a few nightmares, and the occasional flashback, but he was definitely on the mend. Reading a few personal improvement books had helped. Self-hypnosis and meditation had been of benefit too. He had also made a decision about what he was going to do next that had greatly improved his mental state.

He had also refused the treatment offered by his GP, which consisted of anti-depressants and sleeping pills. From what he had read, these medications didn't cure anything, they only masked the symptoms. Sleeping pills, in particular, gave you a few hours of drugged, non-refreshing sleep followed by a hangover. And you could soon become dependent on them so you couldn't sleep without them. No, it was better to sort himself out without drugs. He had refused counselling and cognitive behaviour therapy as well. He had known a few army chums who had received that treatment and ended up feeling worse. He would fix himself without any help from the NHS, thank you very much.

His left arm had healed. Until the previous week, there had been an ache in his elbow when he put the joint under strain. Despite this, he had restarted cycling just thirty days after his near-drowning experience. He was now up to thirty miles a day when weather permitted. He enjoyed racing across Hyde Park on his matt red, lightweight Boardman bike with its skinny Citizen Schwalbe tyres, only slowing down to the 5 mph limit when he saw a policeman or a park warden. He loved the sensation of sun and wind on his face, the sound of the Derailleur gears changing, the gentle, soothing vibration coming up through the handlebars, and the aroma of a London summer. Cut grass, sun-cream and fresh sweat. Hundreds of people slumped in striped, brightly coloured deckchairs or lay on beach towels as they soaked up the strong late summer sun.

Now, with eight weeks having elapsed since his injuries, he hoped he could start work on his upper body muscles. Gingerly, he lifted up a heavy non-stick wok with his left hand and found he could raise it above his head without any discomfort. There was still a slight ache in the left side of his rib cage but that was improving too. All good. Later, he would restart his usual full-body exercise program using weights and various isometric exercise devices. He had four of these compact gadgets, namely a Bullworker X-5, a Bullworker 'Steel Bow', a Bullworker Iso-Bow and an Isokinator. All were designed to build up muscle bulk and strength by using so-called isometric contractions in which muscles contracted against a fixed resistance. They could be particularly effective when combined with conventional muscle-building exercises using weights. He knew he had to get himself as fit and strong as possible before he could carry out his plan.

But his immediate priority was breakfast. Sausage, bacon, fried egg and tomato. Plus a splash of HP brown sauce. Orange juice, two slices of brown toast and filter coffee to finish off.

Thirty minutes later, he was slurping his coffee and munching the last bit of buttered toast when the *Daily Mail* arrived through his letterbox. The front page story was all about new climate change legislation. On page five there was a short article about the ongoing police investigation into the recent drone attack which confirmed that no arrests had yet been made, although police were following up a number of leads. Rick sighed, put down the paper – which he would read more thoroughly later – and padded through to his fully tiled en suite bathroom for a shave and shower. Rick didn't like modern shaving gels and preferred to work up a lather with an old-fashioned Erasmic soap bowl and brush. After a quick shave with a Gillette disposable multi-blade razor, he showered for a few minutes using Pears soap and then lay on the bed with a towel round his waist while he watched *Good Morning Britain* on TV. Ben Shephard was berating a government minister for his inaction on some issue while Susanna Reid looked on, as gorgeous and immaculate as ever in a red summer dress. After thirty minutes, Rick had dried off sufficiently so he sprayed some deodorant under his armpits and got dressed in jeans, white trainers and light blue polo shirt.

Rick was tying his laces when the doorbell rang. He looked at his Rolex watch. 8:45 a.m. Who could be calling at this early hour? The postman rarely delivered anything before 11:00 a.m. these days.

Rick opened the front door. A man who looked about thirty years old stood on the doorstep. He had black plastic spectacles and short dark hair which was slicked back with gel and he wore a dark grey suit and a white open-necked shirt. He showed Rick a laminated photo ID card which hung on a lanyard round his neck. It had the blue NHS logo in the top right-hand corner.

'Mr Fernscale, I presume. Is it all right if I call you Rick?'

'Of course, people have called me far worse things. Particularly in my army days!'

The young man chuckled.

'My name is David. I'm a community psychiatric nurse. We dress in civvies these days. Can I come in?'

'Of course!'

Rick showed David through to the lounge. Rick perched on a comfortable cream leather armchair while David sat on the matching two-seater sofa. Rick remembered that Laura had bought these items at a sale at the DFS furniture warehouse.

'My apologies for this intrusion,' said David. 'But I already have an appointment with another client just down the road and your GP asked me if I might visit. I'll get straight to the point. Your GP is rather concerned that you have refused medication and have also declined counselling and cognitive behaviour therapy.'

'That's true,' answered Rick. 'I don't believe in the efficacy of these treatments. I know some army colleagues who felt worse after counselling and cognitive behaviour therapy. And I have no desire to be turned into a drug -addicted zombie either!'

'Obviously you're perfectly entitled to your own views. But I would point out that cognitive behaviour therapy and anti-depressants are both evidence-based, while the alternative therapies which your GP says you are using, such as hypnosis, meditation and tapping treatments, are all a bit woo-woo as far as the NHS is concerned.'

'You're perfectly entitled to your own opinion as well, but I have to disagree as they work for me.'

'I also understand you attended a self-help group for people with PTSD on just one occasion and never went back.'

'That's correct. I don't see the point of sitting with other PTSD survivors and moaning about how awful it is to have post-traumatic stress. I think it probably makes you feel worse. Besides, there is another reason why I have coped so well. My religion. I have always been a Christian and I have been reading the Bible a lot in the last weeks.'

Rick pointed to the black, leather-bound Bible that was lying on the coffee table.

'As Jesus said in Matthew 5:38-42 in the New Testament: 'That ye resist not evil: but whoever shall smite thee on thy right cheek, turn to him the other also. And if any man will sue thee at the law, and take away thy coat, let him have thy cloak also. And whosoever shall compel thee to go a mile, go with him twain."

David looked stunned. It was not what he had expected to hear from a former SAS soldier who had won the Military Medal fighting insurgents and terrorists in Iraq and Afghanistan.

Rick continued.

'In plain language, the path to healing involves forgiveness. What these people did that day eight weeks ago was horribly wrong, but also understandable. For decades the capitalist West has been exploiting the Third World. And America in particular has supported the State of Israel, a nation which continues to oppress the Palestinians. The people of the Middle East are being controlled by puppet regimes, many of them installed by the Americans. And one percent of the world's population controls all the wealth. If the money was evenly distributed there would be no poverty or famine.

'So I find it quite understandable that a terrorist group wants to change things. I don't support their methods and I don't approve of the killing of civilians but I forgive them for what they did to Laura. If I ever met any of them, I would give them a big hug. You see, me forgiving them is the only way I will ever achieve mental peace and come to terms with what happened.'

'That is remarkable,' said David. 'And I agree with what you say.

Forgiveness is the only way you will ever achieve mental peace. If only more of my clients had these same mental strategies, I would have less problems to deal with.

'But now I must leave because I can't be late for my next client. Rest assured, I will inform your GP that I now have no concerns about you. Just keep on doing what you're doing.'

David rose from the sofa and headed towards the front door.

'Thanks for coming,' said Rick as he showed David out and then closed the door. As the psychiatric nurse headed down the steps, Rick stood with his back against the door and smiled wryly. *How easy it was to fool that tosser*, he thought. Rick had indeed been reading the Bible but he wasn't a Christian and hadn't been to church for thirty years. And the Bible passage he was most interested in was from Exodus 21-24 in the Old Testament:

'*...if there is serious injury, you are to take life for life, eye for eye, tooth for tooth, hand for hand, foot for foot, burn for burn, wound for wound, bruise for bruise.*'

There was another passage from Leviticus 24:19-21 which he also liked: '*He that killeth a man, he shall be put to death.*'

Forgive the terrorists for what they did to Laura? *Not bloody likely!* He was going to track down every member of that evil gang, torture them for information that might prevent further attacks and then kill them in the most inhumane way possible. They would all die in agony after a lengthy period of great pain. They were going to learn the meaning of the word 'suffering'. That was the only way he could properly avenge Laura's death. *Rick wasn't interested in justice, he only wanted revenge and he was going to get it...by hook or by crook!*

CHAPTER 9

DEATH FROM THE SKIES

27 January 1991, 18:57 hours

The City of Hebron

West Bank, Palestinian Territory

Mahmoud Rashid was just nine. But what he knew surprised his teachers. Like his classmates, he understood that if you started off with ten Jews and killed four of them, then you would be left with six. That was the way that arithmetic was taught in many Palestinian schools. He also knew that his people had suffered a great injustice in 1948 when the fascist, illegal State of Israel had been created. What right did they have to take over their land and their houses? He also realised that this move had had the blessing of the United States and Great Britain. The two greatest capitalist countries. The Great Satan and the Little Satan.

But that was no surprise. The American political establishment was controlled by the Jews, both in the Senate and Congress. Jewish bankers had funded the establishment of the State of Israel. And that man Oppenheimer – who had led the atom bomb project – was he not Jewish too?

No, the Jews ruled the roost and that was unfair. His father had told him many stories about what had happened over the last few decades. In 1956, the British, French and Israelis had invaded Egypt and tried to take over the Suez Canal, but had been forced to withdraw. Then in 1967 Israel had inflicted a humiliating defeat on brother Arab states. He knew that the key weapons used by the Israelis in that conflict had been supplied by France and Britain. French Mirage and Mystère fighters and Vautour bombers had proved superior to the Soviet junk that the Arabs had been forced to use. And the Israeli tank armies consisted of a mixture of upgraded American Shermans and British Centurions. The British had also supplied Israel with hundreds of surplus M3 halftracks.

After the war was over, the French had turned their back on Israel and declined to sell that illegal state any more arms, even extending the embargo to several gunboats the Israelis had already paid for. But America had stepped into the breach and supplied Israel with F-4 Phantoms and A-4 Skyhawks to replace its aging Mirages, Vautours and Mystères.

Then on 4 October 1973 – the Jewish holiday of Yom Kippur – the Egyptians and Syrians had launched a surprise attack on Israel. Egyptian troops paddled across the Suez Canal in boats and overwhelmed the weak Israeli defences on the east bank. Hundreds of tanks and thousands of troops had streamed over newly-built pontoon bridges and into the Sinai Peninsula. Any Israeli warplanes that dared to intervene were shot down in droves by the latest Soviet surface-to-air missiles. The Israelis attempted to counter-attack but their Centurion tanks were decimated by the new AT-7 Sagger man-portable, wire-guided, anti-tank missiles. Meanwhile, a vast fleet of Syrian tanks rolled west over the Golan Heights, territory that had been captured by Israel in 1967.

It looked as though Israel was doomed but then President Nixon announced that the United States would supply its client state with the latest weapons. Within hours, every available USAF Lockheed C-5 Galaxy and C-141 Starlifter transport aircraft was heading across the Atlantic, laden with military hardware, including the new TOW anti-tank missiles and M60 tanks.

TOW was an acronym for Tube-launched, Optically-tracked, Wire-guided and was the most advanced anti-tank missile in the world in 1973. Mounted on jeeps, armoured personnel carriers or helicopters, it was devastatingly effective against tanks and had been deployed in Vietnam the previous year.

The M60 was the most modern tank in the US arsenal and was a lineal descendant of the old M26 Pershing which had first seen service at the end of WW2, when it had been designed to counter the German Tiger. The M60 had a very effective M68 A1 105 mm gun – an American license-built version of the British L7 rifled weapon used in the Centurion – which could pierce the armour of any Soviet tank. Along with other American weapons, including replacement Phantoms and Skyhawks, the TOW and the M60 helped the Israelis to destroy the two advancing armies. Eventually the Israelis eliminated the invading Syrian armoured force in the Golan Heights and then launched their own counter-attack across the Suez Canal. They cut off the Egyptian force and even threatened Cairo. The Israelis were on the point of complete victory when international pressure forced them to agree to a ceasefire.

Egypt's President Anwar Sadat was crestfallen. He felt he had been on the verge of defeating Israel and would have done so had the United States not intervened. He could beat Israel but not the United States. So America was to blame for what happened! Here was a chance for the Syrians and Egyptians to liberate Israel and return Palestine to its rightful owners and it had all gone wrong! Mahmoud's father was furious and the whole incident had increased his hatred for America. 'Death to America' became his new slogan.

To make matters worse, a few years later Sadat signed a peace treaty with the Israelis. And who was behind that? The Jew, Henry Kissinger. It must be obvious to anyone that the Jews were pulling the strings. Mahmoud's father was jubilant when Sadat was murdered by dissident army officers a few years later but unfortunately the peace agreement remained in place.

No, thanks to regular pep talks from his father, Mahmoud was very knowledgeable about world affairs. Everything that was wrong with his life was the fault of the Jews and the United States. Britain was no better as it was under the thumb of the Americans. The British Prime Minister was the American President's lapdog. *Maybe that is who we should be attacking*, thought Mahmoud as he relaxed on the flat roof of his family's humble dwelling. Soon it would be too cold to stay outdoors but for the moment he was content to lie on a mat and look at the stars.

As Mahmoud lay on his back studying the Milky Way, he spotted a bright yellow light crossing the sky from east to west. What was it? Was it a comet with a fiery tail or perhaps a meteorite? Or maybe even a satellite re-entering the atmosphere? Then a second light appeared, followed by a third. What were they? Could they be alien spacecraft? The other night he had had a strange dream about a huge flying saucer with a giant brain inside landing in the Qattara Depression in Egypt. Could this be the explanation?

A rusty, white Toyota pick-up with a holed silencer and a missing front bumper pulled up outside the family house in a cloud of dust. Chickens scattered in every direction, clucking loudly. Three young men wearing *keffiyehs* jumped out and pointed their AK-47 assault rifles at the sky as they loosed off unaimed bursts on full auto and screamed with joy. Brass cartridge cases landed on the ground.

'Saddam! Saddam! Saddam! Our saviour. Freedom for Palestine!'

In a flash, Mahmoud understood what was happening. He had heard that Saddam Hussein had started bombarding Israel with Scud missiles a few days ago in an attempt to break up the anti-Iraq coalition which was attempting to liberate Kuwait and destroy Iraq's military machine. They hoped to achieve this by bringing Israel into the war as no Arab country could be seen to be fighting on the same side as the Jews.

The lights he had seen crossing the sky must be the tail-flames of Scuds and now they were heading for Israeli cities, maybe even Tel Aviv. In a few minutes there would be a lot of dead Jews. Mahmoud was elated. He and his father had approved of the invasion of Kuwait as the inhabitants were rich, decadent puppets of the west. But why had Saddam not attacked Israel as well? That would have been an even better idea. It might even have led to the liberation of the Palestine people and a return of occupied territory to its rightful owners.

As Mahmoud watched, the three Scuds headed west until they were just glowing pinpricks of light above the horizon. Suddenly, there was a yellow flash on the ground in the far distance, accompanied by a loud bang, and a glowing white ball of light rose in the sky taking a curving path towards the leading Scud. An orange explosion bloomed in the sky with a loud *boom* as the projectile struck home and bits of flaming Scud missile fell to the ground. Within a minute the two other Scuds were despatched in a similar fashion. What had happened? Why hadn't the Scuds hit their targets?

There was a collective wail of despair from the crowds which had gathered in streets and on rooftops. Someone said the word 'Patriot' and Mahmoud realised what had happened. After the first Scud attacks, America had rushed MIM-104 Patriot surface-to-air missile batteries by air to Israel along with trained crews to operate them. It was the very first time American servicemen had been deployed on Israeli soil. Just as had happened in 1973, America had saved Israel and preserved the anti-Saddam coalition. Mahmoud was despondent. *The Great Satan would pay for this crime. And the Little Satan as well.*

CHAPTER 10

AMBUSH

Southern Israel, near the border with Gaza

6 April 2005, 10:07 hours

Mahmoud Rashid lay in a patch of brown desert scrub as the rising sun warmed his body. The gentle, warm southerly wind smelled of olive trees. He glanced at his watch. If his informant was correct, the Israeli Army patrol vehicle should be along any moment. Just yards away, his trusty assistant Abdul wiped his AK-47 assault rifle with an oily rag and inserted a curved thirty-round magazine. They were expecting four soldiers in the truck, equipped with automatic weapons, so they would be outnumbered two-to-one. But both insurgents were well-trained and armed with AK-47 assault rifles and a single RPG-7 rocket launcher with three missiles. They also had the advantage of surprise. Both men wore desert camo fatigues and beige *keffiyehs* to help them blend into the terrain.

It would have been less risky to set up an improvised explosive device (IED) by the side of the road and detonate it from a distance using a command wire. Some HAMAS fighters had even started using cheap mobile phones as wireless remote detonators.

But Mahmoud preferred to do things the old-fashioned way, using a manually-aimed rocket. He wanted to hear the screams of Jews in pain. To see his hated enemies engulfed in flames, dying in agony. And smell their roasted flesh. He wanted to riddle their bodies with 7.62 mm rounds, see them lying in pools of blood and then imagine their grieving families drowning in their own tears. They didn't cry when Palestinian children died in Israeli bombing raids, did they?

Mahmoud had not eaten breakfast earlier that morning when he had slipped over the border into Israeli territory. Now he regretted his decision as he felt hungry and light-headed. He opened his canvas backpack and retrieved two plastic Tupperware boxes with green lids. One contained eight falafel and a large dod of hummus, the other a few fresh dates. Mahmoud dipped three falafel in the hummus and then wolfed them down. Then he took a swig of water from his metal canteen and passed the plastic container over to Abdul. The young man smiled, showing a flash of bright white teeth which contrasted with his dark complexion and black curly hair, and devoured the remaining falafel. Abdul always had a good appetite but remained as thin as a whippet.

Within minutes, Mahmoud's blood sugar level rose and he felt more alert. Then he sensed a gurgling sensation in his lower abdomen and realised he needed a shit. A doctor friend back in Gaza had once told him that it was a physiological phenomenon known as the gastro-colic reflex of McEwen – if you ate something it would often trigger defaecation. Well, that would have to wait. The Israeli patrol would be along in a minute and he didn't want to be caught with his trousers down…literally.

As if on cue, the noise of a vehicle engine reverberated across the sun-scorched, rocky landscape. An experienced HAMAS fighter, Mahmoud could identify most military vehicles by their distinctive engine sound. This one had a petrol engine, not diesel, and six cylinders. Most armies had moved over to diesel motors so it was probably an Israeli AIL 325 Command Car. Mahmoud could picture the HAMAS intelligence file on 'weapons of the enemy.' Built in a factory in Nazareth in the hated fascist State of Israel, the 325 had a 3.7 litre slant-six petrol engine and was based on the vintage American Dodge weapons carrier which had seen extensive service in the Second World War. No protective armour, but up to three 7.62 mm machine guns. Yet, provided the two of them acted boldly, it would stand no chance against an RPG-7.

Mahmoud inserted a PG-7VL armour-piercing rocket into the front end of his rifle-sized RPG-7 launcher, lay on the ground and waited. When the best opportunity to fire came, he would stand up, aim and pull the trigger. A risky move, but a bold one that often produced results. Then they would riddle the Israeli vehicle with bullets, check they had killed all the soldiers and return to Palestinian territory.

At last, the two fighters could see the pale green AIL 325 open truck as it winded its way slowly along the narrow, potholed tarmac road which passed close to their hiding place. Bright early morning sun glinted off its windscreen. It was just a hundred yards away now, well within range of an RPG-7 but Mahmoud knew he would have a better chance of a 'kill' if he let the truck get closer. The two HAMAS fighters had chosen their position carefully so that the rising sun was behind them, making them hard to spot. The truck driver had pulled down his sun visor while the three other soldiers on board swivelled their pintle-mounted machine guns as they nervously scanned the landscape, searching for any threat.

Eighty yards away...seventy yards...sixty yards. As the truck slowed down further to negotiate a sharp bend, Mahmoud stood up, aimed his weapon at the vehicle's radiator using the crude metal sight and pulled the trigger. There was a loud bang and a bright flash as the small rocket streaked through the desert air, leaving a white smoke trail behind it. Almost immediately the three Israeli machine gunners spotted the flash and slewed their weapons round to engage the target...but they were too late! A second later, the rocket's powerful hollow-charge warhead struck the truck's radiator and blew a huge hole in it, causing hot green sticky coolant to spray everywhere. A white-hot jet of molten metal pierced the engine block and started a petrol fire which engulfed the front end of the vehicle. An orange fireball climbed into the sky and the front tyres caught fire. Even from sixty yards away, Mahmoud could smell burning paint and rubber as a large pall of sooty black smoke climbed high into the sky. The bespectacled driver bailed out of the truck with his uniform on fire and rolled on the ground but he had already suffered ninety percent burns to his body and had only minutes to live.

One of the three remaining Israeli soldiers had been blown clear of the truck by the blast and was lying on the rough ground, nursing a broken arm. The other two were shocked, but unharmed, and fired short controlled bursts through the smoke and flames at the patch of scrub where Mahmoud and Abdul were hiding. But with smoke blowing in their faces, the Israelis couldn't aim well and their rounds went wide of the target.

Mahmoud pushed another rocket onto the end of his RPG launcher and fired again, this time aiming at the main troop compartment behind the cab. The RPG wasn't an ideal anti-personnel weapon but the blast from the explosion sent wooden splinters flying everywhere, seriously wounding the two Israeli troopers and blinding them.

With no return fire to worry about, the two Palestinian fighters raced towards the truck and pumped a few rounds from their AK-47s into the three wounded Israeli soldiers. Then Mahmoud walked several yards to where the seriously burnt driver was lying. His body was blackened and smoking and he was muttering something incomprehensible in Hebrew. *Probably wanting his mother*, thought Mahmoud as he unholstered his Soviet 9 mm Tokarev pistol.

'Death to Israel!' said Mahmoud as he fired two bullets into the young soldier's head from a range of three feet. Blood, brains and cerebrospinal fluid splattered over the desert floor.

Mahmoud was just putting his Tokarev back into its holster when he heard the sound of a powerful diesel engine and the clank of tracks. He looked to the north and saw a huge metal behemoth coming over a rise in the ground. It was a tank, and a big one at that, with three pintle-mounted machine guns on top of the turret and a huge main gun the size of a telegraph pole. It was a 65-tonne Merkava (chariot), built in Israel, and the only armoured vehicle in the world specifically designed for desert warfare. It also had a reputation as the safest tank in the world with its extra-thick frontal armour. The Israeli designers had even placed the engine at the front to give extra protection.

During the Second World War, the Allies had feared the German Tiger tank because of its thick armour and powerful 88 mm gun but the Tiger was like a toy compared with the Merkava, which was designed to withstand a direct hit from a Soviet 125 mm gun. And it was well armed too. Early versions had the superb M64 105 mm rifled tank gun – based on the weapon used in the Centurion and M60 – while the newer models had an even better MG253 120 mm smoothbore, probably the best tank gun in the world. But it really made no difference to Mahmoud whether he was facing a 105 mm or a 120 mm. Either way he was screwed!

All he had to defend himself was an RPG-7 with a single remaining rocket. Mahmoud knew that the RPG-7 was ineffective against the

Merkava – especially from the frontal arc where the armour was thickest – but he had to try. The Israeli tank was just a hundred yards away as Mahmoud slotted his last round into his launcher, balanced the weapon on his right shoulder and aimed at the area where the turret met the hull. This was a weak point in most tanks.

Mahmoud pulled the trigger. The rocket shot through the desert air and hit the angled front glacis plate with a loud clang. The tank was enveloped in a cloud of white smoke. When it cleared Mahmoud could see an area of blackened paint on the front plate, but no hole. The Merkava had lived up to its formidable reputation.

Now a second tracked vehicle drew up beside the Merkava. It was a boxy American-made M-113 armoured personnel carrier. The Israelis called them the *Bardehlas*. Thinly armoured, it would have been a juicy target for an RPG-7 but that was an academic point now, as Mahmoud had no missiles left. There was only one thing to do now and that was run! There was an olive grove just two hundred yards to their south and if they could make it there, they might elude their pursuers as the two armoured vehicles couldn't follow them into the trees.

Mahmoud dropped the RPG-7 and shouted to Abdul:

'Run, my friend! Drop your pack but keep your rifle!'

The two young Palestinians raced for the safety of the olive grove as the two armoured vehicles followed, firing short bursts from their machine guns. Mahmoud knew the Israelis would prefer to capture them alive if possible so they would be aiming wide in the hope that they might surrender. He could feel his chest tighten as his breathing speeded up and his heart pounded away in his chest. His throat and ribs hurt and his legs felt like jelly. For a moment he had the odd thought that HAMAS fighters running away from Israeli tanks must have broken Olympic sprinting records. He had already dropped his pack but was still carrying his heavy AK-47. It weighed nine pounds.

Did he really need it or should he throw it away? He would go a lot faster without it.

Now the two men were just fifty yards from the olive grove. Mahmoud could hear the clank of tracks and the whine of diesel engines behind him and sniff the acrid smells of cordite and exhaust fumes. Soldiers shouted in Hebrew. Bullets whizzed past his ears.

Twenty-five yards to go! They were going to make it! Then there was another sound. The slow whumph…whumph…whumph of rotor blades and the distinctive whistle of gas turbine engines. Mahmoud looked back and saw two helicopters in the distinctive markings of the Israeli Defence Forces. Both were painted in sand, brown and green camouflage with blue and white circular Star of David markings on the fuselage sides. Each had a chin turret mounting a triple-barrelled Gatling-type 20 mm cannon and short stub wings with rockets. At first Mahmoud thought they must be AH-64 Apaches but then he realised they were late model Bell UH-1 Cobras. They were designed to knock out tanks, so two lightly-armed insurgents would be an easy target.

Abdul raised his AK-47, selected full auto and fired a long burst at the cockpit of the nearest Cobra. The rounds bounced off the armoured glass. The helicopter's gunner, sitting in the rear cockpit, adjusted the aim of the chopper's chin gun and fired a one-second burst at the young insurgent. Abdul fell to the ground dead, his body cut to pieces by the heavy 20 mm rounds.

Mahmoud was enraged. He had promised Abdul's mother that he would take care of him so he was determined to destroy the Cobra if it was the last thing he did. He remembered what one of his HAMAS instructors had told him: *'All helicopters have a fatal weakness. The rotors. It is the one part of a chopper that cannot be armoured. An RPG shot through the rotors will bring down the toughest attack helicopter. If you don't have an*

RPG, then multiple rifle or machine gun rounds fired at the tail rotor will often bring it down.'

It was worth a try. Mahmoud slapped a fresh magazine into his AK-47, selected full auto and fired a long burst at the whirling tail rotor of the nearest Cobra. Most of the rounds passed through the blades without hitting anything but a few struck home and destroyed the rotor. Bits of the blades flew off at high speed and struck the ground nearby. Deprived of the lateral thrust from the tail rotor, the chopper spun around its vertical axis and struck the other Cobra. Immediately, both aircraft lost lift and plummeted fifty yards to the ground where they exploded. The blast from the detonating jet fuel nearly knocked Mahmoud off his feet. An orange fireball rose high into the sky. Then he felt a blow to the back of his head. Everything went grey and Mahmoud fell to the ground, stunned.

'Radio HQ,' said an Israeli sergeant. 'Tell them we've got one of them alive and we're bringing him in for interrogation. Whatever it takes, we'll make him talk!'

CHAPTER 11

REVELATIONS

6 April 2005, 19:27 hours

A bucket of cold water poured over his head brought Mahmoud back to full consciousness and washed away the blood that had trickled from his scalp wound into his eyes. A naked hundred-watt light bulb dangled from the wooden ceiling above his head. There was a noise like a petrol lawnmower outside the window, combined with the whirring sound of a fan. A blast of cool air dried his wet combat shirt and his sweat-soaked body. Then Mahmoud twigged. He was in a hut which had electricity and air conditioning, courtesy of a petrol-driven generator. Air conditioning! He knew that most Palestinian homes didn't have that luxury and yet the Israelis fitted it in Army huts! He tried to move and discovered he was sitting on a hard, wooden chair with both hands tied behind his back.

Two young helmeted Israeli soldiers in desert camo battledress and full webbing kit stood on either side of him. He could smell their fresh sweat. Both had short black curly hair and tanned skin. The one on his left clutched a 9 mm Uzi submachine gun, the other held a Galil 7.62 mm assault rifle. Mahmoud knew the Galil well. It was an Israeli design based on the AK- 47, but with a few additional features such as a bottle opener. The soldier on his left put his Uzi on a table, grabbed Mahmoud by the shoulders and spoke to him in passable

Arabic with an Israeli accent:

'You killed four of our men. The crew of two Cobras. And now you're going to talk! Who sent you? Where is your base? How did you get over the border? Who is your leader? Where do you store your arms? Who are the other members of your group?'

The soldier slapped Mahmoud across his mouth so hard that he split his lip. The young Palestinian felt the salty taste of warm, fresh blood. *If only he wasn't tied to the chair, he would kill these two Jews with his bare hands!*

'Talk my friend or things will get very bad for you!' The soldier pointed to a towel that was lying on a table beside a large jug of water. 'You know what that's for, don't you? We'll get you on the table, put a towel over your face and then pour lots of cold water over it. You won't be able to breathe and you'll feel as though you're drowning. The Americans call it *waterboarding*. It's one of the most frightening tortures ever. Even the toughest of fighters have been broken with this method. Talk now you bastard or you will die!'

The soldier got so close that the Palestinian could smell tobacco, garlic and coffee on his breath. Their faces were just inches apart. Mahmoud couldn't use his fists or his feet but he still had his teeth. Stretching his neck forward suddenly, he bit a chunk out of the soldier's nose and then spat it out. The squaddie let out a scream and staggered back, clutching his maimed nose which was bleeding heavily.

The other soldier reacted by smashing the butt of his Galil against Mahmoud's jaw. The Palestinian fell back in his chair and cracked his head on the wooden floor. As the first soldier attempted to staunch his bleeding nose with a towel, the other cocked his rifle and took aim at the Palestinian's left knee. At that range the bullet would destroy the knee joint and cause enough damage to make an above-knee amputation necessary. Mahmoud would be crippled for life.

'Stop!'

The soldier turned round to see an officer of the Israeli Army standing in the doorway. He had the rank of *Seren* (Captain) with a small neatly trimmed black moustache, shiny hair and olive skin and facial features which looked Arabic rather than Jewish.

'Have you taken leave of your senses! Abusing a prisoner and denying them food, water and medical care is a violation of their human rights! It is also contrary to the principles of the Geneva Convention, which states that prisoners should be removed from the battlefield and taken to a safe rear area for processing. Enemy soldiers are only required to give their second name, rank and serial number. Physical violence or the threat of it should never be used to obtain information.'

'This man is a terrorist, sir. He shot down two of our helicopters. All four crew were killed. He is not classified as an enemy soldier under the terms of the Geneva Convention. Rather he is what is commonly known as an illegal combatant. He doesn't have any rights under international law.'

'I disagree. In my opinion, even captured terrorists and insurgents deserve to be treated according to the terms of the Geneva Convention. Otherwise, we're as bad as them. I don't condone their actions, of course. Killing women and children is wrong. But if we want to stand on the moral high ground then we must treat captured enemy with reasonable humanity.'

The Israeli *Seren* turned to the door just as two Military Policeman arrived.

'Arrest these two soldiers! I want them charged under Israeli Military law. And make sure the one with the nose injury receives urgent medical attention. He may need plastic surgery. And I want our prisoner here to have his wounds seen too.'

One of the MPs took away the two Israeli soldiers while the other remained on guard inside the hut, clutching his Uzi. A female army medical orderly arrived and dabbed at Mahmoud's wounds with a brown, iodine-based antiseptic and closed his lacerations with Steri-Strips, while an army nurse cleaned him with a washcloth and untied the ropes that were securing him to the chair.

'I must apologize for my colleagues,' said the officer. 'But they do get carried away a bit. They have seen so many of their friends killed in ambushes that they do get a bit heavy-handed in their approach. I don't expect you will want to tell me your name but that is fine. We will find out in due course. The Mossad files are very extensive. The organisation has a legendary reputation, you know.'

'A reputation for killing innocent people,' said Mahmoud, with a sneer on his face. Then he continued:

'I know all about Mossad operations in neutral countries. If anyone is breaking international law, it is them!'

'You're perfectly entitled to your views but I have to disagree with you on that point. Our country has been fighting for its survival since 1948. A few years before that, six million Jews were killed by Adolf Hitler's Germany. Since our country's inception we have always believed that we should strike at our enemies wherever they are found. Sometimes we have to play dirty. I myself am not even Jewish. I'm actually an Arab but am proud to be an Israeli citizen. My name is *Seren* Haddad and I'm a Muslim.'

'A Muslim? I thought you didn't look Jewish. So why do you work for this pariah state?'

'Oh, but there are nearly two million Arabs who live quite happily in Israel and are free to practise their religion, and there are four hundred mosques in Israel. In 1948, Israel – or Palestine as you still call it – was just a strip of desert with few natural resources. The only country in the Middle East with no oil. But we worked hard to turn desert into cultivated land. We found ingenious ways of providing water for our people. We have diverted rivers and built desalination plants. And we now have thriving industries. Factories which turn out tanks, missiles, aircraft, guns, patrol boats, vehicles and even satellites. A few decades ago we were nothing. In 1956 our army used second-hand Sherman tanks left over from the Second World War. Now we have one of the most powerful militaries in the world. We have ten times as many tanks as Great Britain. And yet your people refuse to make peace with us. Yasser Arafat had the opportunity to do a deal with us on many occasions but every offer we made was turned down.

'Yet, there is an opportunity here to achieve lasting peace in the Middle East. At the moment most Arab countries spend much of their considerable wealth on huge military forces. So do we. But if there was a comprehensive peace agreement across the whole Middle East, we could all scale down our armed forces and spend our money on improving the living standards of our people. Is that too much to ask? We must forget what happened in the past and focus on the future. We must forgive others for past crimes and help each other to build a better world based on love not hate, peace not war.'

Mahmoud's face fell. This is not what he expected to hear from an Israeli Army officer.

'My organisation will never make peace with Israel. Never! The only solution to the problems of the Middle East is the total destruction of the fascist Zionist state.'

'Well, I am afraid we will have to agree to disagree on that point, my friend.'

The door of the hut swung open on creaking hinges, letting in a blast of balmy air which smelled of flowers. A female Israeli soldier, her dark hair pinned back, entered carrying a large wooden tray with two glasses of hot mint tea, some *baklava*, two plates of hot *shakshuka* and some bread with olive oil dip.

'Would you like to join me for a late breakfast?' said Haddad. 'Our cookhouse has prepared some fresh *shakshuka*. A traditional Israeli breakfast dish which is also popular in Egypt. The bread is fresh. It comes from a local bakery and is still warm. Even though I am not Jewish, I love the Israeli tradition of large cooked breakfasts. It all started in the early days of our state in the *kibbutzes*. Workers would get up at four a.m. to avoid the burning heat of the sun, work for a few hours and then devour a huge buffet. What we are having today is a mere snack by comparison. But I must confess that I am a little peckish after all the excitement earlier. Come my friend, sit down at the table.'

Mahmoud was apprehensive. Was this an attempt to poison him or drug him? He had seen enough American police movies to be aware of the 'good cop, bad cop' routine. He didn't trust the Israeli *Seren*. Yet he was hungry. And that fresh bread and hot *shakshuka* smelled divine. He remembered what his HAMAS instructors had once told him: if you are captured and you are offered food or water then you should accept, unless you think it may be poisoned. After all, you don't know when you will eat again.

Mahmoud sat down and inspected the *shakshuka*. He knew it was made with red peppers, tomatoes, onion, spices and garlic with fried eggs on top. Just to be on the safe side he swapped plates so Haddad was forced to eat the one that might be poisoned.

Haddad laughed. 'You have a suspicious mind my friend. Here, have some bread.'

Haddad passed a plate of bread over to the young Palestinian who grabbed a large slice, dipped it in olive oil and put it in his mouth. It was warm and delicious. The *shakshuka* tasted pretty good as well. He had to admit that – although he hated Israel – their food was excellent and not that different from Arab cuisine.

Soon Mahmoud had gobbled up the *shakshuka* and was wiping the plate clean with the last piece of bread which he then popped in his mouth. Then he attacked the sugary *baklava*, washing it down with hot mint tea. Who would have thought that he would ever have breakfast with an Israeli Army officer? But such were the fortunes of war.

As Mahmoud was finishing his last piece of *baklava*, he heard the sound of two vehicles drawing up outside. The door opened and an Israeli sergeant entered.

'Transport to take the prisoner to the interrogation centre, sir! One jeep and a patrol truck.'

A look of fear came over Mahmoud's face. What tortures awaited him at this interrogation centre?

Haddad wiped his mouth with a napkin and spoke:

'The sergeant is correct. You will be taken to a specialist interrogation centre at a remote location an hour's drive from here. I will be coming with you as you are classed as a high-value prisoner. I wouldn't think of escaping. You will be handcuffed to me in the back of the truck, which will have two armed guards. Four soldiers will be travelling in a jeep in front. But now we must leave.'

*

Mahmoud sat on the hard bench seat in the rear of the AIL 325 truck as it trundled along the smooth tarmac road which traversed the desert landscape. He had to admit that the Israelis had done a great job of improving their infrastructure. The roads in Palestinian territories were rutted and potholed, while those in Israeli territory were up to European standards. And the Jews had made the desert bloom and built cities and holiday resorts which were the envy of the civilised world.

He was handcuffed by his left wrist to *Seren* Haddad who was now wearing a pair of sunglasses. Above him was a canvas roof which gave some protection from the fierce desert sun. The sides had been rolled up to give better visibility. From where he sat, he could see the driver and next to him a single machine gunner who was standing up as he scanned the landscape for any threat. On the opposite bench seat were two Israeli soldiers armed with Uzis.

As he looked forward through the windscreen, he saw an Israeli jeep travelling fifty yards in front. Then there was a loud bang. The windshield crazed and he felt a hot blast wave pushing him against the side of the truck. The jeep travelling ahead rolled over, crushing the soldiers inside. Debris from the blast peppered the AIL-325 as it screeched to a halt to avoid a large crater. Haddad screamed orders:

'Don't stop! We're facing an ambush! Get on the radio and report the incident. Steer round the bomb crater and keep going!'

The driver of the AIL-325 engaged first gear, stamped on the accelerator and swerved round the burning, overturned jeep. The heavy vehicle gained speed slowly as the driver worked through the gears but was soon up to thirty miles per hour. As the truck rounded a bend, the driver discovered that the road ahead had been blocked by two old cars which had been set on fire. There was a river to the right and large boulders to the left, which would both prevent any vehicle going off-road. The ambushers had chosen the location well. The Israeli truck slowed to a halt. Twelve insurgents wearing *keffiyehs* emerged from the bushes on both side of the road and raced towards the vehicle. Most of them carried AK-47s and one had an RPG-7. They all had Tokarev pistols in holsters.

Haddad unholstered his 9 mm Browning Hi-Power pistol and shot one of the insurgents. The two Israeli soldiers sprayed a few bursts from their Uzis at the attackers, killing three of them. Then the truck's machine gunner slumped dead, hit by a sniper.

Soon the truck was overwhelmed by the remaining attackers, who pumped two rounds into each of the soldiers' chests. Blood splattered everywhere in the rear of the truck. Haddad was unharmed and still handcuffed to his prisoner.

Ali, the leader of the attacking force wore a chequered *keffiyeh*. Pointing his pistol at Haddad, he barked out orders in Hebrew:

'The keys for the handcuffs. Give them to me now!'

Haddad complied with the order and a moment later Mahmoud was free.

'Now get out of the truck and stand at the side of the road. We're going to shoot you in the head. You will be found dead in a ditch. A suitable humiliation for an Israeli officer.'

'No,' said Mahmoud. 'I want to kill him myself. You have no idea what he put me through. Give me your pistol!'

Mahmoud led Haddad to the side of the road and walked him at gunpoint until the two men were thirty yards from the damaged truck. As he pointed his Tokarev at the officer's head at a range of two feet, the leader of the rescue squad could just see his lips moving but couldn't hear what he was saying. What was he saying to the Israeli? Probably something like 'Death to Israel.'

Mahmoud pulled the trigger, there was a muzzle flash and a loud bang and Haddad fell into the ditch, blood streaming from a head wound.

The members of the insurgent gang slapped Mahmoud on the back and made their way to two old stolen Toyota pick-ups which were hidden in a nearby olive grove. They would make their way to the border and cross into Palestinian territory using one of the many tunnels which the Israelis had failed to detect. It had been a good day's work. Nine Israeli soldiers killed and one of their best fighters rescued. It would be in the Palestinian newspapers tomorrow.

As the insurgents drove off in a cloud of dust, Haddad recovered consciousness in the ditch. He felt his scalp and found he had a bleeding wound where a bullet had just grazed his skull without penetrating. Just before he had been shot, the Palestinian had quietly told him to fall in the ditch as soon as he heard the gunshot. As it happened the bullet's impact on his scalp had caused him to pass out momentarily. So the Palestinian had spared his life...but why?

CHAPTER 12

REFLECTIONS

25 August 2022, 10:17 hours

Rick cut the engine of his dark grey metallic 2009 Jaguar X-Type automatic estate and opened the driver's door. A fine yellow dust had settled on the paintwork, which was heating up rapidly in the morning sun. That old car had been a good buy, he thought. A powerful three-litre, six-cylinder engine delivering 235 bhp lay under the bonnet. As one of the rare Sovereign variants, it had every conceivable extra, including sat nav, heated seats, front and rear parking sensors and an electrically heated front screen. One of the previous owners had used it to tow his caravan and had not bothered to remove the rear towing hook. Most importantly, it had permanent four-wheel drive which meant it could be driven fast in adverse weather conditions. It was exactly the car Rick needed to execute his plan.

The lock-up was in a rural location, deep in the Kent countryside. Originally a farmer's barn, it had been converted into a secure storage facility for agricultural equipment and then became surplus to requirements. The farm buildings now lay derelict, a victim of the economic crash which had followed the coronavirus pandemic. No-one visited the area. And nobody noticed that the old barn had been kept in good condition, its few windows strengthened with steel bars and its main doors reinforced with metal panels on the inside. The structure had been given a fresh coat of dark brown Butinox wood preservative. It was miles from anywhere and a considerable distance from the nearest CCTV cameras, which Rick knew were at a BP filling station seven miles down the main road. There were no travel surveillance or speed cameras on that section of road either.

Rick reached into the right trouser pocket of his dark green combat trousers and pulled out a set of keys. The barn's main doors were secured by two high-security mortice locks concealed behind moveable wooden flaps, plus two chunky Chubb padlocks. *Just like in a prison*, thought Rick as he swung the doors open.

The barn lacked artificial lighting but enough sunshine streamed through the few barred windows to let Rick see what he was doing. There was hay everywhere, both loose and in bales but Rick knew where his stuff was stored and after a few minutes work he had cleared the hay to reveal four wooden crates, each five feet long. Taking a jemmy from his backpack, Rick prised open the first box.

As an only child, Rick had been left some money and a house when his father had died from non-Hodgkin's lymphoma eleven years before, but one thing that was not mentioned in the legal paperwork about the will was what Rick referred to as the 'Fernscale arms cache.' His father had first started it in the summer of 1982 when he had brought back some captured Argentine weapons from the Falklands. He was looking at some of these munitions right now, which included a Belgian-made 7.62 mm FN-FAL rifle and a 9 mm Browning Hi-Power pistol. There were also three 66 mm LAW one shot anti-tank rocket launchers, various grenades, and a huge quantity of ammunition. Rick had no idea how his father had smuggled all this contraband back to Britain. But with thousands of troops coming back to Britain in the summer of 1982 aboard the *Canberra*, the *Queen Elizabeth* and other vessels, and RAF VC-10 transport aircraft, things tended to get through customs. The Military Police and Customs Officers often turned a blind eye to all this as they knew that such weapons tended to become harmless war trophies on the walls of regimental messes. He had seen a photo of the Stinger launcher used by his father to down an Argentine Pucara on 21 May 1982, which now had pride of place on a wall at the SAS headquarters in Stirling Lines, Hereford. The RAF Regiment had even brought back several 35 mm Oerlikon GDF twin-barrelled anti-aircraft guns, complete with Skyguard radars, which they then used for airfield defence, and he had seen TV news footage of some Argentine Pucaras being transported to the UK as deck cargo. One was even test-flown at Boscombe Down and some were now in museums. So, who was going to bother about a few captured guns, which were nothing more than war trophies?

Rick picked up the heavy FN-FAL rifle and held it up to the light. It was coated in protective grease and wrapped in protective polythene sheeting. Before mothballing it, Rick had stripped it down to its constituent parts, cleaned, oiled, and then reassembled it. After degreasing and further lubrication, it should work perfectly. It was a heavy gun but fired a powerful 7.62 mm cartridge which had far greater stopping power than the 5.56 mm round used in the British Army's current rifle, the SA-80. He remembered that when he had served in Afghanistan in the 2000s, some of his fellow soldiers had wished they had an FN-FAL or its British version, the SLR. In their experience even a few 5.56 mm rounds would often fail to stop a drug-crazed Taliban insurgent. A single 7.62 mm round would stop them in their tracks. Permanently.

Over the years, Rick had added to his arms cache whenever he could, finding more modern weapons from various sources. He had a couple of Heckler and Koch MP5 submachine guns and a futuristic-looking Finnish Jatimatic SMG. His most recent acquisition was a modern Glock 17 pistol. In addition, Rick had a copious supply of plastic explosives, detonators and timers.

Rick had no idea why he had felt compelled to create an arms cache. Perhaps he had a form of OCD. He had read of people who had huge collections of all sorts of things. Empty jamjars, beer mats, manhole covers, vintage comics, sewing machines, toilet seats, old newspapers and so on. Was he any different? There was another factor though. He was following his father's orders. Before he died, his father had told him all about the arms cache and its location.

As his dad handed the keys to Rick, he had whispered his last words into his left ear. 'Here are the keys to the barn, Rick. You know where it is. Look after these weapons. One day you may need them. We live in a sick society where terrorists are allowed to win. But we will hit back, won't we son?'

*

Mahmoud Rashid opened the window of his shabby high-rise council flat in Newham and stared at the London landscape. The view was hazy because of air pollution but he had heard it had been much worse in the 1950s before the introduction of the Clean Air Act. Thousands of Londoners were making their way to work by bus, train and tube. Others chose to walk or use a bicycle. A lot of them were wearing facemasks. He wasn't sure if this was a legacy of the virus pandemic or to counter air pollution.

It was a typical late August day in the capital. About 22 degrees centigrade with a burning sun and patchy cloud. There was that characteristic smell of a London summer. Sweat, diesel fumes, rotting rubbish from punctured black bin bags. Broken glass in the gutters and graffiti spray- painted on walls. Several takeaway restaurants were visible. All were protected by steel shutters and grilles until opening time. Patches of vomit and urine were drying in the hot summer sun. Black FX4 taxis with noisy diesel engines scooted about everywhere.

Mahmoud heard the sound of throttled-back jet engines high above him and looked up to see a twin-engine jet with its gear down orbiting the capital prior to landing at Heathrow Airport. There was always an airliner circling the city during daytime hours. What a juicy target that would make for an SA-7 *Strela* missile! Its infra-red seeker head would home in on the hot engine exhaust and blow the wing off. And, if the aircraft subsequently crashed in Central London, the carnage would be enormous. He wondered why no terrorist group had ever done this.

As he looked at the densely populated metropolis, he felt nostalgia for all the Arab capitals he had visited over the years. Damascus, Beirut, Cairo, Amman. All teeming with people getting on with their lives. He had visited Edgware Road in London many times and when he was in a Lebanese restaurant eating mezze, lamb shawarma, pickles, hummus, spiced rice and flatbread, he could almost believe he was back in the Middle East. Sometimes he would sit outside a restaurant enjoying a smoke from a hooka pipe and re-assessing his life.

So much had happened in the last two decades. After his capture by the Israelis in 2005, and his subsequent escape, he had travelled to Afghanistan to help the Taliban in their fight against British and American imperialism. He had supported the attacks on the Twin Towers and regarded Bin-Laden as the saviour of freedom fighters everywhere. Yes, the struggle with Israel was important but it was really America and Britain that were behind it all. Britain had created the conditions for the establishment of Israel with the hated Balfour Declaration. They had sold it arms. And America was funding Israel and supplying it with the latest weapons. These were the countries he had to hit.

After some years in Afghanistan, he had joined ISIS and had taken part in many battles in Syria and neighbouring countries. He had racked up many kills of Western soldiers and participated in bombings, kidnappings and beheadings of hostages. Then in 2017 he had been invited to become part of a group of international terrorists, now known as *The Seven,* who were planning to attack Western countries who had fought ISIS. Britain and America were top of their hit list.

He had never forgotten his encounter with *Seren* Haddad but he had rationalised what had happened. Haddad must have been a sympathiser to the Palestinian cause all along. A true Israeli would never have treated him with compassion like Haddad had. In reality, Mahmoud was suffering from what psychologists called *cognitive dissonance.* He had certain beliefs about Jews and Israelis and when he was presented with facts which conflicted with these beliefs, he rejected the new information.

He now regarded his sparing of Haddad's life as being a temporary error of judgement which would never be repeated. He had been wounded and traumatized at that time and wasn't thinking straight. But now he would return to his former ruthlessness. No lives would be spared. The British and Americans would find out what it was like to cry over their dead children.

For the past three years he had been working as a waiter in a Lebanese restaurant and had refrained from any terrorist activity. But he was not a changed man. In the parlance of the world of espionage he was a 'sleeper'. Soon he would awaken and carry out his mission. He was going to kill the British Prime Minister!

CHAPTER 13

LOVE ACTUALLY

After years of heartbreak, little Molly was in love with a man who felt the same about her. And Mahmoud loved her the way she was. He didn't care that she was a post-menopausal forty-nine, with broad hips, chunky thighs, bingo wings, cellulite, thick ankles and a protruding stomach. Mahmoud adored her blue eyes, five-foot two inches height, West Country accent and shoulder-length golden hair, although Molly was not a natural blonde, as Mahmoud had already discovered.

It had not always been like that. Twenty-four years earlier, when she lived in Falmouth, she had been married. But it had all gone wrong. Robbie was a young, fit plumber with a lithe body but was rather lacking in the brains department. Still, they had enjoyed a happy marriage for a few years before it went tits up. Robbie couldn't cope with Molly's neurotic traits, her obsession with cleanliness and tidiness and her irrational jealousy. When he was late coming back from work, she assumed he must be seeing another woman. Indeed, Robbie had a few longstanding female friends – *but was he really bonking them behind her back?* Molly feared that he was, despite his denials.

After a few years, their marriage broke up. Then her OCD got worse. Her GP prescribed anxiolytic drugs and referred her to an NHS clinical psychologist but her treatment (if you could call it that) was laughable and ineffective. She was required to keep a diary of her obsessive thoughts and actions, and at every clinic appointment the psychologist would read them aloud and laugh. It was supposed to give her insight into how ridiculous her obsessive thoughts were but they actually made her feel ashamed and humiliated. When she complained about this and how the treatments didn't help, she was told that there was 'no cure' for her condition.

Then one day she read about a former NHS hospital doctor who practised hypnotherapy at a private clinic in Harley Street. He had helped many people who had been deemed 'incurable' by psychologists and psychiatrists. Could he possibly help her?

After just one session, Molly discovered that her OCD had gone. And she also realized that she had developed strong feelings for this doctor. She didn't know it at the time but she had been affected by *transference*, a phenomenon first described by the great psychiatrist Sigmund Freud, in which the patient falls in love with their therapist.

A few months after this life-changing treatment session, Molly learned that the doctor was holding a weekend training session in the techniques he had used to cure her. Could she – a former patient – be allowed to enrol? She worked as an NHS nurse but had always been interested in alternative therapies. No problem, said the doctor. She was a past patient – not a current one – so there were no legal or ethical issues.

A few weeks later, Molly attended the training weekend and found she couldn't keep her eyes off the doctor. He was in his early forties with short, dark, greying hair, Harry Potter-style specs and a little overweight. Hardly a matinee idol, but clearly an honourable man and intellectually brilliant. And he was witty. Then, halfway through the training weekend, the doctor said something that destroyed Molly's hopes. *He mentioned his wife.* Molly felt a knife plunging into her heart. *A wife! He was married! Why didn't he wear a wedding ring? How could he deceive her like this? And was his wife younger, slimmer and better looking than her? Maybe the bitch should die and then he could marry her! How could he do this to her? Did he not realise how many nights she had lain awake, unable to sleep, thinking about him and how they were going to get married one day?* For months she had fantasised about the wedding and the dress she was going to wear. She had chosen the venue and the menu for the wedding breakfast. She had even visited a clairvoyant who had confirmed that he was indeed the man of her dreams and how they would be together one day.

Molly felt a surge of panic rising within her. *OK, he wasn't available right now but maybe things would change in the future.* Over the next few years Molly saw the doctor a few more times for the treatment of various issues including a spider phobia and a fear of clowns. But she still had her jealousy problem. That was something that seemed to be hard-wired and resistant to treatment.

All the same, she used these private hypnotherapy appointments as a way of expressing her feelings for the doctor. In addition to paying his fee, she showered him with presents. Books, DVDs, even a pricey Parker pen set. And then there were the 'Thank You' cards and letters in which she praised his beautiful voice and stated that he was 'very special' to her. He had already accepted her request to be a Facebook friend. *Did that mean he really loved her?*

Then in 2017 she learned through Facebook that he had suffered a severe heart attack. *Maybe this was the opportunity she had been waiting for?* If she could prove to the doctor that she really loved him, that she was the only person in the world who really cared for him, then perhaps he would see sense and leave his wife to be with her.

Molly would never forget the day she visited him. *The day of the great trauma* as she later called it. She drove thirty miles to the hospital where the doctor lay seriously ill after an unsuccessful heart operation. She chose her visiting time very carefully. 1:00 p.m. The patients' lunches would be over but visiting didn't start officially until 2:00 p.m. so there would be no chance of her bumping into his wife. Almost as soon as she entered the room, she blurted out the words she had been wanting to say to him for years:

'I've been in love with you for the past eleven years!'

Molly would never forget the look of horror on the doctor's face. *That was not supposed to happen!* Then he delivered a withering put-down, a sentence so crushing that Molly would replay it over and over in her head for years to come:

'I'm never going to leave my wife, I have no feelings for you and I think you should go now, Molly.'

Molly drove home in her red Ford Fiesta – considerably over the speed limit – with tears streaming down her cheeks. *How could he say these things? Did he not realise that she was the only person in the world who truly cared for him?* She had bought him presents and sent him cards. *Surely that would make him love her?*

Like many people who were in the grip of unrequited love, Molly was deluded and believed that this doctor must really love her too. *It was just that he didn't want to say.* So she would give him one last chance.

The following night, after three glasses of red wine, she felt she had enough Dutch courage to do what was required. She rang the Cardiology ward at 9:45 p.m. on the phone line which was reserved for patients. The on-duty charge nurse answered the call and took the cordless phone through to the doctor's room.

'A call for you,' said the nurse.

The doctor took off his oxygen mask and accepted the phone.

'Hello!'

'I don't usually throw myself at married men!' said Molly, her speech slurred with alcohol.

'I don't want to speak to you,' said the doctor, before pressing the red 'end call' button.

On the other end of the line, Molly burst into tears. Her whole world had collapsed around her. As she glugged down the rest of the wine, she wondered what she should do. *How could he do this to her?* Perhaps she should slit her wrists or take an overdose of the anti-depressants her GP had prescribed? For a few hours Molly cried so much she used up two whole boxes of Kleenex. Then she came to a decision. She would resign herself to living alone. No more men. No more relationships. She would live by herself in her tiny flat in Lambeth with her two cats and concentrate on her job. After all, as the saying went, 'A woman needs a man like a fish needs a bicycle.'

As her tears dried, Molly put on a CD of *The Carpenter's Greatest Hits* and selected the track *Goodbye to Love*. The lyrics seemed so relevant to her current situation:

I'll say goodbye to love
No one ever cared if I should live or die
Time and time again the chance of love has passed me by
And all I know of love
Is how to live without it
I just can't seem to find it

*

But all that is behind me now, thought Molly as she sat in a coffee shop in Edgware Road. Five years had passed since the 'great trauma.' And now her life was wonderful, thanks to Mahmoud. It had all started a few months earlier when she had lunch in a Lebanese restaurant just a couple of blocks from where she was sitting now. Her dining companion was her old friend Penny, a fellow NHS nurse with short dark hair and blue eyes whom she had trained with, thirty years earlier. Unlike Molly she was fit, with a stunning figure and long, slim legs. Molly had only wanted a cheap sandwich meal in *Pret a Manger* but Penny had suggested a good Lebanese eatery which did the best lamb shawarma in London.

It was a sweltering summer day in London but the restaurant was cool thanks to several ceiling-mounted fans. Many of the eateries in the capital were grubby, but this one was spotless, its marble floor mopped daily. There was a smell of flowers, wax furniture polish and Middle Eastern spices. Outside the restaurant several middle-aged Arab men smoked hookah pipes and quaffed glasses of hot mint tea as they read Middle Eastern newspapers.

Molly chose lamb shawarma with spiced rice, pickles and flatbread, while Penny had *soujok*, a particularly delicious Lebanese sausage which was served with tabbouleh and fried potatoes. No alcoholic drinks were available, as was the norm in most Middle Eastern restaurants, so the pair washed down their meal with delicious fruit juices which were freshly made on the premises.

As the two women finished their meal by quaffing glasses of hot cinnamon tea served with complementary *baklava*, Penny related amusing tales of what her husband Richard got up to in his spare time, his various DIY disasters, how her two kids were doing and how they were all going on holiday to Benidorm the following week.

But it was the waiter serving them who really caught Molly's eye. About forty years old, but in great physical condition with healthy dark skin, brown eyes, a flat stomach, slim waist, and toned arms with bulging biceps. Black shiny hair which was slicked back, a thin well-trimmed beard and perfect white teeth. And a lovely natural body smell mixed with soap and a little cologne.

'Anything else I can get you two beautiful ladies?' said Mahmoud as he clutched his little note pad and pencil.

'Just the bill please,' said Penny. As both women retrieved their purses, Mahmoud spotted NHS identity badges on lanyards in both handbags.

Molly giggled and blushed. It was a long time since a man had given her a compliment. But although Mahmoud had served both of them, it was her that he was most interested in. Every time he delivered another delicious course to the table, he would make eye contact with Molly and 'accidentally' brush against her. Molly felt a frisson of excitement. She was sure there was a bulge in his crotch. Did he really fancy her? She was forty-nine years old. He was much younger, but she knew that a lot of Middle Eastern and Turkish men had married British women who were in their forties, fifties and even sixties as they found them 'beautiful.' According to some cynical British newspapers it was really their bank balances and credit cards that they found 'beautiful.' But Molly's heart was overruling her head.

Mahmoud brought the bill to the table along with two small cards which the two ladies could complete with their ratings of the restaurant, including the quality of the food and the service. They were also invited to put down their email addresses so the restaurant could send them details of special offers, although this section was optional, for data protection reasons. Penny declined to complete this part in case she got a lot of spam but Molly was quite happy to do this and she observed a twinkle in Mahmoud's eyes as he picked up the cards.

The two women said goodbye with mutual pecks on the cheeks and then Molly went shopping in Oxford Street. Two hours later, as she was standing outside Marble Arch Tube station, she checked her Samsung smartphone and discovered that she had an email from that charming waiter whom she now learned was called Mahmoud. He wondered if she would like to meet him for dinner in a couple of days in a little Italian restaurant which was close to Kensington High

Street Underground Station? Molly replied 'Yes' and said she would contact him again later when she got back to her flat.

*

Two days later Molly was sitting in the *Rimini* restaurant waiting for Mahmoud to arrive. She consulted her watch. It was three minutes to eight. Mahmoud should be here any minute.

She had spent the last two days fretting over what she should wear for this crucial first date. Eventually she had opted for a long, loose-fitting black dress which concealed her protruding stomach and ample hips. Her chunky calves were covered with fishnet tights and she wore high-heeled black shoes. Her face was well made-up with foundation, false lashes and bright red lipstick. Not too shabby for a woman of forty-nine, she thought.

At exactly eight o'clock, Mahmoud entered the restaurant carrying a bunch of red roses. Molly felt her heart race as he approached the table. God, he was so handsome. So much better looking than British men of the same vintage who tended to be fat and bald with bad teeth and halitosis. Mahmoud handed her the roses and kissed her on her left cheek.

'You look so beautiful tonight, Molly.'

Mahmoud wore an expensive dark grey Italian suit with a white, open-necked silk shirt and highly-polished black Gucci shoes. He smelled of expensive cologne.

Mahmoud drank only mineral water that evening but was quite happy for Molly to enjoy a bottle of Chianti. To start, Mahmoud had a bowl of minestrone soup while Molly had bruschetta. For mains Molly chose lasagne and Mahmoud had spaghetti carbonara with a side-salad. To finish, they both had the restaurant's highly-acclaimed home-made ice cream with chocolate sauce and wafers followed by café lattes. After all, everyone knew that Italians made the best ice cream and coffee in the world.

Over dinner Molly learned more about Mahmoud. Before he had been born, his family had lived in Tripoli. Then they had moved to Morocco in 1970 after Colonel Gaddafi came to power. His father, Anwar, owned a large hotel in Tangier so the family was rich. Mahmoud himself was studying at the London School of Economics and only worked as a waiter at the restaurant part-time to supplement his income. But he didn't really need the money because his father gave him a generous allowance. He loved the British and didn't mind the Americans either. And his views on Middle Eastern politics seemed moderate. He felt that all the region's problems should be sorted out with negotiations rather than military action. And he accepted that Israel had a right to exist and the Palestinians should accept the best deal that was available.

Molly was relieved because she was concerned that Mahmoud might only be interested in her for reasons of financial security. She had read horror stories in the press about middle-aged British women who had fallen for young men while on holiday in places like Egypt and Turkey. They had subsequently married them and then everything had gone wrong. But that didn't appear to be the case with Mahmoud. He was genuinely solvent and didn't need her money.

Mahmoud also seemed very interested in her. He asked her everything about her job and Molly explained that she worked in a surgical ward at St Thomas's hospital. She was particularly knowledgeable about the post-operative care of patients who had undergone abdominal surgery.

He also praised her looks, saying he liked mature women with fuller figures, not the brainless mini-skirted stick insects he had seen in nightclubs.

'You have the most beautiful blue eyes I have ever seen, Molly.

And your lips look very kissable.'

Molly smiled and blushed. *Was this really happening to her?* Or was she really dreaming? Was she going to wake up any moment and find herself back in her tiny flat with only her cats for company?

At 10:07 p.m. the waiter brought the bill. Mahmoud insisted on paying and added a £20 tip.

'And what would you like to do now, my beautiful Molly? The night is still young. We could go to a nightclub in the West End…or alternatively we could go somewhere where we can have some private time together, if you know what I mean.'

Molly' s pupils dilated and she blushed. 'You mean go back to your flat?'

'Oh, that is some distance from here, but I have something even better in mind. You see I took the liberty of booking a luxury suite at the Dorchester Hotel. It is only about ten minutes by cab from here. You will probably have heard of the Dorchester. It is frequented by celebrities and is very plush. As I speak, a bottle of Dom Perrier champagne is sitting in an ice bucket in the room. And I have pre-ordered a room service breakfast. That is right Molly, I want to make love to you tonight. And that is what I have always wanted since I first saw you in the restaurant.'

Molly's heart raced. She had never been propositioned like this on a first date. What kind of woman did he think she was? Yet she couldn't resist. Despite being an overweight, menopausal woman of forty-nine, she was about to go to bed with a younger man who could get anyone he wanted. *She would go for it!*

'Very well, I accept your proposal. But first I need to powder my nose. Excuse me a moment.'

Molly headed off to the ladies' toilet while Mahmoud reached into his right jacket pocket and pulled out a circular pill box containing a single light blue tablet. It was Sildenafil, better known as Viagra. It would take an hour to work so he would have to chat with Molly for a while once they got to the hotel room. A combination of the drug and thinking about the porn he had viewed earlier on the internet should fire up his engine. He was delighted at how easy it had been to fool Molly about how he actually felt about her. Did that fat English bitch really think he was genuinely interested in her? *She was going to be just a small part of a very large jigsaw and by the time she realised it, it would be too late!*

CHAPTER 14

THE NIGHT BEFORE

Molly awoke after seven hours of deep, refreshing sleep. All around her was darkness with just a thin line of light beneath the thick blackout curtains. The only noise was the faint hum of air conditioning. Her body was relaxed and she felt more content than she had been in years. There was still wetness inside her and in an instant she remembered what had happened the night before. *The Night Before!* Wasn't that a song by the Beatles? She smiled as she realised that one night of smouldering passion had eradicated all her insecurities.

After they had gone back to Mahmoud's suite at the Dorchester, the wiry Arab had served her a couple of glasses of ice cold champagne while he stuck to chilled fresh orange juice. As they sat on a comfy settee, they talked about life in London. Molly had told Mahmoud about her job as a Charge Nurse at St Thomas's Hospital. Her specialty was post-operative care of patients who had undergone general surgery, particularly abdominal operations. Mahmoud asked her a few questions about this and then chatted about his idyllic life in Morocco, where the sun shone almost every day, even in winter.

'Maybe one day when I have finished my studies at the London School of Economics you could come back to Morocco with me, beautiful Molly? There are plenty of jobs for experienced nurses or, if you prefer, you could become a lady of leisure. My father is wealthy and drives a Bentley. He has a huge house with servants to take care of all his needs. We could live in a beach-front villa, swim in the warm Mediterranean every day and enjoy the delicious local cuisine.'

Molly blushed. She had never known a man who was so forward on a first date. Making plans for their future together when they had only just met. *Yet somehow it all seemed so exciting. A dark, mysterious stranger from a foreign country who clearly wanted her like no man ever had.* Molly just couldn't resist his charms. And he always smelled so divine with fresh breath and a lovely natural body scent, mingled with expensive cologne. No, Mahmoud would never have BO or halitosis.

A moment later, Mahmoud leaned over and planted a kiss firmly on her lips. She could feel his tongue searching inside her mouth. Molly's body responded instantly for the first time in years. Then after a minute, Mahmoud ended their first kiss and smiled at her, his lips still wet from her saliva, his teeth gleaming.

'I want you now Molly. I cannot wait a moment longer.'

Using his great physical strength, Mahmoud carried Molly from the lounge to the bedroom, laid her gently on the king-sized bed and undressed her slowly. Molly didn't resist as she was enjoying every moment of this romantic adventure. No British man she had ever known had wanted her with such passion. Mahmoud unzipped her dress, pulled it off and placed it on a seat. Then he unclipped her bra, pulled off her tights and dragged off her huge Bridget Jones-style knickers. Molly would have preferred to have worn a thong, but her arse was too big for such a garment.

Then, as Molly lay naked on the bed, with Mahmoud lying beside her, she unbuttoned his Italian white silk shirt, unfastened his black leather belt and pulled off his trousers. His torso was firm and muscular with six-pack abs, his biceps bulging. He also sported a few scars. Some day she would ask him how he had got them. Then

Mahmoud was inside her, stretching and stimulating her like no man had ever done before. For the first time in years she felt truly loved and wanted.

And Mahmoud could keep going for hours, using his tongue, his penis and his fingers to satisfy her again and again. He seemed oblivious to her fat, cellulite and stretch marks, and kept telling her how beautiful she was and how she had the bluest eyes he had ever seen. Finally, at 1:15 a.m., exhausted by their passionate lovemaking, they both fell asleep in each other's arms.

*

All that was now a pleasant memory as Molly lay between fresh Egyptian cotton sheets in the comfort of the king size bed at the Dorchester. It was a brilliant late summer's morning outside but barely a chink of light got through the thick blackout curtains. She reached out her hand to touch her lover's hair on the adjacent pillow and realised he was not there. *Oh no, he was gone! Had he left her? Was he married? It was all too good to be true! Or had it all been a dream?*

Molly sat up in bed and saw some light beneath the door. She could hear the faint sound of someone speaking in Arabic in the adjacent lounge. It was Mahmoud. *Of course, he was next door!* Molly switched on the brass bedside lamp, put on a white cotton towelling bathrobe which hung in the bathroom, and gently opened the door to the lounge.

Mahmoud stood with his back to her, wearing a white dressing gown, holding what looked like some kind of mobile phone. But it was larger and chunkier than any she had ever seen, like one of the early brick-sized mobiles that had first appeared in the mid-eighties. And it had a long antenna, which projected from the top.

Molly couldn't hear everything that was being said but she did catch a few words *'qatal rais al-wazra'*. She had no idea what that meant.

Mahmoud turned round and greeted her with a flash of white teeth. If anything, his early morning stubble made him more handsome.

'Good morning my love. You slept well I hope?'

'I did, thanks to you. But who were you speaking to? And what is that device? It doesn't look like an ordinary mobile phone.'

'It's a satellite phone, my darling. Very expensive. A present from my father. It can be used anywhere in the world even if there is no mobile phone mast in the vicinity. In fact, I was just phoning my family in Morocco.'

'Morocco? Is there something wrong?'

'Not at all, my love. But I need to have some surgery carried out very soon. Don't worry, it is not cancer or anything like that. It is what doctors and nurses call an elective procedure. You see I have some problems with my gallbladder and I need to have it removed. I think the procedure is known as a cholecystectomy. A routine operation with a very high success rate and little risk.'

'So how soon is this and where are you getting this operation done? Are you going to be admitted to St Thomas's?'

'No, much as I would like to be treated in the hospital where my beloved works, my father has arranged for me to be admitted to a private hospital here in London. He will be paying the bill. I expect to be in hospital for no more than a week. The stitches will have to be taken out after ten days but that will be done at the outpatient clinic.'

Molly's brow furrowed with anxiety.

'Oh my darling, I had no idea you had health problems. Let me make a suggestion. Once you have been discharged from hospital you can stay at my flat. I can sleep on the folding Z-bed and you can have my double bed. I will take care of you, cook for you and help you to wash. And I can take out your stitches. You will recover much quicker with my help.'

'But my family have already offered to fly over from Morocco to help with my recuperation.'

'But I insist, Mahmoud. No disrespect to your family but I am a highly trained specialist nurse and I know how to look after someone who has had abdominal surgery. You will be in safe hands.'

'Very well, I accept your offer. We can discuss the details later. But first we must eat. Our room service breakfast arrived just before I made the phone call.'

Mahmoud pointed to a mahogany trolley with brass wheels which was standing in the corner of the room. It was piled high with gleaming white crockery, a glass jug of orange juice and an aluminium coffee pot.

'Smoked salmon and scrambled eggs for two. Brown toast. Butter. Marmalade. Jam. Freshly squeezed orange juice. A selection of fresh fruit and a pot of coffee. Will you join me?'

The smell of the fresh coffee was divine. Molly felt her stomach gurgling and realised how hungry she was after the previous night's exertions.

'Of course I will, my darling. It's not often that I have a cooked breakfast.'

British Army Monitoring Station

Troodos Mountains, Cyprus

Sergeant Ben Andrews saved a copy of the mystery signal to the hard disc of his computer and then turned to his superior officer, Major Harry Calman.

'It's an encrypted satellite transmission all right, Major…sent as a compressed GMR-2 file in less than a second. I will send it through to GCHQ for decrypting and translation. It was too brief to get an accurate triangulation but we believe it originated from somewhere in London.'

'London,' said Major Calman as he sipped a glass of iced tea, glad that this facility had effective air conditioning and was located in the cooler mountains of Cyprus.

'There have been a few of these transmissions in the last few weeks. And then there was that drone attack in London. Better inform the CIA at Langley in addition to MI5 and MI6. We don't want our American friends to be left out of the loop. I have a funny feeling that something is going to happen soon and it isn't going to be pleasant!'

Atlas Private Hospital, Edgware Road, London

9 September 2022

'This is the first time I have been asked to carry out an operation on a fit, healthy man, which will result in his death,' said Consultant Surgeon Mr Anwar, as he scribbled with his silver Parker fountain pen in Mahmoud's case notes. 'It goes against all known medical ethics and the well-known Hippocratic Oath. If the General Medical Council were to find out, then I would be struck off. And there would be a criminal prosecution as well.'

'I know,' said Mahmoud as he buttoned his shirt and knotted his tie. 'Your dedication to our cause is admirable. And I am sure the $2 million fee you will receive will make it all seem worthwhile. And just remember that if you renege on our agreement then we will make sure the Mossad are tipped off about your role in this operation.'

Anwar shuddered. Even a brief mention of Israel's lethally

effective security service sent a shiver down his spine. The Mossad had killed many of Israel's enemies in various countries around the world with little concern for diplomatic repercussions. If Mahmoud had intended to frighten him then he had certainly succeeded. So he had no option other than to go ahead with the procedure.

Anwar knew exactly what was going to happen. In just a few days time Mahmoud would come back to the clinic and be given a general anaesthetic. While he was unconscious, a standard laparotomy incision would be made in his abdomen, allowing the removal of his entire spleen and part of his liver. After cauterizing all the bleeding blood vessels with diathermy, two powerful plastic explosive charges studded with steel ball bearings – and installed inside non-immunogenic silicon pouches – would be placed in the cavities created by surgery and fitted with electrically-operated detonators connected to a long-life battery. A tiny two-pin socket would be implanted over Mahmoud's breastbone and a press switch would be mounted beneath the skin in the xiphisternum, the small depression at the lower end of the sternum. To arm the firing circuit, Mahmoud would have to insert a plug into the two-pin socket and then detonate the bomb by pushing his fingers hard into the depression over the xiphisternum. The blast would rip his body to pieces and anyone within twenty-five feet would suffer fatal injuries. The armoured windscreen of the Prime Minister's car would be easily penetrated by such a powerful charge.

'It' s a brilliant system,' said Anwar. 'I can only admire the ISIS scientist who invented it. The ultimate suicide bomb. The problem with backpacks and suicide vests is that they are bulky and easily spotted. But with this new type of bomb, the explosive is carried inside the human body and thus impossible to detect. All you have to do is arm the circuit, spread-eagle yourself on the windscreen of the target vehicle and then press the firing switch. The most important thing is to move fast and act quickly before a marksman can get you. You can really only be stopped by a head shot. A bullet hitting the abdomen will activate a trembler switch which will set off the bomb. The switch can also be activated by a high voltage electric current going through the body, even without the two-pin plug in place. When this thing goes off, ball bearings will fly in every direction. We estimate it will kill everyone within a twenty-five-yard radius. The British Prime Minister will be only three or four feet away when it detonates, so he won't stand a chance.'

'It will be a glorious martyr's death for me,' said Mahmoud. 'And well worth the sacrifice to kill the leader of a country which has long supported the illegal Zionist State of Israel.'

'Indeed,' said Anwar. 'And it is pioneering surgery as well. For decades, doctors have suggested that artificial organs might be created and implanted inside the body. For example, in the future there could be an artificial pancreas to cure diabetes and a mechanical heart which might make cardiac transplants redundant. But this is the first time in history that a bomb has been placed inside the human abdominal cavity. You will be remembered forever as a martyr. And once you reach Paradise, the seventy-two virgins will be waiting for you.'

'Are there likely to be any side-effects of the surgery?' asked Mahmoud.

'That's a good question. As your spleen is being removed to create space for one of the two explosive charges, you will have to take penicillin every day to prevent bacterial infection. You will also have a painful abdominal wound which will need to be looked after very carefully. In the long-term there is a risk of post-operative adhesions developing and that is why we recommend that you carry out the attack two to three weeks after the surgery. Any longer than that and there is a risk of complications developing.'

'Don't be concerned. I have already picked a date. The British Prime Minister's days are numbered and there is nothing anyone can do about it! To quote President Franklin D. Roosevelt, it is a date that will live in infamy!'

CHAPTER 15

PREPARATIONS FOR BATTLE

29 August 2022, 08:01 hours

22 SAS Barracks, Stirling Lines, Hereford

Nothing tastes as good as real coffee first thing in the morning, thought Captain Andy Harrington as he sipped an Americano from his white china mug and contemplated another cup from the Bosch Tassimo machine. The recent heatwave had ended with a violent thunderstorm. Outside the rain-streaked window, a dozen SAS soldiers wearing sodden DPM camo battledress and black woollen hats jogged round the grounds carrying Bergens filled with stones. Heavy rain pattered off a line of olive green DAF trucks and long-wheelbase Land Rovers. But it wasn't the weather outside which occupied Harrington's attention. Instead, it was the display of photos and other memorabilia – commemorating the history of the regiment – mounted on the wall around the fireplace.

There was a gilt-framed sepia photo of the founder of the regiment, Colonel David Stirling, in full dress uniform, and another of him sitting in a jeep in the Libyan desert with sand goggles pushed up his forehead. The SAS had been the first British Army unit to receive this versatile American four-wheel drive vehicle in June 1942, and mechanics had modified it for desert conditions. Some of the bodywork in front of the radiator had been cut away to increase airflow around the engine and a simple coolant recycling system – consisting of a rubber hose and a condenser can filled with water – had been installed, as had a Bagnall sun compass.

Machine guns – twin Vickers K 0.303s and one heavy American M2 fifty-calibre weapon – had also been installed, giving the vehicles awesome firepower against parked aircraft. Harrington knew that at one point in 1942 the SAS was destroying more enemy aircraft than the RAF's Desert Air Force. The vehicle was heavily laden with jerrycans of petrol and water, leaving little room for the occupants.

There was also a photo of a bearded, tough-looking officer wearing a *keffiyeh*. It was none other than the legendary Major Blair 'Paddy' Mayne. There was a rumour that he had participated in a couple of classified missions during the war. And the next faded photo was supposed to have been taken during one of these very operations. It showed Mayne standing beside a stripped-down Chevrolet patrol truck, as used by the Long Range Desert Group. There was also a young RAMC officer beside Mayne. He had a thin moustache and slightly bandy legs. Looked a bit like Peter Sellers. And in the background was a British tank which Harrington recognised as a Valentine. But it was like no other Valentine Harrington had ever seen as it had a big turret and a largish gun which Harrington estimated was a 75 mm. He was interested in the history of armoured vehicles and knew that the Valentine started with a two -pounder 40 mm QF gun, was then upgraded to a six-pounder 57 mm, and was finally fitted with a 75 mm in the Mark XI version in 1943. Yet this photo was dated June 1942. What was a Valentine doing with a 75 mm in 1942? When he got time, he must email a scan of the photo to his old mate David Fletcher of the Bovington Tank Museum and get his opinion.

Harrington's gaze then moved over to another set of photos which depicted the regiment's post-war successes in places like Northern Ireland, Iraq and the Falklands. There was a photo purchased from the Press Association which showed three SAS troopers in black combat suits and respirators on the balcony of the Iranian Embassy in Princes Gardens, Kensington, in 1980. The success of that operation had inspired the 1982 Lewis Collins movie *Who Dares Wins*. Hamilton knew that Collins had wanted to join the SAS at one point but had been rejected as he was too well-known.

Another photo depicted several burnt-out Argentine propeller-driven aircraft on a windswept grass airfield. A second Falklands snap showed a grinning, unshaven SAS trooper wearing standard British Army DPM camo battledress in front of a couple of wrecked Argentine Pucaras. One was missing a canopy. The other had collapsed on its nose, its fuselage riddled with cluster bomb fragments. The caption revealed that this photo had been taken at Port Stanley airfield on 15 June 1982, the day after the Argentine surrender. He knew the identity of the soldier in the photo. It was Jack Fernscale, who had become a legend in the SAS when he had downed an Argentine Pucara on 21 May 1982. And right in the centre of the display – mounted on brackets – was the Stinger launcher that Jack had used that day. Someone had painted the small white silhouette of a Pucara on the side to indicate a single kill and it had obviously been dusted regularly. Jack Fernscale. What a guy! And his son Rick was a great soldier too. A colleague had once described him as 'the best sergeant in the best regiment in the best army… in the world. Period.' What a pity he had retired from the SAS three years ago. The regiment could do with him right now as the country was facing a new terrorist threat.

'Captain Harrington. Colonel Stewart will see you now!'

Harrington turned round to see another SAS captain (or 'Rupert' as they were known in the SAS) holding a sheaf of papers. He was wearing a green wool army pullover with fabric patches on the shoulders and elbows, combat trousers, a blue Sam Browne belt and a beige beret complete with the famous 'winged dagger' SAS badge which had been designed by David Stirling himself in 1941.

'Follow me, Captain. The Colonel apologizes for keeping you waiting. He was on the phone to the Metropolitan Police. Big flap on at the moment in the capital as you know.'

Colonel Stewart's small office was packed with filing cabinets and smelled of wood and Pledge furniture polish. On one wall was a large, specially commissioned painting by a well-known aviation artist depicting an RAF C-130 Hercules aircraft discharging two open Land Rovers packed with SAS troopers from its rear loading ramp during *Operation Mikado*, the night-time suicide attack on the Argentine airbase at Rio Grande, Tierra del Fuego, in 1982, which was planned but never executed. The painting depicted considerable action. Each Land Rover mounted a single Milan anti-tank guided missile launcher and two 7.62 mm general purpose machine guns. Tracer rounds crisscrossed the night sky. Three Argentine Dassault Super Etendard strike aircraft burned fiercely in the background after being riddled with hundreds of bullets and wrecked by multiple anti-tank missiles

The Colonel seemed engrossed in his laptop as Harrington entered and then gazed at him over the top of the machine's screen.

'Sit down, Captain. I have news for you. The PM has ordered 22 Regiment SAS to relocate to Central London ASAP. We've received a tip off from MI5 that a terrorist attack is imminent. Our monitoring station in Cyprus picked up an encrypted signal which was decoded by GCHQ. I want your men in London within twenty-four hours. We've arranged accommodation at some army barracks in the capital.

We'll be taking our sniper teams with us, plus our latest surveillance drones. I also want preparations to be made for resolving possible hostage situations.'

'Very good sir. The government must know they can always rely on the SAS. As Paddy Mayne once said: 'Most problems can be sorted with high explosive.''

'Excellent quote, Captain. Tell your men to pack their Bergens and await transport. You'll be leaving at 11:00 hours. That's all for now. I'll keep you updated.'

*

Rick lay on his bed in his flat near the South Bank in Central London, still damp from his shower, with his towel round his waist. He had completed his daily thirty-mile bike ride plus a muscle-building routine. His Jaguar X-Type estate (plus weapons and equipment) was safely stored in two adjacent lockups at the rear of the block of flats. He had moved everything from the barn three days earlier, arriving at the flats at 4:00 a.m. when few people were around. For additional security he had concealed all his weapons in tarpaulins and sprayed graffiti over the lens of the CCTV camera which covered the rear of the property.

All he had to do now was wait until the terrorist group, *The Seven,* made an attack and he would respond. And there lay the weakness in his plan. He had no access to any intelligence about the gang. He had no idea what any of them looked like or where they were going to strike. So how could he wipe them out? All he had was a burning desire for revenge, to make these evil people pay for Laura's death, not once but many times over. And it was that which gave him the drive to get up every morning. No, he was sure that if he fixed this great desire in his mind then an opportunity would present itself. *It was just a matter of time.*

ATLAS Private Hospital, Edgware Road, London

12 September 2022

Mahmoud sat up in bed as Anwar listened to the back of his chest with his Littman stethoscope.

'Well, your chest sounds completely clear. And your abdominal wound is healing nicely. You are now eight days post-op so I think you could get home tomorrow. What's his urine output like, nurse?'

'Good,' replied the Lebanese staff nurse. 'Urine testing is normal and bloods taken yesterday show a haemoglobin level of 13.0 with no leucocytosis. Normal Us and Es and LFTs. Mahmoud is also eating and drinking normally.'

'Excellent,' said Anwar. 'In that case you can go home tomorrow. Take it easy for the next week. Gradual mobilisation. Stitches out in six days. You can perhaps start a little walking every day in a couple of days. I understand someone with nursing qualifications will be looking after you for the next couple of weeks?'

'Yes, that is correct.'

'Good. And I take it that the balance of my fee will be paid to me now?'

'Of course it will. Paid directly into your Swiss bank account. Your support for our cause will not be forgotten. I am now on the road to becoming a martyr for our cause and for that I will be eternally grateful. You will be reading about my heroic mission in the papers before too long.'

Lambeth, near the South Bank, London

27 September 2022, 06:27 hours

Molly pulled her enormous knickers over her huge arse, slipped on a bra and donned her blue uniform consisting of baggy trousers and a loose top. Earlier in her nursing career she had worn a traditional nurse's dress but these had now been phased out in favour of more practical, loose-fitting clothing similar to theatre scrubs. The modern outfits were also more flattering to her fuller figure.

On the double bed near to her, Mahmoud was still sleeping. He didn't snore and slept very deeply. She remembered that night at the Dorchester when he kept going all night, satisfying her again and again. What a stud he was! A British man of the same age would have come after two minutes, and then rolled over onto his fat belly and snored all night, keeping her awake.

Mahmoud's laparotomy wound had healed quickly. But why was it so long? Molly understood that cholecystectomies were usually done by keyhole surgery these days, resulting in a small wound which healed rapidly. And why had he been prescribed long-term penicillin tablets?

'I have to take these for the rest of my life, Molly. They stop me from getting sick,' he had said. She had wondered about this. The only patients she knew of who were required to take penicillin every day were those who had undergone a splenectomy, which was usually carried out if the spleen was damaged in an accident. Perhaps the doctors at the private hospital had their own protocols for post-operative medication which she was unaware of.

Molly put on her flat-heeled black shoes, grabbed her bag and let herself out of the flat to begin her early shift at St Thomas's Hospital. Mahmoud's eyes opened. Good, she was gone. After a quick breakfast of coffee and buttered toast, he would phone Khalid and get the latest update on the Prime Minister's movements. *Soon that evil man would be dead and the world would be a different place! There would be celebrations across the Middle East. It would be the start of a New World Order!*

CHAPTER 16

DEATH WISH

2 September 2022

Rick munched a slice of buttered wholemeal toast with peanut butter and sipped his third cup of milky coffee as he contemplated his problem. He had little information about *The Seven* and no idea where to find them. In his SAS days he would have had a 'Chinese Parliament' of several soldiers who would pool ideas, but that was not possible now. He was on his own. He didn't even have Laura any more. Perhaps he should go for a walk, get some fresh air and then something might occur to him? He knew many people got their best ideas when they exercised.

Rick let himself out of the flat, bounded down two flights of stairs, and stepped out into the street, heading northwest along Waterloo Road towards the Thames. It was cooler now as summer turned to autumn and the sun was less intense. Just as well he'd slipped a dark blue fleece over his white T-shirt, jeans and trainers. That particular fleece was one of his favourites and he had fitted two large square pockets inside – secured with Velcro strips – so he could carry his smartphone and wallet with ease.

Rick's route took him just north of Waterloo Station and he chuckled as he remembered how the French President Charles De Gaulle had baulked at having to pass through that transport hub on his way to Winston Churchill's funeral in 1965. *Waterloo*. That name had a lot of negative connotations to any patriotic Frenchman and he wondered how Abba had managed to sweep the board at the Eurovision Song Contest in April 1974 with a song with that very title. Did they get any French votes?

Rick negotiated Tenison Way – which surrounded the IMAX cinema near the National Film Theatre – and headed west towards Waterloo Bridge. Rick didn't cross the Thames but instead descended a set of concrete steps which took him to the river walkway that led south west past the London Eye, the huge Ferris wheel near County Hall which had proved massively popular with tourists. Hundreds of people were taking advantage of the good weather to walk or cycle, or just sit on benches and enjoy the view of the river. Rick bought a plastic pot of steaming hot sweetcorn from a stall and continued his walk.

His plan was to continue on the South Bank for another couple of miles and then cross the river at one of the many bridges, head back on the other side and then return to his flat via Waterloo Bridge. It was a round trip of five miles which would take him about eighty minutes at a fast pace. As he looked down, he noticed that that his left trainer lace was undone. How many times had his SAS instructors told him to tie a double knot? Having your laces come undone during a fight could cause you to trip, or worse.

There was an empty wooden bench to his left so he sat down for a moment to secure his laces with an approved army knot. Rick was just about to restart his journey when a man of Middle Eastern appearance walked past, heading towards Westminster Bridge. Rick sized him up. Estimated age: forty. About six foot tall, 170 pounds, medium-build with a slim waist and well-toned biceps. Dark hair and olive skin. Thin beard. Clearly a fit-looking specimen. Yellow T-shirt, blue jeans and white trainers. But there was something else. *He looked familiar. He had seen him before. But where?*

Rick recalled 'selection,' when he had first applied to join the SAS. It was one of the most gruelling experiences of his life. Several days in the freezing winter cold of the Brecon Beacons, while wearing a WW2 greatcoat and battledress as a hunter group of paras searched for him was one of the hardest experiences of his life. Most people got caught eventually and were forced to undergo a humiliating mock torture session in which they were stripped naked and taunted about the size of their penis by a female officer. No food. No water. No sleep. Lots of slaps and kicks. And a cloth hood would be placed over his head while he was forced to stand in a stress position with legs apart and both hands flat against a wall. Most people found this very uncomfortable though more experienced SAS soldiers had learned to sleep in this position.

But there was another part of the training which was not so widely known. You would be woken up after just two hours in bed and shown a monochrome film about something boring like flower arranging. Then you would have to answer a number of detailed questions about the film even though you were dead tired and craving sleep. If you didn't get the answers right you would be rejected and sent back to your unit because a very important part of being an SAS trooper was the ability to remember even the smallest of details, sometimes for years.

Yes, he had definitely seen that man before. But where? Northern Ireland? Unlikely. Iraq? No, he didn't think it was Iraq. Syria? Sierra Leone? Afghanistan? Yes, it was Afghanistan. He couldn't remember the exact date but it was in the mid-to-late 2000s when the regiment had been deployed in Helmand Province. One day, two troopers had brought in a young insurgent who had been captured. What was his name? The young man had refused to talk but he had been fingerprinted and a name had come up on the MI6 database back in London.

Mohammed something. Mohammed Rashid. No, it was Mahmoud. *Mahmoud Rashid*. That was it! *Mahmoud Rashid*. Once his identity was known, it was clear that they had captured someone of importance. The Yanks wanted to speak to him and so did the Israelis. A compact one-person cell at Camp X-Ray beckoned, complete with orange jump suit and shackles.

A USAF C-17 Globemaster rendition flight was leaving from Kabul the following day and Mahmoud was going to be on it. Unfortunately, he escaped by overpowering his guards and jumping off the truck taking him to Kabul airbase. Hundreds of troops were brought in to search for the missing prisoner. Helicopters and drones scanned the ground, but Mahmoud was never seen again. The consensus of opinion was that he had escaped over the border into Pakistan.

But what was he doing in London all these years later? It was obvious that he was up to no good. With his background, he obviously wasn't collecting for the Red Cross! Rick made a snap decision to follow him and see what he was up to. After tossing his partly-eaten pot of sweetcorn into a bin, Rick set off in hot pursuit at a brisk pace.

Mahmoud was only wearing a T-shirt, jeans and trainers. No rucksack and no suicide belt so he wasn't carrying a bomb. No obvious firearm either, although he could have a weapon under his trouser leg, attached to his calf. Rick closed the distance and then kept ten yards behind Mahmoud, ensuring at least three people were between him and his target. To do this sort of thing properly he really needed a team of people on foot and others in parked cars, all talking to one another by radio, but he didn't have that luxury. Hopefully

Mahmoud wouldn't be expecting a tail and wouldn't look back.

Now Mahmoud was passing the London Eye where a large crowd of tourists had gathered. Many of them patiently waited in a queue, still observing one metre social distancing and wearing masks, a legacy of the recent coronavirus pandemic. Two armed police officers wearing black Kevlar bulletproof vests and carrying Heckler and Koch MP5 submachine guns in slings looked on. Some tourists were stopped and subjected to spot checks on their backpacks.

For a moment Rick considered approaching the police and telling them his suspicions. Two armed officers would be a great help in apprehending Mahmoud. But it was too risky. He had no ID with him and it was unlikely they would believe his story – that he was an ex-SAS man on the trail of a known terrorist. Lots of people claimed to be former members of the SAS when they were clearly nothing of the sort. The regiment even had a name for them – 'Walts', named after Walter Mitty. No, Rick would follow Mahmoud, find out what he was up to and then capture him. The rule of law didn't apply in this case.

Now the London Aquarium was on their left with Westminster Bridge ahead. Rick felt a lump in his throat as he realized he was close to the spot where the drone wreckage had landed on his wedding boat some months before and burned Laura.

Mahmoud ascended steps to the pavement on the north side of Westminster Bridge and started to cross the river. Where was he going? After traversing the bridge, Mahmoud continued west along Bridge Street. Big Ben and the Houses of Parliament were to his left, and Westminster Underground station to his right. Then he turned right into Parliament Street heading north towards Whitehall. There were many juicy targets in this part of London including the Ministry of Defence buildings and the Prime Minister's residence at 10 Downing Street. Was he about to launch an attack? But how could he do this as he didn't have an obvious weapon? Maybe he was just carrying out a recce?

After a few minutes Mahmoud reached the pavement across the road from Downing Street where a group of tourists had gathered with cameras and phones, hoping to catch a glimpse of the Prime Minister. The entrance to Downing Street was barred by ornate metal gates painted gloss black, in front of which stood two armed policemen carrying MP5s. In addition, several soldiers stood around wearing berets and standard British Army battledress. They all carried compact SA80 automatic rifles.

A Warrior tracked armoured personnel carrier stood to the right of the entrance, its rear doors open. Even from across the road, Rick could hear the sounds of soldiers inside the Warrior speaking on a tactical radio. The vehicle commander stood upright in the turret hatch. Sunlight sparkled off the shiny, well-polished barrel of the turret-mounted 40 mm cannon which was the Warrior's main armament.

Rick looked up and saw a surveillance drone circling high above. An RAF Boeing CH-47 Chinook helicopter crossed the sky at low altitude with the familiar whumph…whumph… whumph sound that Rick knew so well. No other helicopter sounded like a Chinook. London was obviously well prepared for a terrorist attack. So what was Mahmoud up to? Was it possible he had renounced his violent past and was just sightseeing?

At exactly 10:50 a.m. the glossy black front door of 10 Downing Street opened and the Prime Minister exited, followed by a man Rick recognised as the Junior Defence Minister. They got into the back of the Prime Ministerial limousine, which was currently a silver Jaguar XJ Sentinel with a 5 litre engine. Rick knew that it had been fitted with bulletproof glass and Kevlar armour. Another man wearing an overcoat got into the front passenger seat. Rick guessed he would be the Prime Minister's personal bodyguard and would be carrying a handgun.

The two policemen at the entrance to Downing Street opened the gates and the car moved forwards slowly while flashing its indicators to signify a right turn. The Prime Minister was heading towards the Houses of Parliament.

Just a few yards away – on the other side of the road – Mahmoud knew the time had come to make his move. He had already inserted the two-pin plug into the socket over his lower sternum. All he had to do to detonate the bomb was to press one finger into the depression over his xiphisternum and press hard till the switch clicked. He had visited the area near Downing Street a couple of times while posing as a tourist and knew the layout. His plan was based on the successful attack on SS Reichprotector Reinhard Heydrich in Prague on 27 May 1942 by members of the Czech Army who were working for the British Special Operations Executive (SOE). The two soldiers had waited until Heydrich's car had slowed to take a bend. Then one of them, Jozef Gabcik, had attempted to kill Heydrich with a burst from his Sten submachine gun. Unfortunately, the gun had jammed, but while Gabcik escaped on foot, his colleague, Jan Kubis, had tossed an anti-tank grenade into the passenger compartment, severely wounding Heydrich and eventually causing his death from septicaemia a few days later.

Mahmoud knew he had to act quickly. Speed, aggression and surprise were vital. As the Jaguar turned slowly, Mahmoud vaulted over the metal crowd control barrier and flung himself at the bonnet of the car, landing on his stomach with such force that the bonnet buckled. Then he turned over and used the soles of his trainers to push himself up the windscreen. The car screeched to a halt as the driver's view was blocked. Then Mahmoud put his right hand under his T-shirt, his fingers searching for the little depression at the bottom of the sternum where the push switch was hidden. All he had to do was put one finger into the depression, press hard for a second or two and the British Prime Minister would die!

A short distance away, in an army mobile headquarters vehicle in St James's Park, Captain Andy Harrington watched events unfolding on a laptop screen. The screen showed footage which had been captured by a drone fitted with a TV camera with a telephoto lens. A man was sprawled on the windscreen of the Prime Minister's car.

Why had the army and police not placed men on the other side of the street opposite Downing Street? He had advised them to do this but his recommendation had been ignored. However, Harrington had placed several SAS snipers on rooftops between Downing Street and the House of Parliament. They were all equipped with American-made Barratt sniper rifles which fired a hefty fifty-calibre round, could penetrate thin armour and had an effective range of a mile.

Harrington could hear one of these snipers speaking to him through this headset.

'Charlie Four calling. Possible X-ray on windscreen of Prime Minister's vehicle. Permission to shoot please.'

Harrington froze. The mystery man could just be a protestor. On the other hand, he could be a terrorist. Could he have a concealed explosive charge somewhere in his body? Harrington made a snap decision.

'Shoot now! That's an order!'

Charlie Four squeezed the trigger. A powerful fifty-calibre round sped through the air heading for Mahmoud's skull. In one second he would be dead.

CHAPTER 17

PURSUIT

A thin layer of car polish saved Mahmoud's life. As he struggled to push himself further up the windscreen, his trainers slipped on the shiny, waxed bonnet and he slid down the glass just as the SAS sniper pulled the trigger.

It was enough to spoil what would have been a perfect shot. Instead of hitting the centre of his forehead, the bullet grazed Mahmoud's scalp and punched through the Jaguar's armoured windscreen, which was only designed to withstand 7.62 mm and 9 mm rounds. The driver died instantly as the heavy fifty-calibre bullet split his heart in two, passed through his left lung and back muscles and landed in the rear passenger footwell, where it just missed the Prime Minister's right foot, penetrated the thinly armoured floor and lodged in the tarmac road. The driver's blood splattered everywhere inside the passenger compartment but he was the only fatality.

Mahmoud slipped off the bonnet and landed on the tarmac, spraining his right wrist. The terrorist felt under his T-shirt for the two-pin plug and pulled it out as bullets started pinging on the ground all around him. He inserted the plug back into his jeans pocket, got to his feet and started running south, ignoring the pain in his wrist.

Rick reacted instantly and leapt over the barrier in hot pursuit. Soldiers and police at the entrance to Downing Street fired their automatic weapons at the two men as they raced south. They had no idea who the second person was, but it was a fair guess that he was an accomplice, perhaps a lookout. Accurate shooting was impossible because the crowd of onlookers had panicked and were fleeing in every direction, spoiling the chance of a clear shot at the two attackers. One soldier had a bead on Rick with his SA80 but refrained from pulling the trigger when a young woman pushed a pram in front of him. People screamed and the London air smelled of sweat, burnt cordite and fear.

Rick slowly gained on Mahmoud as bullets whizzed past his ear, the 9 mm and 5.56 mm rounds smacking into the windscreens of parked cars and a couple of heavy fifty-calibre Barratt bullets punching holes in the tarmac next to his feet. The SAS snipers on surrounding rooftops didn't realise he was on their side and were trying to take him out, but the best marksman in the world would find it hard to hit a fast-moving target. A surveillance drone buzzed loudly above Rick's head, relaying TV pictures back to tactical HQ.

A white BMW 535 police car with a flashing blue light and screaming siren screeched to a halt in front of him and an armed police officer jumped out the passenger seat. He pointed a Glock 17 at Rick's head at a range of four feet.

'Get on the ground now you fucking bastard! Do it!'

Rick didn't have a weapon so he thought a little mind trick might help.

'I'm just a *Big Issue* seller. I was on my way to the climate change protest in Trafalgar Square when all the shooting started. Please don't kill me!'

Rick could see the officer look down and to the right as he processed this new information. From his SAS training in basic neuro-linguistic programming (NLP), he knew this indicated he was accessing an emotion. Good. The policeman's grip on his pistol slackened as he wondered what to do. Rick moved closer, within striking distance. The policeman had made a big mistake in allowing Rick within grabbing range but he was momentarily confused.

Rick grabbed the Glock with his right hand and pushed it violently to his left with all his strength to remove the immediate threat. Then he wrenched the pistol from the policeman's grasp and shot him in his right thigh. The officer collapsed on the ground in agony, blood spraying everywhere. He would need emergency surgery and months of rehabilitation but he would live.

Rick advanced on the BMW. A terrified female police officer wearing a high-viz fluorescent vest clutched a black microphone with a coiled lead as she attempted to summon help using the vehicle radio. Rick pulled open the driver's door and pointed the Glock at the officer's head. She was young, blonde and pretty with her hair tied back. If circumstances had been different, thought Rick, he might have asked her out on a date.

'Get out of the fucking car and lie face down on the ground with your hands behind your head! I don't want to hurt you, but I will shoot if you don't do as I say. I know you won't believe me but I'm on your side and I need your car to pursue a dangerous terrorist!'

The WPC exited the car at speed, her face white with fear, and lay on the ground as Rick had instructed. Rick took her baton, handcuffs and keys, jumped into the car, which still had its engine running, engaged first gear and tore off with his right foot flat on the accelerator pedal. Through the open window he could smell burning rubber from the tyres. He raced through the gears and got up to sixty miles per hour as he bombed south along Parliament Road, searching for Mahmoud. *Where the hell was he?*

He thought he had lost him but then he spotted a man with jeans, yellow T - shirt and a bloody scalp wound running into Westminster Tube Station. He guessed that Mahmoud's plan was to get on an underground train and then change at another station. He might even repeat the process to foil anyone following him

Rick drove into the kerb at high speed, bursting the nearside front tyre, smashing the left front wing on a concrete bollard and puncturing the radiator. Then he jumped out of the car, avoiding the rapidly expanding puddle of hot sticky green engine coolant, and raced into the station ticket hall just in time to catch a glimpse of Mahmoud swiping his Oyster card, going through the barrier and onto the descending escalator which would take him to the Circle Line heading east.

Rick didn't have his Oyster card with him so he vaulted over the barrier and raced down the escalator steps – ignoring all the verbal abuse that was being directed at him – as he pushed people aside. All that mattered was to keep his eye on the man with the blue jeans and yellow T-shirt.

His quarry arrived at the eastbound Circle Line platform just as a train pulled away. The overhead display showed that the next train was in three minutes. His best chance to capture Mahmoud was right now. He had the captured Glock 17, the police baton and the handcuffs all stuffed in the inside pockets of his fleece. But where was Mahmoud? He couldn't see him right now because of the mass of people on the platform.

The passengers who had got off the recently departed train started to disperse but others arrived. As Rick elbowed his way through the crowds, he spotted Mahmoud at the west end of the platform next to the tunnel entrance, with blood streaming down his face. He had to grab him now but first he had to clear the platform. Rick pulled out his Glock and screamed at the top of his voice:

'I need to apprehend a dangerous terrorist! Everyone leave the station now!' Rick ended his address by firing two shots from his Glock into the ceiling. Immediately there were screams of terror and everyone rushed for the exits in a panic. Only Mahmoud remained by the tunnel entrance, staring directly at him. Just a hundred feet away.

'Mahmoud Rashid. I know who you are. You're a terrorist. I'm a plain-clothes police officer and I'm arresting you,' shouted Rick, hoping his bluff would work.

'A team of armed police have already arrived at this station and are making their way down the escalators. They will be here any minute. You cannot escape. Lie face down on the platform and put your hands behind your head and you will be well treated. If you resist arrest, you will be shot.'

For a moment Mahmoud looked perplexed. Then he jumped off the platform onto the rails. Rick aimed and fired. The bullet missed and buried itself in the wall. Rick cursed. If he had aimed at the centre of Mahmoud's body rather than his legs, he would have got him. But he didn't want to kill him. At least not yet, because he had to extract important information from him.

Rick ran to the end of the platform as Mahmoud disappeared into the darkness of the tunnel. He would have to follow him but that would be dangerous. There were two live rails between the main traction rails giving a total of 630 volts, more than double the British domestic voltage. If he touched one he would be dead. The tunnel was fitted with lights but they were only switched on after 1:00 a.m. when maintenance work was carried out.

Rick rummaged in his trouser pocket for his keyring, which was fitted with a tiny torch. That would have to do. Rick put his Glock back into his fleece inside pocket, slipped over the edge of the platform and headed into the tunnel, guided by the torchlight. If he kept well to the left, he should be safe from electrocution, and if a train appeared, he could flatten himself against the tunnel wall. He also knew there were many alcoves built into the tunnel walls to protect workers. There was just one thing that bothered him. Even if he managed to overpower Mahmoud, how was he going to get him out of the Underground when the Metropolitan Police, the regular army and the SAS were on their way? He had no idea but he would think of something when the time came.

British Army Tactical HQ, St James Park

SAS Captain Andy Harrington had just received a briefing on the latest incidents. There had been an attempt on the Prime Minister's life just outside Downing Street. A man had leapt over a security barrier and jumped on the windscreen of the prime ministerial car. He wasn't wearing a suicide vest or carrying a backpack but there was a suspicion he had an explosive charge inside his body. Eye witnesses had seen him putting his hand inside his T-shirt. Was he trying to set off a bomb? The attack had been foiled by an SAS sniper. Then the terrorist had ran off, apparently injured, followed by another man. Was he an accomplice? The second man had then stolen a police car and a pistol and had been seen entering Westminster Underground Station.

Captain Andy Harrington made a preliminary review of the CCTV footage which had been captured from various sources, including a couple of surveillance drones which had been fitted with ultra-high-definition TV cameras. One piece of footage particularly interested Harrington. It showed a fit-looking man with dark hair overpowering an armed police officer, then hijacking a police car and driving off at high speed.

Harrington felt a certain admiration for the skill shown by this man.

'That's the way we're taught to do it in the SAS. Get in close to an assailant armed with a pistol, grab it forcefully and then push it to one side. Then snatch it. And his driving technique. It's just the way we learned back at Hereford. And he spared the policewoman's life.'

Harrington spoke to the CCTV technician who was sitting next to him.

'Zoom in on his face and enhance the picture.'

The technician worked his mouse and clicked on a couple of icons on the computer screen. Within a minute a pin-sharp image of Rick's face appeared on the screen.

'We can send this shot to MI5 and MI6 for scanning with facial recognition software,' said the technician.

'There's no need,' said Harrington. 'I recognise him. It's Rick Fernscale. He was a sergeant in the SAS at the time I joined the regiment. One of the best men we ever had. Could he be working for the terrorists? If so, we are facing a very dangerous opponent. We may have to tell our men to shoot him on sight!'

CHAPTER 18

TUNNEL BATTLE

St James' Park Underground Station

Captain Andy Harrington raced down the escalator steps three at a time, followed by four SAS troopers. Harrington and his men were dressed in the 'black kit' and Kevlar helmets which had been the standard SAS outfit for anti-terrorist operations for over four decades. Respirators dangled from their necks. All four troopers carried Heckler & Koch MP5 submachine guns with spare magazines in pouches, plus Sig Sauer P226 pistols and G60 Flash Bang grenades, which also contained CS gas. All the MP5s were fitted with Maglite torches under the gun barrels. The last passengers had been cleared from the station by the police just two minutes earlier. One busker had departed in such a hurry that he had left behind his guitar and case, which was filled with small change.

Just two minutes later the five men stood on the platform next to the eastbound Circle Line. Harrington spoke briefly on the wall-mounted, corded emergency phone and then replaced the handset.

'OK men, listen up. London Transport has switched off power on this section of the line. All trains on the Circle Line have been stopped. The tunnel maintenance lights have been switched on. So the only risk comes from the two X-rays. One is of Middle Eastern appearance. Estimated age forty. Name unknown. The other is forty-three. His name is Rick Fernscale. Ex-SAS. He may be working with the terrorists, we're not sure. The bad news is that he is an expert in firearms and unarmed combat and is someone who cannot be underestimated.'

'So do we capture them or kill them?' said Trooper James McIlroy, who hailed from Falkirk.

'The plan is to capture both X-rays as we need to interrogate them. But if it looks as if they are going to escape, or your own life is threatened, then you have permission to shoot to kill. Who knows what other atrocities these two may be planning? If there are no other questions, then we must go now. A four-man SAS team is leaving Westminster Underground Station right now, heading west along the same tunnel so we should meet about halfway, by which time we should have snared the two terrorists. Once we have caught them, they are to be disarmed, cuffed and taken to Westminster Station, where the police will take over their processing. Now let's go. We don't have a moment to lose. It's quite a short tab to Westminster Station. Less than two clicks.'

The five soldiers slipped over the platform and headed east with Captain Harrington leading, Sig Sauer pistol in hand.

'This is just like that old *Doctor Who* story *The Web of Fear*,' said Trooper Dean Collins, who had worked as a London black cab driver before joining the army. 'Watched it last night on DVD. Six-part story but Episode Three is missing. Patrick Troughton is the Doctor and it's all about an alien entity called The Intelligence which invades the London Underground using robot Yetis and a deadly fungus. The British Army is called in to fight the creatures but bullets won't stop them, though they can be destroyed by grenades and bazooka rounds. First appearance of Brigadier Lethbridge-Stewart, but he's just a Colonel in this story. Much prefer it to all the PC crap the BBC makes now. They should call it *Doctor Woke* rather than *Doctor Who*!'

'Why did you ever join the army, Dean?' said McIlroy in his broad Scottish accent. 'You're such a nerd. You should wear glasses and spend all day playing computer games. And how on earth did a geek like you get through selection?'

'Oh, but I did wear glasses. I had corneal refractive surgery when I was eighteen, didn't I? So I don't need specs now.'

'When you're in the SAS your hobbies should be beer and women,' said McIlroy. 'Watching old *Doctor Who* DVDs is for tossers.'

'OK you two, pipe down,' said Harrington. 'Dean, you can tell us all about *The Web of Fear* when we get back to Hereford. Just keep your mouths shut until we've captured the terrorists. And stay alert.'

*

Just a few hundred yards east of Harrington's squad, Rick was gaining on the injured Mahmoud. All the weeks of cycling and muscle-building exercises had paid off as he was making a brisk pace despite the uneven ground. The tunnel maintenance lights had just come on and he could now see quite clearly where he was going. He had a pistol and he was sure his quarry was unarmed and wounded so there was no question that he would catch him. Shooting Mahmoud would be easier than an abduction but he had to interrogate him. The only problem was that there was likely to be an SAS or police hunter force behind him and maybe a second one ahead of him. That is exactly what he would have ordered if he was in command of the anti-terrorist forces. Even if he captured Mahmoud, how were the two of them going to get out of the Underground without being detected?

Rick sprinted along a sharp bend and caught sight of Mahmoud, who was limping badly and still bleeding from a scalp wound. Rick reckoned the terrorist had sprained his right ankle when he had jumped from the platform but had walked through the pain with his adrenaline keeping him going.

Rick pulled his Glock from his inside fleece pocket and aimed at Mahmoud's head, holding the pistol with both hands. The range was fifty feet.

'Stop right there or I fire! I'm a trained marksman. Get down on the fucking ground with your hands behind your head or I shoot.'

Mahmoud turned round, flashed his white teeth and stared at Rick. Then he turned about and ran as fast as his sprained ankle would allow, zig-zagging to make Rick's task harder. Rick's best option would have been a 'double tap' — two rounds in quick succession — aimed at the chest, but he needed the terrorist alive, so that wasn't possible. Rick held the gun with both hands, aimed low and pulled the trigger. Bang! The noise reverberated around the tunnel as the bullet tore a piece out of Mahmoud's right calf muscle and the terrorist collapsed face down on the ground, bruising the right side of his face on a rail.

Rick advanced on the wounded terrorist, put his pistol back in his fleece inside pocket and retrieved the handcuffs and keys he had stolen from the WPC. Then he cuffed Mahmoud's hands behind his back and searched him thoroughly for any concealed weapons. Standard SAS procedure.

'You have violated my human rights,' said Mahmoud. 'I demand medical attention and the services of a Human Rights Lawyer.'

'Human Rights,' said Rick, astonished. 'What about the rights of my wife Laura? Burned to a crisp by one of your drones. Yes matey, we're going to have a little conversation but it won't be in a cosy police station. You see, you're coming with me!'

'So this is what this is all about! You're not police or SAS. You want revenge. But I will never tell you anything! The members of *The Seven* keep their secrets forever.'

Rick smiled. Mahmoud had just admitted he was part of *The Seven*. So far so good.

Rick had just got Mahmoud to his feet, and had tied a clean handkerchief to his right calf as a field dressing, when he saw five shadowy figures approaching from the west. They were led by an officer holding a Sig Sauer pistol. Behind him were four black-clad SAS troopers carrying MP5s. The officer spoke:

'Rick Fernscale. I know you. We met at Hereford. My name is Captain Andy Harrington. I'm familiar with your service record and I don't know why you're working with the terrorists. You're outnumbered and another four troopers are approaching from the east. Lay down your weapon and surrender and then your friend can get the medical attention he requires.'

'This man is a terrorist but he's not my friend. Can't you see I've cuffed him? I'm on your side.'

'Surrender, Rick, and come with us to Westminster Station where the cops are waiting. You will be taken to a police station where you can explain your side of the story. All we want is to get to the truth.'

Rick's face fell. This is not what he wanted. If he went with the SAS squad he would be arrested and charged with multiple offences. He would very likely spend the next ten years in jail. No, that was not acceptable. He had to find out more about *The Seven* so he could take them down. He had to think and act fast to get out of this situation.

'OK, I surrender. I have a pistol inside my fleece jacket. I'm going to take it out very slowly and then place it on the ground. I will then lie on the ground on my stomach and you can cuff my hands behind my back and take me into custody. Is that acceptable to you?'

'Yes it is,' said Harrington, as he raised his Sig Sauer pistol and aimed it at Rick's forehead. 'Any tricks though and I'll blow your brains out! Now do it slowly!'

Rick pulled the pistol out of the inside pocket of his fleece and raised it into the air.

'Good,' said Harrington. 'Now put it on the ground.'

Rick slowly lowered his pistol as though he was complying. Then without warning he pulled the trigger. Rick was aiming at a plastic circuit breaker box on the wall of the tunnel which he had spotted earlier. The bullet struck home, smashing the box into a dozen pieces. There was a blue flash and the tunnel was plunged into darkness.

Even though it was pitch dark, Rick had already memorised the position of two people, namely the nearest trooper, who happened to be Collins, and Mahmoud. He launched himself at Collins and grabbed an object about the size of a food tin from his belt. It was a G60 stun grenade, also known as a flashbang. Rick shoved it in his fleece pocket, grabbed Mahmoud by the hair and pressed the muzzle of his pistol against his head as he pushed him forward, heading east.

'Move or I'll shoot. As fast as you can.'

Mahmoud was in agony from his sprained ankle, but complied. He didn't know what was worse – being captured by the SAS and then jailed for life, or being taken hostage by a crazed ex-soldier who wanted revenge for the death of his wife. Just a few yards behind them, Harrington attempted to take command of the situation.

'Switch on the Maglite torches on your MP5s, men. And then get after these two. They won't get far. They're heading straight for the other hunter force!'

Rick took the G60 stun grenade out of his fleece pocket, pulled the circular wire loop attached to the pin and threw the grenade back down the tunnel towards the pursuing SAS troops. A couple of seconds later the flashbang exploded, temporarily deafening, disorientating and blinding the troopers. There was worse to come as a cloud of CS gas burst from the G60 casing causing the troopers to be temporarily blinded. Their throats and noses stung and tears poured from their eyes.

'Get your respirators on,' screamed Harrington. 'The effects will pass in a moment!'

About fifty yards ahead, Rick and Mahmoud had been minimally affected by the G60 grenade as they had put sufficient distance between themselves and the munition. Rick felt his eyes and nose sting but the symptoms passed in a moment. But he knew he had only bought a few minutes. Soon the troopers would recover from the effects of the flashbang and would be racing after him. And another SAS squad was heading directly towards him. Unless he could think of something very soon, he would be trapped between the two advancing forces!

CHAPTER 19

TALK OR DIE!

Rick pushed the muzzle of his Glock 17 into the back of Mahmoud's head and urged him to walk faster. But he knew he was doomed. With every second that passed, the five-man SAS team behind him was closing the gap. Mahmoud's injured ankle was slowing him down. And in any case, the quicker they went, the sooner they would bump into the other SAS squad which was heading towards them from Westminster Station. He had to think of something... fast!

Just ahead of them, the traction and power rails gleamed with the reflected light of four gun-mounted Maglite torches. The approaching troopers were just around the next bend in the tunnel and would be with them any minute.

Then Rick spotted it. A safety alcove on the right. Rick knew that Underground tunnels were fitted with many of these recesses to enable maintenance workers to shelter when a train was passing. They had been built when the London Underground was first constructed, though weren't used much now as maintenance was usually carried out between 1:00 a.m. and 6:00 a.m. when the trains weren't running. Rick knew this because he had watched a Channel 4 documentary about the Tube.

This particular alcove had an old, stout wooden door at the back. Rick pulled on its handle and it creaked open on rusty hinges. By the light of his mini-torch, Rick saw a set of moss-covered stone steps leading up to a passageway. Where did that lead to? Another Underground tunnel? Perhaps a disused one? A maintenance tunnel? The sewers? Rick knew there was a rabbit warren of disused tunnels under the streets of London, some dating back as far as the 18th century.

Rick pushed Mahmoud through the doorway and then urged him up the steps by pressing the muzzle of his Glock into the small of his back. Then he closed the door behind him and secured it with the two stout bolts that had been fitted, top and bottom. Rick ascended the steps, keeping Mahmoud in front of him. Where would he end up? He had no idea but he would soon find out...

*

The two SAS hunter squads recognised each other immediately. By the light of nine Maglite torches they exchanged greetings. But almost immediately there was a feeling of collective disappointment. What had happened to the two fugitives?

Captain Harrington spoke to his tactical HQ using the wall-mounted emergency phone which had been patched through to the SAS radio network by MoD technicians:

'We've carried out a sweep of the tunnel from both ends but there's no sign of the X-rays. The tunnel maintenance lights have gone out, thanks to a wrecked circuit breaker box. We need some electricians down here ASAP to get them working. In the meantime, some more powerful battery lights would help. We also need to do a thorough search of the tunnel. In particular, all the safety alcoves need to be checked. And we need more men. The Green Army will do or even the police. We must find out if there is any way the X-rays could have escaped.'

*

Rick pushed Mahmoud ahead of him as he walked along the uneven stone pavement to the left of the canal-like sewer. The stench was overpowering, a mixture of urine, faeces and rotting food. Used tampons, condoms and soiled toilet paper floated on the stinking liquid. In places, the flow of foul sewage was partly obstructed by 'fatbergs', big lumps of grease consisting of used cooking oil and baby wipes. He remembered that council workers had to clear these out periodically. A couple of squeaking rats scurried past his feet as he pushed onwards relentlessly.

Rick knew it was only a matter of time before the SAS teams worked out what had happened. They would draft in extra men, get better lights and check every inch of the tunnel, including the safety alcoves. Eventually they would discover the door and blow it open. At best he had gained an hour on his pursuers, maybe less. He had to find a way to the surface and then get lost in the vastness of London. He also had to get Mahmoud to the special interrogation cell he had prepared and subject him to the hospitality he deserved. It was a tall order.

*

'That's the only way they could have escaped,' said Trooper Collins as he pressed his gloved hand against the thick, oak door. 'We've searched the entire tunnel with the help of the extra men from the army and police. There are no hidden compartments under the rails and all the alcoves are empty. This is the only one with a door. It's immovable. No sign of a lock so I guess it's bolted on the other side.'

'OK Dean,' said Harrington. 'We'll have to blow the hinges off. Alec, use your 870.'

Trooper Alec Gordon stepped forward carrying a large, heavy American-made Remington Model 870 pump-action shotgun, which the SAS also called the L74A1. It fired a special munition called the Hatton round which could blast a door off its hinges using multiple chunky plastic pellets.

Gordon wore his respirator mask to protect his eyes and face. The other soldiers stood well back as he took aim at the upper door hinge from point-blank range and pulled the trigger. The blast blew a fist-sized hole in the door around the top hinge. Then he re-cocked the weapon, ejected the used cartridge, aimed at the lower hinge and gave it the same treatment. Again, the blast from the powerful round tore a large chunk out of the door, which was now held in place by just two bolts.

The smoke soon cleared. Alec rested his gun on the tunnel wall and wrenched the door off with his gloved hands. It fell on the rails with a loud thump.

'Well done, Alec,' said Harrington. 'Now let's get after them. Red Troop, follow me.'

Harrington and eight SAS troopers, all wearing newly acquired headband-mounted torches on their helmets, walked up the steps to continue their pursuit.

*

Mahmoud's eyes flicked open. His head was pounding and his mouth felt as dry as the Negev desert. He was drowsy but it was not the pleasant, healthy sensation he had experienced when he had contemplated bed after hours of exercise. Instead, it was the nauseating sensation of sleepiness caused by a powerful hypnotic drug. When he moved his head, he felt a spinning sensation. What had happened to him and where was he?

There was a strong smell of old wood and hay. To his right, a naked 100-watt filament light bulb hung from the ceiling, which consisted of rough-fitting wooden planks. He tried to move and discovered he was not in a bed but was secured to a large wooden table by leather straps round his wrist and ankles. The table was slightly inclined at about twenty degrees with his head below his feet. His right trouser leg had been cut off below the knee and he could see that the wound in his right calf had been expertly stitched. He could also feel the slight discomfort of an intravenous drip pouring saline into his left arm through a green Venflon cannula which was secured by white Micropore surgical tape. How had he got here? What was going on? He remembered being pushed forward in that dark tunnel with a pistol pushed against his head. But he had no recollection of what had happened after that.

Over to his left a trapdoor opened in the ceiling and a fit-looking man in his early forties with dark hair descended a set of creaking wooden steps. The sound of a petrol-driven electric generator was just audible. The man munched a sandwich before speaking:

'Like *Pret a Manger* sandwiches, Mahmoud? Many of their branches closed down because of the Covid-19 crisis but there's one still open near Charing Cross. Sorry I don't have any food for you but believe me you won't feel like eating once you discover what I have in store for you. In fact, you'll probably throw up.'

Rick finished his sandwich, wiped his mouth with a paper napkin and then continued:

'You're probably wondering where you are and why you can't remember what happened in the last few hours, so I'll tell you. Eventually we escaped from the tunnel via a manhole and found ourselves on the banks of the Thames near some old warehouses. I handcuffed you to some railings and then came back for you with my car. Fortunately, the pursuing SAS team must have taken a wrong turn in the labyrinth of tunnels and got lost.

'I then drugged you and put you in the boot of my car. I used two compounds, the sedative Rohypnol and the anti-cholinergic drug Hyoscine, better known as Scopolamine. In small doses Scopolamine can be used as a travel sickness pill but in higher doses it causes disorientation and makes people more compliant and easier to handle. You've probably got a hell of a headache right now and can't remember much of the last few hours. That's because of the Rohypnol. It causes retrograde amnesia.

'A lot of people think Scopolamine is a truth serum. That's because they've seen the movies *The Guns of Navarone* and *Where Eagles Dare*. Unfortunately it doesn't work like that, so I am going to use more traditional methods to get information out of you. Alastair MacLean may have been very knowledgeable about naval matters and the inside of a whisky bottle but his knowledge of pharmacology sucked.

'I've sutured your wounds and put you on a drip so you're not at risk of dying, but I haven't given you any painkillers. It would be counter-productive in view of what I'm about to do.

'Yes, you' re going to talk my friend. It may be five minutes from now or an hour from now but you will talk. I guarantee that. You're going to experience more pain and discomfort than you ever thought possible. You will feel as though you are about to die. There's no person on earth who can withstand the level of pain I am going to put you through. I am an expert in the delivery of pain. I know how to break people. As part of my SAS training, I experienced torture myself.'

'But you are British,' said Mahmoud. 'You always do the decent thing. During the Second World War you never tortured captured Japanese servicemen even though they treated Allied prisoners worse than animals. You British believe in honour and treating people with compassion. Gentlemen officers. David Niven. That kind of thing.'

'Oh, but I'm not working for the British Government,' answered

Rick. 'I was in the army and the SAS, but I retired. You might call me a freelance operator. And I have a very special personal reason for doing this to you, as you already know.'

Rick pulled a well-worn photo from his right jeans pocket and held it in front of Mahmoud's eyes. It was the picture of Laura that he carried everywhere. She was wearing pink lipstick and a matching short-sleeved top.

'Beautiful, isn't she? You won't recognise her, but she was my wife. Laura Fernscale. Unfortunately she was only Mrs Fernscale for about forty minutes. She was killed three months ago when your organisation launched a drone attack on London. Burned to death when the drone wreckage landed on a river boat.'

'Civilian casualties are to be expected in any war,' said Mahmoud. 'No-one bothers when Arab children die as a result of Israeli or American bombs. We are merely paying back the West in kind for their crimes. The only solution to the world's problems is the total destruction of capitalism.'

'I'm not interested in your political views. All I want is justice for Laura. And I'm going to achieve this by destroying your organisation. So, I want the names of *The Seven*. I already know your name because we have met before. You may not remember me, but I was there when you were captured in Afghanistan. Your name is Mahmoud Rashid. I want the names of the other six and their current location. In particular I want the name of your leader and also the person who operated the drone.'

'I will never tell you. I would rather die, you capitalist pig!'

Mahmoud spat in Rick's face with all the energy he could muster. Rick wiped off the saliva and mucus with his *Pret a Manger* paper napkin and grinned.

'Bad move, Mahmoud. You're going to have to learn to obey me.

Just for doing that I'm going to make sure the torture lasts longer.'

Rick picked up two thick, rubber-covered electrical leads with large crocodile clips at the end. They lead to a large blue metal box with a red light and a meter on the front.

'That's an isolating transformer by the way. It enables me to deliver high voltage, high amperage current to your body without blowing a fuse. The pain will be excruciating, especially when I apply current to your genitals, as I will do if you don't talk. Great skill is required to administer this torture correctly as there is a risk of causing cardiac arrest. The last thing I want is for you to die without telling me what I want to know. To avoid this, I will start off by putting current through your lower limbs. If that doesn't produce the desired result, I will attach small electrodes to your genitals. The pain is said to be off the Richter scale because that area of the body has so many nerve endings,'

Mahmoud shuddered. He was a brave fighter but experiencing unbearable levels of pain while being strapped down was something he was not prepared for. Then he realised the pain would only last a second or two as the current would trigger the bomb. It had been designed that way. Mahmoud knew he would die a martyr and a feeling of calmness came over his body.

Rick flipped a switch on the front of the transformer box and then pulled up Mahmoud's left trouser leg. Both calves were now bare. He held both chunky leads with thick rubber gloves as he contemplated his next move.

'Now you're going to give me some answers. Let's start with two easy ones. Who is the leader of your organisation and where can I find him?'

Mahmoud smiled as Rick prepared to apply the crocodile clips to his body. *Why was he smiling?* thought Rick. *Something wasn't right here.*

He was going to have 500 volts through his body and he was smiling. Surely he couldn't find the prospect of electrocution appealing unless...

Rick evaluated the situation. He had seen Mahmoud jump onto the windscreen of the Prime Minister's car. But he had no backpack, no suicide belt, no obvious bomb. How did he intend to kill the Prime Minister? There was only one explanation...

Rick put down the leads, switched off the transformer and pulled up Mahmoud's T-shirt. There was a thin red vertical line on his upper abdomen. It was a recent laparotomy scar.

'You're carrying a bomb inside your abdomen...and an electric shock will set it off. That's the reason you look so calm. Well, I'll just have to resort to Plan B.'

Rick filled a blue metal watering can with cold water from a jerrycan and picked up a large white cloth from a wall-mounted rail.

'Do you know what I'm going to do to you Mahmoud? It's called waterboarding and it is one of the most unpleasant tortures known to man. Even the toughest terrorists have given information after being subjected to the technique. That's how the Yanks found the location of Osama Bin Laden, leading to a successful assassination mission. Now one last time before the fun begins...who is the leader of your group and where can he be found?'

'Fuck you, infidel,' screamed Mahmoud. 'I'm glad your wife died. She was a Western whore.'

Rick resisted the temptation to smack Mahmoud across the jaw. If he injured him too much it might impair his ability to talk. Instead he put the towel over Mahmoud's face as he lay on the table and poured some water over his head until the cloth was saturated.

Mahmoud shook with fear and let out a gurgling noise. Rick had only used a small quantity of water and yet the terrorist felt that he was drowning. Rick kept the cloth on for forty seconds and then whipped it off. Mahmoud gasped for air. Rick let him have a minute to recover and then repeated his questions:

'Who is the leader of your group and where can I find him?'

'Fuck you and fuck your dead wife!'

Rick refilled the watering can from a jerrycan and repeated the process again and again. Mahmoud still refused to talk but Rick could see that his resolve was weakening. He had subjected many terrorists to 'enhanced interrogation techniques' over the years and knew they all broke eventually. Every human being had an innate instinct to survive and that superseded any conditioning instilled by their fanatical beliefs.

Mahmoud finally broke after seven cycles of waterboarding:

'Khalid is our leader,' he gasped. 'He has a base at Merlaux. Old Maginot Line fort. But he moves around a lot. He could be somewhere else. The man who fired the drone is called Maurice L'Arconne. Ex-French Army. He's a missile expert. Lives in Dinard, France. Runs a computer shop near the seafront. Used to be in charge of a French Army Roland surface-to-air missile battery. That's all I know about these two, I swear. It was too dangerous for all the members of *The Seven* to know too much about one another.'

'Very interesting, Mahmoud. Now I want you to give me the names of all the other members of *The Seven* and their location. As much as you know.'

'I'm not telling you anything else! That's all you're getting!'

Rick was disappointed, but not surprised. He had seen this before with torture subjects. They would give a little information to placate their interrogators and then clam up. The only solution was another round of waterboarding.

Rick placed the soaking cloth on Mahmoud's face and poured more water over it. Mahmoud screamed as he struggled for breath. A minute later he went limp. Rick pulled the cloth off and checked for a carotid artery pulse in his neck. There was none. Then he listened to his chest. There was no heartbeat. No breathing. He had arrested. Rick hit the left side of Mahmoud's chest in the hope it would restart his heart. Nothing happened. Then he carried out CPR, compressing Mahmoud's chest to the imagined rhythm of the Bees Gees hit *Staying Alive* and gave him the kiss of life. After five minutes of fruitless effort, Rick gave up. Mahmoud had died under torture without giving him all the information he needed. Still, he had two names and possible locations. That was a start. He could pass this information on to the authorities but that wasn't part of his plan. The man who ordered the attack and the terrorist who controlled the drone were next on his hit list! Soon they would be dead. Then it would be three down and four to go!

CHAPTER 20

COURT MARTIAL?

3 September, 2022

SAS Tactical HQ, St James Park, London

Captain Andy Harrington stood to attention inside the temporary building which had been erected at St James Park. He was still wearing his black combat suit and Kevlar helmet. His superior officer, Colonel Stewart, sat at his desk dressed in a green army sweater with fabric patches and matching combat trousers. He wore his brown plastic half-moon reading glasses as he consulted a sheaf of papers. Outside the half-open window it was a glorious early autumn day. Regular army sentries wearing DPM camo battledress and black berets carried SA80 rifles as they patrolled the perimeter of the SAS compound. Three four-ton DAF army trucks were being cleaned with a power-washer. Two SAS troopers wearing the regiment's beige berets surveyed the landscape with binoculars from the newly-constructed watch tower. In the far distance Harrington could see joggers, cyclists and walkers taking advantage of the fine weather.

'Not very good. Not very good at all, Andy.' Unlike the regular army, the SAS had a tradition of using first names.

Stewart continued:

'You were pursuing just two terrorists with one handgun between them. One terrorist was wounded. And yet they managed to give you the slip, not once but twice. There was the first incident in the Underground tunnel when one of the terrorists blew the lights and then incapacitated your men with a flashbang. Then it took a full hour for you to resume pursuit at which point you lost both X-rays. What happened?'

'One of the men we were tracking was Rick Fernscale, sir. He's ex-SAS. Was a sergeant in 22 Regiment back at Hereford. His combat skills are exceptional.'

'Yes I know. I've worked with him before.'

'And the flashbang wasn't the standard version. It was the model containing CS gas, designed for dealing with hostage situations. That was the version we were carrying.'

'Things might have gone differently if all your men had been wearing their respirators instead of having them dangling around their necks,' said Stewart. 'And you should have had your gun Maglites switched on the moment you entered the Underground Station, just in case there was a power cut. And when you eventually pursued the terrorists through the sewers you should have taken a police tracker dog and handler with you. That way you wouldn't have lost them! What the hell did they teach you in your basic counter-insurgency training?'

'I know, sir. As the saying goes, experience is the name we give to all our mistakes. I sincerely apologise for what happened. The way I handled these incidents did not meet the very stringent standards of the SAS and I am prepared to accept whatever disciplinary measures you consider appropriate, sir.'

Stewart looked down at the opened leather-bound book that was in front of him and then took off his glasses and put them on the desk.

'I've consulted Queen's Regulations and I am in no doubt that I would be justified in ordering a Court Martial, at the end of which you would probably be returned to your original unit, which in this case would be the paras.'

Harrington tensed up. Return to Unit (RTU as it was known) was the punishment every SAS soldier dreaded.

'However, we are currently facing a national emergency and this country needs good soldiers. I'm aware that your previous service record has been exemplary and you were facing an exceptional opponent. I am therefore prepared to forget about this whole incident. I hope you will learn from this experience, Andy.'

'That's very generous of you, sir. And I can assure you that I won't slip up again if you will give me another chance.'

'Good, that is all, Andy.'

Colonel Stewart took a red box file off a shelf and replaced his reading glasses just as Harrington was heading out the door.

'Oh, one last thing Andy. Do you think it's really likely that Fernscale is working for the terrorists? From what I hear they are all Marxist radicals. Fernscale was a *Daily Mail* man. Left-wing extremism isn't his thing.'

'I was thinking that too, sir. I trust the police are looking into this?'

'They are indeed, Andy. Good luck and good hunting.'

Lambeth Police Station, near the South Bank

DCI McAllister bit into his second bacon roll with added HP sauce and slurped a large mug of tea with three sugars. It was only three hours since his usual fry-up breakfast and he felt peckish. Only two hours till lunch though. At the next desk DS Brown sipped a green tea and munched an apple as he perused *The Guardian*.

*

There was a knock at the door and a dark-haired WPC entered.

'Sorry to disturb you during your tea break, sir, but a woman's turned up at the front desk. She's a nurse at St Thomas's hospital. Wants to report a missing person. He's her boyfriend.'

'OK. Just put her into Interview Room Two. We'll be down as soon as we've finished our tea.'

*

Molly had never been in a police station before and was surprised at how bleak an interview room was. Four plain walls painted with shiny magnolia paint. No paintings or photos. No pot plants. One window with vertical venetian blinds. A fluorescent strip light. Cheap thin brown carpet tiles and a simple wooden table with four uncomfortable plastic chairs. Even after sitting on one of them for just five minutes her back felt sore.

McAllister entered, followed by DS Brown who was carrying a yellow A4 pad, a biro and some forms. The two men sat down at the table.

'I understand you want to report a missing person,' said McAllister. 'Tell me more.'

'I haven't seen Mahmoud since early yesterday morning. He was recovering from an abdominal operation, you see. I work as a nurse, specialising in post-operative care and I suggested he spend a couple of weeks at my flat to get his strength back. I even took out his stitches.'

'I take it you've tried phoning him,' said McAllister.

'Of course. All my calls go straight to voicemail. I've also sent him texts, emails and messages via Facebook Messenger. I've been to his flat in Newham and its empty. The neighbours haven't seen him either.'

'So, what's Mahmoud's full name?'

'Mahmoud Rashid. He came from Libya originally but his family now lives in Morocco. They're very wealthy. Mahmoud's doing a course at the London School of Economics but he has a part-time job at the *Palms of Beirut* Lebanese Restaurant in Edgware Road.

Before you ask, I have checked with the restaurant and he hasn't turned up there either.'

'Mahmoud Rashid. That's a very common Arab name. Sort of like John Smith in English. Do you have a photo of him?'

'I don't have any prints but I have a few photos on my phone.'

'That's very helpful. We'll upload these pictures from your phone and get them distributed to all the police stations in London, and then nationwide if we deem it necessary. All the details of your case will go on our IT system. We'll let you know as soon as we hear anything. And we may need to speak to you again. Make sure you leave all your contact details including your work phone number.'

'Thank you, Inspector. I will feel much happier knowing he is not six feet under!'

*

Rick carried Mahmoud's body with a fireman's lift and dumped it into the makeshift shallow grave he had prepared, fifty yards behind the barn. The area was screened by trees and could not be seen from the road. Using a shovel, Rick threw in all the earth he had previously excavated and then carefully replaced the squares of grass he had meticulously removed with an army entrenching tool. One of the first things he had learned in basic training was how to dig a slit trench. The SAS took excavation to a higher level as troopers were often required to create carefully camouflaged dug-outs in which two men could live for weeks while they spied on enemy positions. They were expected to pee into jerrycans, defaecate into plastic bags, eat cold rations and sleep on a shift system while maintaining constant watch and avoiding detection. Compared with that, digging a simple grave was child's play.

Rick patted down the last square of grass and admired his work. Only an expert could tell that the ground had been dug up. Soon, grass and weeds would grow and conceal the scars in the ground. The grave might be found eventually by sniffer dogs but by then he would have completed his task. One down and six to go. His next target was Maurice L'Arconne, the man who had operated the drone. He now had the address of his shop in Dinard, France. Would L'Arconne be there? He had no idea. But wherever he was, he would track him down. The days of that evil organisation, *The Seven,* were numbered. After what Rick has just done, they would have to call themselves *The Six.*

CHAPTER 21

RED DAWN

Maurice L'Arconne was radical. His political indoctrination started when he was a child. His father, Gaston, was a trade union representative at the massive Renault works at Billancourt, near Paris. Gaston loved nothing better than bringing all the workers out on strike over some petty grievance. He saw such actions as his personal contribution to the war against capitalism.

Gaston had a combative attitude, shaped by years in the military. As a captain in the Foreign Legion in the 1950s, he had served in Algeria where he was engaged in regular battles with freedom fighters who wanted independence from France. Gaston secretly sympathized with these guerrillas because he disapproved of colonialism and found himself torn between his loyalty to the French flag and the Foreign Legion, and his political convictions. Deep down, he believed that countries like France, Britain and the USA should leave the Middle East, and he strongly disapproved of the State of Israel and its persecution of the Palestinian people. He was aghast at the Anglo-French Suez operation in 1956 – carried out with the collusion of Israel – and incensed when President Charles De Gaulle agreed to sell the latest French weapons to that pariah state, including the AMX 13 tank, Mystère and Vautour strike aircraft and the supersonic Mirage III fighter.

In 1964, Gaston resigned his commission and became an assembly line worker at the giant Renault plant at Billancourt. It was something of a demotion for the former Legionnaire officer but he had a family to feed and his wife Brigitte wanted more children. She had two daughters, Lisa and Anne-Marie but really desired a son to make the family unit complete.

Gaston worked long hours on the production line – doing all the overtime that was available – and in his spare time read every book on Communism he could find. Gaston believed that the solution to all the world's problems lay in a totalitarian Marxist state. Ideally, just one world state and one world government. All private property should be confiscated, houses should be sold and people would be forced to live in apartments where they could be kept under surveillance. Of course, as a party member – and hopefully one of the elite – he would receive extra privileges as was the norm in socialist paradises like North Korea and Cuba.

By 1966 Gaston was a shop steward at Billancourt and had already brought the men out on strike three times over wages and working conditions. Then in 1967 he suffered an injury when a Renault 10 tumbled off the production line and crushed his left ankle. It took several months to heal and left Gaston with a permanent limp. He attempted to sue his employer but the Renault company brought in the best lawyer money could buy. Despite the best efforts of his trade union, Gaston only got a small out-of-court settlement. The whole incident had a lasting effect on him as it amplified his conviction that big corporations were evil and all factories should be owned by the workers.

In May 1968 Gaston participated in the Paris riots, which had been initiated by students. There were many factors behind this event. Anger at capitalism. Anger at Charles De Gaulle's French

Government. Anger at rising unemployment. Anger at the escalating and seemingly never-ending Vietnam War. Some Paris academics had pointed out that the French had really started that war in the first place as they had refused to pull out of French Indo-China in the 1950s.

Gaston felt exhilaration as he flung pieces of broken paving stones at the Paris police. To him, the gendarmes represented the embodiment of state control, of suffocating capitalism. Confronted with tens of thousands of protesters, the Paris police could only respond with water cannon, tear gas and baton charges. Eventually the riot police defeated the crowds but Gaston felt the people had won a moral victory. By 23 May they had brought about a general strike involving ten million people. If it had continued it might have caused the downfall of the government. Socialism had triumphed over the forces of evil. What might have been achieved if the protestors had guns and tanks? They could have stormed the presidential palace and installed a new Socialist leader who would declare France a Marxist State. It might have been the beginning of a 'New World Order', the end of capitalism, a 'Global Reset'. Gaston relished the thought.

Gaston continued to read widely. His favourite book was *Das Kapital* by Karl Marx, and he vowed that if he ever had a son he would make sure he became indoctrinated in its contents. Marx himself had recommended that children start learning the principles of extreme socialism at an early age. In 1977 Gaston's wish came true when Brigitte had a son, Maurice, at the age of 39.

As soon as Maurice was old enough to understand, Gaston started his overt brainwashing. Little Maurice learned that all the world's problems were caused by capitalist countries like Britain and America, which exploited the working class. France was no better as she was a puppet of America and was stoking up trouble by selling arms to the illegal State of Israel. She had also adopted a capitalist system in which poorly-paid workers lived in hovels while fat cat bosses resided in mansions with their wives and children, wined and dined their mistresses, drove expensive cars and made obscene profits by exploiting the workers. They ate oysters, steak and *pâté de foie gras,* and drank champagne while poor people survived on bread, cheese and water.

Gaston foresaw a time when capitalism would be defeated by force of arms. According to his calculations, 'The Great Reset' would begin in 2022 so it was essential that his son made the necessary preparations, which included skill in handling weapons. As soon as he was old enough, he should join the French Army, preferably the Foreign Legion, which had always seen a lot of action in foreign trouble spots. It was essential that Maurice received military training in preparation for 'The New World Order'. As a former soldier, he might be required to suppress any dissidents and his duties might include lawful executions of those who disagreed with the state. Although Gaston had mixed views about the military and the way it had supported corrupt governments in the past, he knew it offered the easiest and cheapest way of training his son for the forthcoming challenges he would face.

In 1995, at the age of 18, Maurice joined the French Army. After basic infantry training, he chose to become a missile operator with an Air Defence Regiment equipped with the Franco-German Roland surface-to-air missile (SAM) system. This was equivalent to the British Rapier SAM system which had been deployed in the Falklands in 1982 with limited success. However, the manufacturers of Roland believed their system was far superior to the Rapier. Indeed, one unit deployed at Port Stanley airport had been credited with a single Sea Harrier kill during the 1982 conflict.

Maurice excelled in his new role and soon gained a reputation as the best missile operator in his regiment. His skill was so great that a few years later he was chosen to be the first person in the French Armed Forces to be offered the chance to train as a drone controller. The French had been impressed by the use of drones by British, American and Israeli military personnel since the early 1980s. These pilotless aircraft were cheap and simple and didn't put the lives of aircrew at risk. Ideal for surveillance duties with their high-definition TV cameras, and armed with four Hellfire guided missiles each, in case they came across a juicy target. From now on, no terrorist in the world was safe from attack. Even if he were residing in a friendly country like Iran or Syria, he could be spotted from the air and then taken out. Drones were hard to detect and could often infiltrate enemy airspace without being picked up on radar. They were every terrorist's nightmare.

Initially the French Armed forces bought several unarmed MQ-9 Reaper drones for surveillance duties. Maurice was relieved because he didn't want to kill any terrorists unless absolutely necessary. For the moment he had to maintain his cover, to give the impression that he was a patriotic French soldier who hated terrorists and would do anything to eliminate them. He even pretended to be jubilant at the election of Donald Trump in November 2016, adopting a mock gung-ho attitude in the mess as the election results were announced on French TV.

'Good man, that Trump,' he said as he quaffed a half-litre glass of Kronenbourg 1664. 'Any problems in the Middle East and he'll send in the B-2s and B-52s to carpet bomb the lot of them. I hope we get a chance to do our bit for the West as well. Down with communism! Capitalism always triumphs in the end! Bomb the bastards, that's what I say!'

Maurice laughed and took another mouthful of beer as his colleagues looked on in horror. L'Arconne was clearly right-wing. If only they had known his real views, they would have been shocked. Like all sleeper agents, Maurice had to keep his true opinions secret in order to maintain his cover.

While he was pretending to be pro-American and learning about drones, Maurice kept up contact with a number of radical organisations which were dedicated to the overthrow of Western civilization. They were in no rush for him to leave the French Army and become a fighter in the Middle East. Instead, they were quite happy for him to remain a sleeper agent, learning about Western methods and weapons. One day they would call upon his services, but not just yet.

Then on 4 March 2019 Maurice received an encrypted email message on his home laptop. A new terror organisation was being established in Europe and his military expertise was required. He was to resign from the French Army as soon as possible. A flat had been purchased for him in Dinard on the west coast of France. As cover, he would be given a computer shop to run in the town and two of the employees – both computer engineers – were committed members of the cause. He would receive an initial payment of 500,000 US dollars into a Swiss bank account to compensate him for any inconvenience. His orders were to run the shop as a *bona fide* business and await further instructions.

The battle for 'The New World Order' was about to begin.

CHAPTER 22

MASTER OF DISGUISES

4 September 2022, 10:55 hours

Rick connected the power lead of his Bosch spray gun to the red Honda petrol-driven electric generator and inspected his Jaguar X-Type estate. He had driven it into the barn and kept the huge wooden doors open for ventilation. All the car's windows, trim and chrome were covered with masking tape and newspapers, the wheels draped with old sheets. The car had already been washed down with detergent, rinsed and meticulously dried in the sunshine with micro-fibre towels.

Rick was glad he had built Airfix models in his youth, and had even learned to use an airbrush, which was really just a miniature spray gun. He had grown up with the smell of Humbrol enamels in his nostrils and knew how to get a good paint finish. Stir the paint well, thin it to the consistency of milk, set the correct air pressure, and spray a series of light mist coats at the optimum distance while taking care to keep the spray gun moving.

After forty-five minutes the job was done. An hour to let the paint dry and then he could remove the newspapers and tape and change the number plates. A few weeks earlier, he had cycled around London until he had come across another Jaguar X-Type estate parked at the side of the road. This one was also a three-litre automatic, though not a Sovereign variant. Rick took a smartphone photo of the front of the car to get the registration number and later checked the exact paint colour on the internet. It was Jaguar Pacific Blue. It was a straightforward process to get a can the right colour from eBay. If his repainted vehicle was subsequently spotted by a number plate recognition camera it would be mistaken for the car Rick had seen parked in the street.

Rick reflected on the latest developments as he sat in a folding wooden chair, ate his last sandwich and drank coffee from a Thermos flask. Captain Andy Harrington had recognised him so it wouldn't have taken long for the police to find his address and raid his flat. It wouldn't be safe to return there as the cops would probably be keeping the property under observation. Fortunately, he had already removed everything he needed from the apartment, including his laptop and a large black leather holdall containing several thousand pounds in cash, four false passports, three cheap mobile phones and some spare clothes and toiletries. He had taken the battery out of his usual smartphone so he couldn't be tracked. The next thing he had to do was change his appearance. There would be a photo on file from his army records and that would by now have been circulated to every police station in Britain.

Rick sipped the last of his coffee and walked over to a plastic basin filled with water which stood on a wooden trestle table. One thing Rick had never learned in the SAS was the art of hairdressing. Yet he was sure that if he followed the instructions on the bottle of hair dye then he could turn himself into a blonde. With the addition of a false moustache and glasses he could radically alter his appearance without resorting to plastic surgery.

The next problem was how to get to Dinard, capture L'Arconne and then bring him back to Britain for interrogation. He could go there in the Jaguar and then bring him back in the boot, drugged, gagged and trussed up. But that would be risky. The chance of L'Arconne being discovered during the journey was high and he might die of suffocation before he could be interrogated. What he needed was a more subtle approach. Rick considered his dilemma and had an idea...

*

Maurice L'Arconne sat at a table outside the *Café Paris* and enjoyed the view of Dinard bay. The early autumn sunshine warmed his body as he enjoyed a steaming hot cappuccino accompanied by a fresh croissant with Normandy butter and strawberry jam. Several cyclists wearing helmets, black Lycra shorts and yellow fluorescent tops rode past and rang their bells. An old grey Citroën 2CV van drew up outside, air-cooled engine ticking over noisily. The driver, an elderly man wearing a black beret, opened the rear doors and unloaded two wooden boxes of onions. Then he carried them down an alley to the back door of the café. A smell of garlic and fresh ground coffee emanated from the front doors and carried in the light warm autumn breeze. An old Charles Aznavour song played on speakers inside the café while smoking patrons sat outside in the mild sunshine and enjoyed multiple Gauloises and Gitanes cigarettes.

Maurice ordered a second coffee from the waiter and then finished his croissant as he reflected on what had happened in the last few weeks. Yes, running a computer shop wasn't such a bad deal. He had two highly-qualified assistants to run the business and attend to repairs while he could really do what he liked. In the evenings he kept in touch with his terrorist colleagues by means of secure encrypted email but for the rest of the day he could enjoy himself. He had to show up at the shop from time to time but he could go shopping, have lunch out and take long walks. It wasn't such a bad life but he knew that everything would change very soon. Once *Operation Armageddon* was concluded, life on Earth would change... permanently!

MI5 Headquarters, Thames House, London

4 September 2022, 11:32 hours

DI McAllister's stomach rumbled as he sat outside the office of George Keen, Head of MI5. He had arrived ten minutes before his appointment and had been given a cup of coffee, but no food. Not even a biscuit. If he was back in his native Scotland right now, he would be tucking into one of the many high-calorie products manufactured by Tunnocks of Uddingston. Perhaps one of their delicious teacakes, a Caramel Log or maybe even a Snowball. He could just imagine the coconutty taste of that particular high-sugar Scottish delicacy. Sometimes at this time of day he might even munch on a traditional Scotch mutton pie or a Gregg's sausage roll. That would be magic! He could feel saliva flowing into his mouth as he contemplated this gastronomic fantasy. Some men lived for sex, for others it was alcohol, drugs, cigarettes or gambling. McAllister's thing was food.

McAllister's reverie was interrupted by the sound of a heavy wooden door opening. A slim, attractive blonde woman who looked about thirty walked into the corridor. She was wearing a wireless headset.

'Detective Inspector McAllister, sorry to keep you so long. Mr Keen will see you now.'

'No problem, hen.'

The first thing that struck McAllister was the smell – wooden panelling combined with the pleasant odour of a new green wool carpet. Above the fireplace was a portrait of the Queen and there were framed photos on the wall showing Keen meeting various officials.

Keen looked up from his laptop screen and then closed the lid, smoothed back his grey hair and polished his spectacles with a cleaning cloth. His huge oak desk was largely empty apart from the laptop, a multi-button corded phone and a silver-framed photo of his wife and two children. He got up from his desk and greeted McAllister with a bone-crushing handshake.

'Please take a seat, Inspector McAllister. I want to talk to you about the latest developments. The Metropolitan Police failed to apprehend a terrorist suspect in the London Underground two days ago. You probably read about the incident on the news. The man attacked the Prime Minister's car. It was probably an assassination attempt using an explosive charge concealed inside his body. We know that organisations like Al Qaeda and ISIS have been experimenting with liquid explosives for some time. That's the reason we introduced the ban on carrying liquids onto commercial airliners some years ago. But this is something new. If what we believe is correct then this terrorist group *The Seven*, as they like to call themselves, could strike again using this new technique.'

'I'm aware of this, Mr Keen. But how does this involve me? I'm only a regular copper. I'm not part of the Anti-Terrorist branch.'

'Oh I know. But the terrorist suspect who we have now identified as Mahmoud Rashid, thanks to information you passed on to us, appeared to be working with an accomplice, a former SAS Sergeant called Rick Fernscale. I know you have expressed doubts about this appraisal of the situation. We have also interviewed the WPC whose car was hijacked. Fernscale told her he was chasing the suspect. Captain Andy Harrington also spoke to him briefly and was of the opinion that he is not working for the terrorists. But you met him when he was in hospital some months back. What did you make of him?'

'If you want my opinion sir, he's not working for the bad guys. No way. His wife was killed in the attempted drone attack on London in June and I think he now wants revenge. Knowing his military record, I think it is highly likely that he wants to kill them all and to hell with the law!'

'That is what I thought. Much as I sympathise with Fernscale's feelings, the British Government cannot condone vigilantes. Locating the terrorists is our job and eliminating them should be left to the military. As it happens, the PM would prefer to see them captured and put on trial.'

'I agree sir. The due processes of law must be observed even though the terrorists have no respect for the sanctity of human life.'

'Absolutely. The first thing we must do then is apprehend Fernscale and find out what he knows. Every policeman in Britain has been asked to look out for him. His flat here in London is under surveillance so if he returns there we will nab him. We have teams sifting through CCTV footage. All ports, airports and railway stations have been alerted. Police are currently hunting for his car and are checking CCTV footage. As soon as Fernscale makes a move we will know. Take my word for it, Inspector, we will catch him. It is only a matter of time.'

The French coast near Dinard

5 September 2022, 05:35 hours

Rick dropped anchor a mile off the coast of Dinard as dawn approached, removed the black rubber dinghy from its stowage locker on the cabin cruiser and started to inflate it using a compressed air cylinder. He knew a lot about boats from his time with the Special Boat Service, certainly enough to make an unauthorized Channel crossing at night in a 12-metre cabin cruiser. After spending some time on the internet researching boat hire businesses on the South coast of England, he had remembered an old friend from his SBS days.

Former SBS soldier Norman Arnott now ran a boat hire business, renting out plush cabin cruisers to wealthy businessman, but had fallen on hard times because of the economic depression which had followed the virus pandemic. Fewer people wanted to hire expensive cabin cruisers as they could get a package holiday for less. So Norman (or 'Norm' as Rick always called him) was delighted to accept Rick's offer of a 48-hour hire for £3,000 in cash. No receipts required. No VAT. No questions asked. Rick stipulated a maximum fuel load. Enough to get to Dinard and back. If there wasn't enough fuel capacity for such a journey, then extra fuel had to be provided in jerrycans. He also wanted fresh water and sufficient provisions for 48 hours plus an inflatable dinghy with both oars and an outboard motor large enough to take two people.

As it happened, Norm had a Nimbus Tender II tied up at his jetty. Just two years old, it was 12 metres long and 3.5 metres wide. A glass-fibre hull and two outboard Mercury Verado V8 petrol engines delivering 300 horsepower each. It could also carry enough fuel to make a return trip to France. And it was fast.

Norm wasn't surprised to see his old friend turn up in a Jaguar. Everyone knew that Rick liked Jags. When he was at Hereford, Rick had owned an old XJ6 and had only got rid of it when it developed multiple electrical problems. He was astonished though to see that Rick now had blonde hair, spectacles and a moustache.

'I expect to be away for forty-eight hours maximum. I would like to leave my car here and if you can stick it in one of your boat sheds away from prying eyes that would be even better.'

'That would be fine. I take it you're going to Dinard for some sightseeing? I won't even ask what's in these bags?'

*

Rick paddled furiously towards the beach with the oars. He could have used the Johnson outboard motor but that would have made too much noise. The sky facing him was glowing orange, the sun just minutes away from rising above the horizon. Salt spray splashed in his face. There was that delicious smell of sea and rubber that he had come to love during his time in the SBS. Then the dinghy grounded on the sand. Rick put his backpack on, jumped out and hauled the dinghy up onto the beach. His boots, socks, feet and trousers were now soaking wet, but getting cold and damp was all part of being a Special Forces soldier.

Rick dragged the dinghy further up the beach, concealed it in some bushes and then draped some camouflage netting over it. As he was cutting some branches and foliage with his Fairbairn-Sykes combat knife to put over the netting, he spotted a pair of headlights coming towards him. A vehicle had driven off the coast road and was heading his way. He didn't have time to drag the dinghy from its hiding place and head out to sea and his pistol was in his backpack, unloaded. He would have to bluff this one out, if that was possible. Rick put his knife back in the backpack and zipped it up.

The vehicle halted just a few yards in front of him, diesel engine clattering and headlights blazing. In the half-light of dawn, Rick could see that it was a white Citroën Berlingo with blue and red stripes on the bodywork. The words *Police Municipale* were written on the sides. Two burly policemen in black uniforms jumped out and pointed Sig

Sauer P022 pistols at him.

'Arreter de lever les mains!'

Even with his limited knowledge of French, Rick knew he was being arrested and they wanted him to raise his hands. Did they know who he was? Unlikely. But if he was taken for interrogation, they would soon work out his true identity. He had to escape, but how? He was outnumbered two-to-one and both his opponents had pistols pointed at him. Rick had been caught with his pants down…and he knew it.

CHAPTER 23

PRISONER

6 September 2022

The two French policemen advanced on Rick, Sig Sauer pistols drawn, as the former SAS man assessed the situation. This was exactly the kind of scenario he had practised for during his counter-insurgency training at Hereford. The good news was that the policemen were members of the *Police Municipale*, the local police force. They were not anti-terrorist experts. In addition, they had probably not spotted the dinghy because Rick had covered it in camouflage netting and branches and hidden it in the bushes. A well-trained search team assisted by sniffer dogs would locate it in minutes, but Rick hoped they would not be called in. The bad news was that both policemen were armed, although they had probably only received minimal firearms training and had never fired a gun in anger.

One policeman stood at a range of two metres and covered Rick, aiming at the centre of his body mass, while the other patted him down after removing his backpack. After confirming that Rick had no hidden weapons, he took a pair of handcuffs from his belt.

Rick's face tightened. If his hands were cuffed behind his back, he would have little chance of escape. His only chance would be to plead with the officers.

'Please officers, I'm only a humble English fisherman. I came across the Channel in a little boat for a laugh after a drunken night out. Please don't put handcuffs on me. I'm terrified of them. When I was at school, a couple of bullies tied my hands together with rope. Ever since then I have had a great anxiety about my wrists being tied. I won't resist arrest. I will go to the police station with you. I will answer all your questions. I don't want any trouble. Please. *Parlez-vouz anglais?*

One of the French policeman understood what Rick had said and spoke:

'OK, *Rostbif.* You do as we say…no handcuffs. Get in the back of the vehicle. Don't try anything or we shoot. We only want to take you to the station and verify your identity.'

'Thank you, officer, thank you!'

Because of his SAS training, Rick knew his best plan was to play the 'grey man', a weak individual who was no threat to them. That way they might take pity on him and make mistakes which would enable him to escape. It was obvious that they thought he was only an illegal immigrant. Once they searched his backpack at the police station, they would discover his pistol and other items of equipment and his cover story would be exposed as the lie it was. If he wanted to escape it would have to be soon.

One policeman re-attached the handcuffs to his belt and ordered Rick into the rear seat of the Citroën Berlingo patrol vehicle at pistol point before flicking a rocker switch on the dashboard which locked the rear doors electrically. Rick was now shut in the back of the vehicle with no means of escape. The only consolation was that he hadn't been hooded or blindfolded, something that would have been standard procedure in the SAS. The other policeman put Rick's backpack in the Berlingo's boot and then sat on the front passenger seat. His colleague started the diesel engine and headed west, directly away from the developing orange glow in the east. Rick had studied a street map of Dinard before he left England and guessed they would be taking him to the *Police Municipale* Station at 16 Rue Winston Churchill.

His situation was grim, but by no means hopeless. If he could just stay calm and exploit any opportunity which developed, he could escape and execute his plan. Only then could he properly avenge Laura's death. His SAS instructors had told him that any breakout had to be done as soon as possible after capture. The longer he waited, the worse his chances would become. Once he was locked in a cell, things would become more difficult. As soon as they looked in his bag, they would find his pistol, and other incriminating evidence. If the French police then did some checking, they might discover his true identity. And if they sent a forensic search team to the beach, they would locate the dinghy. Then he really would be in trouble…

*

Jacques Dubois had a massive hangover. His head throbbed and he felt nauseated. He had only got to bed at 4:30 a.m. after a night of celebrations. Jacques had downed prodigious quantities of beer, cider, Pernod and vodka at an all-night bar to celebrate his birthday with a group of friends. Now, as he gazed at the smartphone by his bed, he regretted his actions. It was 6:45 a.m. He was going to do a shift as a porter at the local district hospital after just two hours sleep. What he really needed was a litre or two of water to rehydrate himself, a decent breakfast with plenty of *café noir*, some paracetamol and at least six hours of deep, refreshing sleep. But that would have to wait. The hospital was short-staffed and his services were needed. He shouldn't really be driving, but it was only a couple of kilometres and he didn't think there would be many traffic cops around at this time in the morning. Jacques picked up a couple of extra strong mints, popped them in his mouth and then retrieved the keys for his ten-year-old silver Renault Clio from the hook by the front door.

The Clio started first time and Jacques set off south east along Rue Gardiner. It was a short drive from his apartment to the hospital and in just three minutes he had arrived at the junction with Avenue Edouard VII which ran in an east-west direction. Commuter traffic was light at this time in the morning and Jacques only had to make a right turn into Avenue Edouard VII before turning sharp left into the car park of the *Hôpital Arthur Gardiner*. Under normal circumstances, Jacques would have spotted the white *Police Municipale* Berlingo which was speeding west at fifty kilometres per hour. But Jacques was sleep-deprived and the Berlingo was hard to see because of the rising sun. A moment later it smashed into the left side of the moving Clio with a loud bang. The impact caved in the driver's door of the Renault, shoved it into a traffic bollard, and smashed all the glass on one side. Cubes of safety glass went everywhere. The Berlingo's radiator burst, discharging sticky hot green coolant onto the tarmac road. The Citroën's two front airbags activated and pushed the policemen back in their seats. They were both stunned and temporarily incapacitated by the airbags, but otherwise uninjured.

It was the opportunity Rick had been waiting for. He unfastened his seat belt and launched himself forward between the two front seats. Then he pressed the dashboard-mounted rocker switch to unlock the rear doors, wrenched the policemen's guns from their holsters and escaped using the right rear door. After opening the boot to retrieve his backpack, he shoved both captured weapons in the bag and raced east along Avenue Edouard VII, heading towards the rising sun. Behind him, an ambulance drove out of the hospital, siren blaring and headed towards the smashed vehicles, followed by some paramedics travelling on foot. He reckoned it would take the police a few minutes to work out what had happened and organise a search.

Even with his heavy backpack, Rick made good progress as he ran east along the Avenue Edouard VII. After a couple of minutes, he turned left and headed north west along the Boulevard L'Hotelier. Rick remembered there was a municipal park on the right called The Parc de Tourelle. He could hide there in the bushes for a while until it was time for Maurice L'Arconne's computer shop to open. Then he could abduct him and smuggle him back to Britain, if all went according to plan.

*

At exactly 10:00 a.m. Maurice L'Arconne tried the front door of his computer shop and found it was open. His two assistants Claude and Marcus had arrived early. Claude was eager to fix an HP computer which was faulty. It was for a rich customer who had promised a substantial cash bonus paid directly to Claude if he could fix it by 5:00 p.m. that day. Maurice didn't know anything about this arrangement but his two employees knew he had little interest in the shop.

It was a lovely day and Maurice thought he could skive off in the afternoon and spend some time on the beach. Even before that, he fancied a trip to his favourite café for a cappuccino coffee and a *croque monsieur*. His two assistants could run the business anyway. First though, he would have to check his emails on his computer in the office at the back of the shop.

Just across the road, Rick observed his quarry from the relative comfort of a Citroën Picasso which he had hired an hour earlier using fake documents and a cloned credit card. He knew the unauthorised transaction would be picked up by the credit card company within 24 hours but by then, if all went to plan, he would be back in the UK. He had no intention of returning the Picasso to the car hire company; it would be left on the beach with the keys under the sun visor, once he had completed his mission.

At exactly 10:27 a.m., L'Arconne emerged from the shop and headed for the narrow dark alley which was his usual short cut to his favourite café. Rick opened the driver's door of his Picasso, picked up his backpack from the passenger seat and followed him. Rick removed a short cylindrical object from the rucksack and closed on the Frenchman as he made his way down the alley. After checking that there was no-one else in the alley and that there were no CCTV cameras around, Rick pulled the telescopic baton out to full length and whacked L'Arconne on the back of the head. The Frenchman collapsed, stunned. Rick caught him from behind and lowered him gently to the ground. Then he rolled up his left sleeve, applied a tourniquet, injected some Propofol from a syringe into a vein in his left ante-cubital fossa. L'Arconne's body went limp. Rick inserted a plastic airway into the Frenchman's mouth to stop him swallowing his own tongue and then concealed his body behind a pile of black bin bags. So far so good. No-one had entered the alley and witnessed the crime.

Rick ran to the Picasso, started the engine and reversed the vehicle into the alley. Then he opened the tailgate, retrieved L'Arconne from behind the pile of bin bags, carried him using a fireman's lift and dumped his flaccid body into the boot of the Citroën. Rick slammed the tailgate shut, ensuring that the load cover was in place to conceal the body.

Only five minutes had elapsed since he had knocked out L'Arconne and as far as Rick knew, no-one had witnessed the crime. The first stage of the abduction of the terrorist had been completed. All he had to do now was stay hidden until darkness fell. Then he could return to the beach, retrieve his dinghy, sail out to his rented motor launch, and return to Britain.

Police Municipale Station, Dinard

11:29 hours

Police Inspector La Salle sat in his office in Dinard's Police Municipale, drank a coffee and looked at his computer screen. He rather fancied having a long boozy lunch that day. After all, nothing ever happened in Dinard, which had one of the lowest crime rates in France.

There was a knock at the door.

'Come in,' said La Salle.

A female police officer entered.

'There's been a bit of excitement today, Inspector. Two of our officers apprehended a male suspect on the beach just before dawn. He claimed to be an English fisherman who had landed in France as a prank. Of course, he could be an illegal immigrant from the Middle East. We get a lot of them in this part of France, as you know, sir. He was being taken to this station in a patrol vehicle when it was involved in a road traffic accident. The officers were stunned but not seriously injured. Unfortunately the suspect stole their guns and escaped on foot. We're still looking for him.'

'Do we know the suspect's name?'

'Sadly not. The officers were planning to establish his ID when they got him to this station.'

'OK, I see. Anything else you want to tell me?'

'There was another incident at 10.30 a.m. A woman pushing a pram was about to take a short cut down an alley when she saw a man with blonde curly hair being dumped in the boot of a people carrier. He appeared to be unconscious. The suspect in this abduction resembles the description of the unidentified foreigner who was apprehended on the beach.'

'I see. Did this woman get a note of the Citroën's number plate?'

'Unfortunately not. It happened too fast.'

'Right, have all available officers taken off routine duties. I want all the relevant CCTV footage for the past few hours checked. We need to get the vehicle's number plate details and also ID the suspect if possible. We may need to use the national facial recognition database. We will find him. It is only a matter of time.'

'Yes sir, I will get onto this right away.'

The police officer left and closed the door.

Inspector La Salle's face fell. He wouldn't be eating out for lunch today.

*

Rick finished his brie sandwich and washed it down with a small bottle of mineral water as he sat in the front seat of the Picasso. It was cool with the front windows open. Above him was a canopy of branches and leaves. After abducting L'Arconne, he had driven several miles into the French countryside and had gone up a rutted track which led to a wood. Somewhere which didn't have CCTV cameras.

He could hear L'Arconne snoring in the boot. The Frenchman now had a green Venflon cannula in a large vein in his right arm, which was secured with micropore tape. This would enable Rick to give him top-up doses of Propofol and Hyoscine during the day to keep him compliant and heavily sedated.

Rick felt dead tired but knew he had to stay awake. He couldn't afford to doze, even for a minute. He was sure that there had been no witnesses to his abduction of L'Arconne, but he couldn't be sure. And police officers could have spotted him on CCTV. The car rental company might have discovered he had used a fraudulent transaction to hire the Citroën. A team of armed police might be on their way to capture him.

Rick even wondered if he had overstepped himself. Contrary to popular belief, the SAS never took risks. They normally planned every operation in great detail. An abduction of a foreign national would normally take weeks to plan and execute. A small team would be sent into the country where they would spend several days observing the suspect and plotting his movements. Only then would a multi-person kidnap team be sent in. The exfiltration or 'exfil' of the subject would be planned in great detail to avoid capture of any team members. They would have several cars, lookouts, walkie-talkies, false IDs and safe houses.

The world experts in this kind of operation were the Mossad who would send a team of anything between six and twenty people to carry out such an operation. Rick wondered if his solo mission was just too risky. Right now, he couldn't see how he could complete it without getting caught.

By 8:45 p.m. it was pitch black. Rick started the Citroën's engine and drove down the rutted track from the wood to the main road. He turned right and headed north towards Dinard. He was quite safe in the country but once he entered the town there was a risk he might be spotted by a number plate recognition camera. He hoped that the police response in a place like Dinard would be slow and that if he acted quickly, he would escape to Britain with his captive.

Rick halted at a set of red traffic lights. There were three more sets of lights between him and the beach where he had left the dinghy. He could just imagine a red warning light blinking next to a TV monitor and a police CCTV operator lifting a phone to summon a patrol car to the scene.

Rick felt his shoulder muscles tense. The next two sets of traffic lights were at green. Then he came to the third, which were red. How long would they take to change? Three minutes passed and they were still red. Were they faulty? Should he crash the lights? No, he couldn't take the chance of being stopped for a minor traffic violation. Not with L'Arconne in the boot.

Another agonising minute passed and then the lights changed. Only two hundred yards to the beach. He had almost made it! Rick drove off the road and headed for the bushes where he had concealed the dinghy. He pulled off the camouflage net and branches and dragged the little rubber boat to the water's edge. Then he ran back to the Citroën, opened the boot and extracted L'Arconne. Using a fireman's lift, Rick carried the Frenchman's limp body to the water's edge and dumped him in the boat. He was just starting to push the little boat into the sea when he was illuminated by a pair of headlamps. He turned round and saw a police car driving onto the sand, blue light flashing and siren blaring. It was another *Police Municipale* vehicle.

Rick opened a waterproof bag that was lying in the base of the dinghy and took out a Finnish Jatamatic submachine gun. Aiming carefully, he fired a couple of short bursts at the lights on top of the police car. Then he took out his Browning 9 mm Hi-Power pistol from his backpack and shot out the headlamps of the police vehicle. The two policemen inside the patrol car panicked and reversed the vehicle off the beach. They would call for armed assistance, but that would take time to arrive and Rick only needed a few minutes to escape.

Rick dragged the dinghy into the sea. When the water reached his thighs, he jumped in and used the oars to take the dinghy a few yards further offshore. When he was satisfied that the water was now deep enough, he lowered the propeller of the powerful Johnson outboard motor into the water and started the engine at the second attempt with the pull-cord. Rick headed further out to sea, heading for the launch which was moored a mile offshore.

Five minutes later, he was alongside the launch. He tied the dinghy to the stern and heaved L'Arconne aboard. Later, he would bring the dinghy on board but for the moment he had to start the engines and put as many miles between him and the French coast as possible.

The powerful diesel motors started first time. Rick hauled up the anchor, pushed the throttle levers forward and turned the bow of the vessel due north towards England. Then he moved L'Arconne to a bunk in the main cabin below the bridge. He was still sleeping with a strong radial pulse of 72 beats per minute. Rick gave him a top-up dose of Propofol and returned to the wheelhouse. It was a fine autumn evening with just a couple of slow-moving bulk carriers in the distance.

A bright light flooded the wheelhouse. Rick turned round and saw it came from a patrol boat which had appeared from nowhere. It was just two hundred yards astern. Commands shouted in French over a loudhailer ordered Rick to heave to and submit to inspection. The police must have called the French Coastguard when they had failed to apprehend him on the beach, thought Rick. The French patrol boat had a good turn of speed and easily outpaced Rick's vessel. After trailing Rick's boat for a couple of minutes it came alongside, its spotlight trained on the wheelhouse.

Further instructions came over the tannoy in French. He was to come to a halt and allow a boarding party to come on board and search the vessel. Rick recognised the French vessel. It was an *Athos*-class patrol boat of the French Coastguard. One hundred and eight metric tonnes displacement and thirty metres long. Armed with a 20 mm Oerlikon cannon for'ard and various small arms. Rick could see that the Oerlikon had a drum magazine fitted but was currently unmanned. Four crew members stood on deck carrying automatic rifles.

Rick had almost made it back to England but now he was being forced to surrender. So near and yet so far. He stepped out of the wheelhouse so everyone could see him and raised his hands. It looked as though he had no fight left in him.

CHAPTER 24

SURRENDER OR DIE!

Rick held his hands above his head. The French Captain put down his loudhailer and ordered the crew to prepare an armed boarding party. While the Captain was distracted, Rick picked up his Jatamatic submachine gun and aimed at the powerful spotlight on the coastguard vessel. He only had a few rounds left but that was all he needed. Rick squeezed the trigger. The glass of the spotlamp shattered along with the bulb and the scene was plunged into darkness.

Rick pulled a tarpaulin from the deck to reveal three L1A1 LAW 66 mm rocket launchers that had come from the arms cache in the barn. He pulled the end caps off the first one, extended it to full length, put it on his shoulder and looked through the sights before sliding the safety catch on top of the weapon forward and pressing the firing button on top of the weapon. A small but powerful rocket with a hollow charge warhead shot out of the muzzle and hit Rick's first designated target – the 20 mm cannon. The explosion bent the barrel of the weapon, leaving it pointing at a crazy angle.

Rick threw the used LAW launcher overboard and picked up a second. This time his target was the boat's radio aerial. The crew scattered in panic as the round exploded above their heads, scattering debris in every direction. His third and last LAW was aimed at the rear hull. Rick smiled in satisfaction as the warhead punched a melon-sized hole just below the waterline. Water gushed into the boat, flooding the machinery spaces.

Rick re-started his vessel and pushed the throttles forward. The French Coastguard vessel was now burning and listing heavily to port. All available French helicopters and ships would be diverted to rescue the crew. Rick turned the wheel and pointed the bow of his boat towards Britain…and safety.

7 September 2022, 10:05 hours

The countryside near Farnborough, England

Rick opened the tailgate of his Jaguar, unclipped the roller blind style load cover and hauled out Maurice L'Arconne. The terrorist was still drowsy from the effects of the anaesthetic agent Rick had administered. His hands were secured behind his back with plastic cable ties and his ankles tied together with nylon rope. As L'Arconne was now semi-conscious, Rick pulled out the plastic airway and cut the ropes securing his ankles with his Fairbairn-Sykes combat knife.

Rick shoved the muzzle of his 9 mm Browning Hi-Power pistol into the small of L'Arconne's back and grabbed the collar of the terrorist's shirt.

'Down these steps. Now! Try anything and I'll shoot!'

L'Arconne muttered an incomprehensible French obscenity and complied. He was still recovering from the effects of the drugs Rick had administered, nauseated from the long sea journey and in pain from being tied up and dumped in the boot of the car. His mouth felt dry from the Hyoscine, and every time he moved his head, he felt his whole world spinning. He was in no condition to put up a fight.

There were a few crumbling moss-covered concrete steps heading down to a rusting iron door.

'Get on your knees and put your hands behind your head,' said Rick, as he fumbled in the right-hand pocket of his combat trousers for the padlock keys. Rick soon had the door open and ordered the Frenchman inside. L'Arconne did as he was told. He obviously knew some English.

'I'm not going to tell you anything!' blurted out L'Arconne. 'You're going to kill me anyway, aren't you?'

Rick didn't answer and shone his torch around the room. The walls, ceiling and floor were constructed of rough concrete, which was now filthy. Two burst plastic bags of fertiliser stood against one wall. A dirty yellowed copy of the wartime *Daily Express* lay on the floor. The only furniture was a simple wooden chair and folding table which stood in the centre of the room. A portable butane gas light hung from a metal hook in the centre of the ceiling. Rick took it down, put it on the table, turned on the gas, lit the mantle with a match and put it back on the hook. Then he ordered L'Arconne to sit on the chair, handcuffed his hands behind his back and used a couple of cable ties to secure the cuffs to the chair.

Rick put his pistol back in his shoulder holster and gazed at the bruised and bloodied face of his captive.

'Now we can talk. You're probably wondering where you are. You're in an old concrete air raid shelter that was built during the Second World War. It was part of a munitions plant near Farnborough. The factory was knocked down decades ago but they couldn't get rid of the shelter as it was built of reinforced concrete. Very hard to demolish. A local farmer used it to store fertiliser but he died and it got overlooked. Not the most pleasant of properties but it will suffice for my purposes.'

A look of fear appeared on L'Arconne's face.

'Who are you? What do you want? Why are you interested in me? I run a computer shop in Dinard. Do you intend to murder me? Or are you a kidnapper? I have friends who will pay you a lot of money for my safe return, unharmed.'

'Oh, I am indeed very interested in you, Maurice. Very interested. It's not every day that I meet the man who was responsible for the death of my wife.'

'What are you talking about?'

'Remember 21 June this year? The River Thames. My wife was on the cruise boat that was hit by the wreckage of your drone.'

'So that is what this is about! We weren't targeting the cruise boat. If the British Army hadn't shot down the drone, your wife would have been unharmed. We were trying to kill the British Prime Minister!'

'Oh I see, it's the army's fault now. But if your attack had gone as planned a lot of people would have died, including many civilians. The missiles your drone was carrying have a large blast radius. No, I don't blame the army's missile operators, I blame you and your depraved organisation *The Seven*. Do you think you can change the world through violence?'

'The purpose of terrorism is to terrorise,' said L'Arconne. 'In a capitalist society, no-one is innocent. People must die to make the world a better, fairer place.'

'Ah, such eloquence,' said Rick. 'If my wife was still alive right now, she would probably disagree with you. But let's get to the point, shall we. There's some information I need to execute my own plan. If you let me have it, then I will spare your life. You won't be set free. I will simply tie you up and leave you where the police can find you. You will spend the rest of your life in prison of course but you will still be alive. Unfortunately this country doesn't hang terrorists any more. On the other hand, if you refuse to co-operate then things will get very unpleasant for you.'

Rick pulled out his torch and shone it at two green plastic fuel cans which were lying at the back of the shelter. L'Arconne turned his head so he could see what Rick was looking at.

'That's right. Two gallons of unleaded petrol. I could have got super unleaded but it's more expensive. A doctor once told me that just one gallon of petrol is enough to cause fatal burns. Gasoline burns at a thousand degrees centigrade, did you know that Maurice? Of course you won't die immediately. You will live for a while until you eventually die from the complications of burns, such as fluid loss, shock, sepsis and kidney failure. And the pain will be horrendous. A huge dose of morphine would help but I don't see any syringes and ampoules lying around, do you?'

L'Arconne let out a wail of despair and started shaking with fear. Then a strong smell of faeces filled the air as he shat himself. Urine dribbled down his left trouser leg and formed a puddle in the floor. Rick had seen soldiers in combat experience the same double incontinence as a result of extreme stress.

'Not so brave are you now, Maurice? By the way I water-boarded your friend Mahmoud Rashid. I never thought he would talk but in the end he sang like a canary. What a pity his heart stopped before I could learn everything he knew. I was planning to use the same method on you but then I remembered that great biblical quote, *An eye for an eye, a tooth for a tooth*. So you will have the same horrific experience as my late wife. She was blonde and gorgeous. Won a beauty contest when she was nineteen. Worked as a model in her early twenties. But when they wheeled her blackened body into the A&E Department at St Thomas's, a couple of the nurses vomited when they saw her. And now you're going to suffer the same fate. That's right Maurice, I'm going to burn you to death unless you talk. And this means your organisation will have to change its name from *The Seven* to *The Five*. You'll have to change your letterheads and your business cards. In fact under British law you could be prosecuted under the Trade Descriptions Act for calling your organisation *The Seven* when there's only five of you left. Ever seen *Blake's Seven*, Maurice? It's a kind of cheap BBC rip- off of *Star Trek*. Created by Terry Nation who invented the Daleks. I prefer *Star Trek* but *Blake's Seven* has its fans. Did you know that in the last season there were only six of them and Blake wasn't in it, but they still called it *Blake's Seven?*'

'You're bluffing. You British are a civilized race. Tea and crumpets on the vicarage lawn and all that. You would never commit such an evil act.'

Rick didn't answer. Instead, he unscrewed the cap of one of the petrol cans and poured the contents over L'Arconne. The Frenchman was drenched in cold petrol. The air in the bunker filled with gasoline fumes. Rick pulled a box of Swan Vesta matches from his trouser pocket, took one out and prepared to strike it.

L'Arconne screamed, tears running down his cheeks:

'OK I'll talk! I'll talk! Just tell me what you want to know!'

Rick dropped the matchbox and pulled a small Olympus digital voice recorder from a trouser pocket.

'Right Frenchie, start talking!'

L'Arconne really did spill the beans. Rick had seen this so many times in his SAS days. Some men resisted interrogation, but once their spirit had broken you could get any information you wanted out of them. After an hour, Rick thought he had everything he needed and put the digital voice recorder back in his pocket.

L'Arconne looked shattered.

'So are you going to hand me over to the authorities now? I need a shower, a change of clothes, food and medical attention.'

Rick didn't speak. Instead he unscrewed the cap of the second petrol can, poured most of it over L'Arconne and used the last dregs of fuel to create a wet trail between L'Arconne and the iron door of the bunker.

'What are you doing?' said L'Arconne. 'You told me that you would let me live if I talked.'

'I know,' said Rick. 'But I lied! And I've always liked bonfires!'

Rick tossed a lit match into the trail of petrol and watched as a moving orange flame sped along the ground and ignited L'Arconne's sodden clothes. The Frenchman screamed in agony as his face caught fire and his hair frizzled. Within a minute his body was a mass of roasted flesh, his hair gone and his clothes burning. L'Arconne's eyelids burned off and then his nose, revealing two gaping oval holes in his face which now looked like a turnip lantern.

'An eye for an eye,' muttered Rick as he closed the shelter door, re-fastened the padlock and then threw the keys as far as he could into the undergrowth. It might be days before L'Arconne's body was found but Rick reckoned he would be dead within an hour. And it would be the most agonising sixty minutes of the Frenchman's life. Laura's death had been avenged but Rick was not stopping now. Not when five members of *The Seven* still remained alive.

CHAPTER 25

POST MORTEM

Lambeth Police Station

9 September 2022, 11:05 hours

DCI McAllister bit off half a chocolate Dunkin Donut and washed it down with a cup of hot sweet tea. In front of him was a cardboard box containing three more of these popular American delicacies. Maybe he should offer one to his skinny accomplice, Brown, as he looked as though he needed a good feed? Did Brown ever eat such things? He usually ate fruit with his tea, which had to be green and unsweetened.

McAllister's gastronomic reverie was interrupted by the sound of someone knocking at the door. DS Brown entered carrying a sheaf of papers.

'I was just thinking about you,' said McAllister. 'Want a doughnut, laddie?'

'I'll pass on that if you don't mind, sir. I've already had my mid-morning apple. Besides, there have been some interesting developments in the last few hours.'

'Tell me more. I'm all ears.'

'I'm just off the phone to the coppers in Farnborough. They're investigating an unexplained death on their patch. Yesterday morning at about 7:00 a.m. a dog walker noticed smoke rising from a patch of undergrowth. When he investigated further, he found it was coming from the air vents on top of an old concrete air raid shelter which was built during the war. The metal door was padlocked shut and hot to the touch so he called the police who came out, along with the fire service. They cut off the padlock, got the door open and discovered a body lying on the floor of the shelter. I've got some photos of the corpse for you to look at.'

McAllister started on his second doughnut as he studied the pictures. He had seen plenty of dead bodies during his career and there wasn't much that could put him off his food.

The colour photos showed a charred black corpse which was lying on a filthy concrete floor, its arms tied behind its back. The scorched remains of a burnt wooden chair were visible.

'The police surgeon and the pathologist have already made a preliminary report. It looks as though the body was dowsed with petrol by another person and then set alight. Definitely not suicide. A mixture of third and fourth-degree burns. As you know, sir, a fourth-degree burn involves charring right down to the bone and is rarely seen in a living person. No recoverable fingerprints so the only options for identification were dental records and DNA. Fortunately the pathologist struck lucky there, sir. There was one area of the body which was unburnt. The perineum. That's the skin and muscle between the anus and the genitals. Because the victim was sitting down, the chair protected that area from burning until it collapsed. Anyway, to get to the point, a pathologist recovered some intact flesh and had it tested for DNA and then checked it against an international police database. They couldn't identify the person from the DNA but it matched some found on a Russian-made, Kornet anti-tank missile fired at the American ambassador in Kabul in 2011. The rocket's warhead failed to explode so it was a gift for the forensic boys.'

'So the mystery corpse is a terrorist, then?'

'Yes sir, he is. And it gets better. A thumb print was recovered from the rocket's tail fins. At that time, it wasn't on anyone's databases so nothing more could be done with the information. But we now know it matches prints taken recently from the body of Mahmoud Rashid.'

'So there is a connection between this mystery corpse and Rashid.'

'Yes sir. It looks as though they have been working for the same terrorist organisation. Furthermore, it is likely they were both killed by the same person… and I am sure you can guess who the most likely suspect is.'

'Rick Fernscale.'

'Precisely. The police have been looking for him for some time.'

'He must be hunting the terrorists who killed his wife. On an emotional level I can understand his motives. Believe me laddie, I hate terrorists. I've seen what they can do. But we can't have people taking the law into their own hands. Otherwise society as we know it will break down. If Fernscale knows where the terrorists are, he should tell us, instead of behaving like a one-man army. We have to find him and apprehend him as soon as possible.'

'I am currently liaising with the anti-terrorist unit at Scotland Yard. If we find out the whereabouts of Fernscale, they will send a Police Armed Response Unit to capture him.'

'Good, keep me posted.'

The old Maginot Line forts at Merlaux, France

10 September 2022, 11:03 hours

Khalid studied the faces of the four terrorists who sat round the table in front of them and sipped a glass of hot cinnamon tea which he held in his left hand. All had glum expressions.

'This should be a time of rejoicing,' said Khalid. 'If things had gone as planned, the British Prime Minister would be dead by now. But he is still alive and well. And Mahmoud Rashid, our brother who carried out the assassination attempt on the British Prime Minister, is missing. Our intelligence indicates he was not captured by the British Police or the Security Services but was found dead after extreme interrogation by an unknown person. And now Maurice L'Arconne has vanished as well. That is a blow to our organisation because he was a missile expert.'

'Do we know who was behind these developments?' said Devlin.

'I don't think the British Intelligence services were responsible,' said Khalid. 'For all their faults, the British are obsessed with correct legal processes. They would not eliminate someone in such a violent way. A more likely culprit would be the Mossad, who strike anywhere in the world against any persons whom they consider a threat to their illegal Zionist state. What has happened bears all the hallmarks of a Mossad operation. However, our own intelligence suggests this is the work of an individual not a team. As you all know, the Mossad tends to use a large number of agents to eliminate just one person. It is the way they operate.'

'So who is this person and how can we find him?' said Devlin.

'I don't know,' said Khalid. 'But I have devised a plan. Instead of waiting for this person to murder us, we must set a trap. He will be captured, tortured, interrogated and killed. Then *Operation Armageddon* can proceed. Whoever this person is, he will soon discover how ruthless we can be.'

CHAPTER 26

SHOOTDOWN

13 September 2022, 07:57 hours

Rick lay on his sagging bed in his cheap, musty hotel room and thumbed through the TV channels. He was bored. So far, he had personally eliminated two of *The Seven*, one of whom was the very person who had controlled the drone which had killed Laura. He had also obtained considerable intelligence about *The Seven*, their members and the location of their European base. All good.

But Rick deduced that *The Seven* would by now have concluded that two of their number had been abducted and probably killed. According to news reports, L'Arconne's incinerated body had been found in the bunker near Farnborough. News reports suggested that the police believed it was a gangland killing, possibly involving a drug deal gone wrong. But Rick knew this was just a cover story as he was sure they now had leads on the true identity of the corpse. Pouring petrol over a body and setting it alight would never destroy it completely. For that he would have needed a proper crematorium.

There would have been enough unburnt tissue left to get a DNA sample and nowadays it could even be recovered from bone. By now the police, MI5 and MI6 would have checked L'Arconne's DNA profile against all their computer databases, including samples recovered from the site of terrorist attacks in the last twenty years.

Did *The Seven* have a mole within the security services who would tip them off? He had no idea. What was certain was that *The Seven* (or *The Five* as they now were) would have realised that someone was hunting them down.

Rick now knew they had a base at the old Maginot Line forts at Merlaux. He could tip off MI5 and MI6, and then the French Special Forces and police could raid the base. But even if the terrorists were there, they would just be arrested, not killed…and that was not acceptable to Rick. It was highly likely they would have vacated that base by now as they would have guessed that L'Arconne might have revealed its existence before he died. It was also possible that the terrorists might take the view that the best form of defence was attack and would come after him. From now on, he would have to watch his back even more than before. Yes, things were difficult, thought Rick, and he had no idea what his next move should be.

Rick made a cup of Nescafé with UHT milk, munched on a ginger biscuit and sat on the edge of his bed as he scrolled through the TV channels. The cheap, metal-framed, single-glazed windows did little to keep out environmental noise, which currently included the sound of an Airbus A320 airliner orbiting London with its undercarriage down. Rick looked out the window and saw the aircraft moving slowly across the sky from right to left. From this distance it looked like an Airfix model.

As Rick studied the slow-flying, airliner he heard a loud bang in the distance. Then a bright yellow flare appeared above the skyline and ascended in a curving path. Rick knew at once what it was. It wasn't just a kid playing with a flare gun. It was a surface-to-air missile. Probably a compact shoulder-launched weapon such as an American Stinger or a Soviet SA-7 *Strela*. Rick felt a gnawing pain in his stomach. Terrorists were about to bring down an airliner over

Central London. They had never done that before. *If they succeeded, the carnage would be enormous.*

Rick held his cheeks between his hands and screamed:

'No! No! No! This can't be happening!'

Rick opened the window and stuck his head out. He wished he could just pluck the projectile from the sky with his right hand or at least warn the flight crew. A violent evasive manoeuvre might just confuse the missile's infra-red seeker head. He had read of US and Israeli air force pilots who had dodged several missiles fired at them just by staying calm and making a sudden change of course at the last moment. But this airliner didn't stand a chance. The crew had no military training, they probably hadn't even seen the missile and the plane had no defensive measures such as chaff and flares.

Three seconds later the missile struck the port engine with a loud thump. For a moment it looked as though the airliner was going to survive the hit but then black smoke spewed out the back of the jet pipe and chunks of metal fell from the engine towards the terrified onlookers below. Within a minute the engine had become a giant blowtorch emitting a plume of orange flame a hundred feet long. As he looked at this horrific spectacle, Rick was reminded of footage he had seen in a TV documentary about the Concorde crash at Paris in 2000.

The Airbus pilot responded by increasing power in the starboard engine and lowering his flaps. He was obviously hoping to make an emergency landing at Heathrow. But he had run out of time. Soon, the engine fire spread to the fuel tanks and the port wing started to droop as the main spars melted. Deprived of aerodynamic lift, the Airbus fell out of the sky and smashed into a densely populated area. A loud explosion was followed by an orange fireball which rose high into the sky. A massive blast wave shattered windows. Then a plume of black smoke ascended from the scene of the crash. Hundreds of car and house alarms sounded.

People screamed in horror. Police cars and ambulances raced towards the site of the crash, sirens blaring. Rick reckoned that everyone on the airliner would have died, plus several hundred on the ground, and many more with severe injuries.

Only one organisation had the audacity to carry out such an atrocity – *The Seven*. But who exactly had fired the missile? They would almost certainly be caught soon, bearing in mind the number of CCTV cameras in London these days. They would eventually stand trial and be imprisoned for decades. But that wasn't a good outcome for Rick. No, he would find out who was responsible, abduct them and then torture and kill them. After all, he now had a reputation to live up to.

For the next few hours Rick watched Sky News. It only took ten minutes for the first reports of the attack to come in. Within an hour, more details were available. Scores of ambulances, police cars and fire engines had been diverted to the scene. Fire crews were struggling to contain the many blazes on the ground. A large number of houses had been destroyed and many families made homeless. The Prime Minister had already made a statement outside 10 Downing Street.

'Our thoughts are with the victims' families,' he said. 'And we will leave no stone unturned in our search to find the perpetrators of this awful crime!'

Sky's Defence Correspondent, Andrew Miller, was interviewed about the attack and how he thought Britain might respond. Miller speculated that military action was likely but the Government's main problem was choosing an appropriate target. The terrorist group *The Seven* was not affiliated to any particular country. Iran had behaved badly in the past but an attack on them might set off a Third World

War and, in any case, with the change of presidency in the USA, the West was trying to cultivate good relations with Iran once more and even reach an agreement on that country's nuclear programme.

Then, three hours after the attack, there was a surprise announcement. A man had been arrested in connection with the atrocity and was now in custody. Apparently he had been caught on CCTV firing the missile. The only other information was that he was a 23-year-old Iranian national who worked in a London restaurant as a waiter. He was currently being held under armed guard at a Kew General Hospital where he was receiving medical treatment. There was speculation that he would be moved to Belmarsh Prison once his condition had improved.

Then another piece of news came through. Reuters had received an official statement from *The Seven*, who were claiming responsibility for the attack. They did it, they claimed, because of recent attacks by Israeli warplanes on Palestinian settlements in Gaza. They held Britain responsible because they had previously supported the establishment of the State of Israel through the hated Balfour Declaration, and had also sold them arms.

Rick was stunned. Arrested after just three hours! That wasn't like *The Seven*. They were highly organised and professional terrorists, rather like the Provisional IRA had been in Northern Ireland. Terrorist groups had threatened to shoot down airliners before but they had never carried out their threats, possibly because the risk of capture was so high. But then again terrorist groups sometimes made mistakes. It could be that they had been so demoralized by their recent reverses that they had decided to stage a 'spectacular', even if it meant the capture of one of their number.

Rick thought for a moment and then decided on a course of action. His next victim was being held at Kew General Hospital. The police would have to charge him within twenty-four hours of arrest or else release him. It would be hard to get at the terrorist while he was in hospital. It was highly likely there would be an armed guard outside his room. There might also be armed police and even troops outside the entrance. Eventually the suspect would be moved to Belmarsh, where it would be almost impossible to get at him. His best option might be to shoot the suspect, Jack Ruby-style, as he was being moved between the doors of the hospital and the police transport taking him to the prison.

Rick reckoned he would have a good chance of killing him if he could get in close and use a head shot or a 'double tap' to the chest. There were would be little chance of abducting and torturing his victim this time, but killing him would be better than nothing. But how would he himself escape after such an audacious crime? He had no idea, but he should at least carry out a recce, as was standard practice in the SAS. He had no time to lose.

Rick walked through to the bathroom, worked up a lather with his Erasmic shave bowl and shaved himself carefully. He would need to wear deodorant and cologne, a shirt and tie and a suit if he wanted to pass as a reporter. He already possessed a fake Press Association card. And his Fairbairn-Sykes combat knife could be hidden in his inside jacket pocket.

Kew General Hospital

13 September 2022, 13.07 hours

Dr Graham Smithers, Consultant in Accident and Emergency Medicine, listened to the chest of his young patient with his Littman stethoscope and then put the instrument back round his neck.

'The only thing wrong with this chap is that he's heavily sedated,' said Smithers.

DS Carter listened attentively as he stood by the bed.

'I've ordered a toxicology screen in case it's anything serious,' continued Smithers. 'His pupils are normal size and reacting to light so he hasn't taken any opiates. No puncture wounds in his veins so I would say he has taken a large oral dose of a sedative such as Temazepam or Rohypnol. As you know, that's a common date rape drug. There's no specific antidote so he'll just have to sleep it off. We've put in an airway to stop him choking, plus a urinary catheter and an intravenous infusion. You'll also notice from his breath that he has drunk a large quantity of alcohol. Rather strange as he is a Muslim.'

'That's very interesting,' said DS Carter as he fumbled in his right jacket pocket for some nicotine gum. 'So if what you're saying is correct, this man fired off a shoulder-launched missile and then swallowed a large quantity of sedatives and alcohol and fell asleep. But why would he do that?

'Normal terrorist practice would be to dump the missile launcher and then leave the area as soon as possible. And I would have expected him to wear latex gloves so he didn't leave any prints. We found his fingerprints all over the weapon. It was almost as if someone wanted him to be found and blamed for the atrocity.'

*

Just a hundred yards from the hospital room where the terrorist suspect was being treated, Rick stood across the road from the hospital entrance. A group of press photographers had gathered near to where he was standing and were taking pictures. A reporter from Sky News was talking to her camera crew.

As expected, there was plenty of security around the hospital entrance. Two white Skoda Octavia estate police patrol cars and three police vans, all decorated with fluorescent yellow stripes. Six policemen wearing black Kevlar vests and clutching Heckler & Koch MP5 submachine guns stood in a semi-circle around the entrance.

Not much chance of getting in that way, thought Rick. His best chance might be to enter via a rear entrance which might be less well guarded. He might have to disguise himself and carry minimal weaponry – or even no weapons – in case he was searched. He had no pistol on him, just his Fairbairn-Sykes combat knife in his inside jacket pocket.

Rick was so engrossed by the hospital entrance that he didn't notice the small electric-powered drone which was circling noiselessly in the sky a couple of hundred feet above his head and was broadcasting HD television pictures to a laptop in a nearby flat which was being operated by a member of *The Seven*.

'I think someone's taken the bait,' said the operative. 'White Causcasian male, early forties. About 160 pounds. Grey suit. White shirt. Blue tie. Blonde hair and moustache. Glasses. All teams move into position. Once he's out of sight of the police, we'll grab him and make him talk. Then we'll kill him…and it won't be quick. We have a little score to settle.'

CHAPTER 27

STAKEOUT

The Streets around Kew Hospital

13 September 2022, 15:17 hours

Rick walked briskly around the streets which surrounded Kew Hospital. As well as the heavily guarded main entrance, he had found two side doors which were each flanked by two armed policeman. Soon he found what he was looking for – a white wooden double door at the rear of the building, guarded by a single armed police officer. If this had been an SAS mission in enemy territory, the guard could be taken out by a sniper team. But Rick had no desire to kill a British policeman, even one who was hindering his mission. The police guard would have to be neutralised by non-lethal means, tied up and drugged. He had suitable pharmaceutical agents back in his hotel room.

Rick waved at the policeman and continued his trek. He wanted to give the impression he was just a reporter sizing up the hospital. There were numerous cars parked at the kerbside. One of them, a blue Volkswagen Polo, contained a driver and passenger who were munching on sandwiches and drinking large cardboard beakers of latte coffee.

As Rick passed the car, the driver spoke into his mobile phone:

'The target has just passed us. It looks as though he has been making a reconnaissance of the hospital. He's now heading in the direction of Kew Gardens Underground Station.'

'OK, we'll bring the van up and nab him before he gets too far. The second vehicle is also in position. Stand by!'

Rick had only walked two blocks from Kew Hospital when a white Transit van screeched to a halt in front of him. The rear doors swung open. Four men wearing nylon stocking masks, black fleece jackets and carrying 9 mm Uzi submachine guns on slings jumped out of the back and pointed their weapons at him.

'Get in the back of the fucking van right now or we shoot,' said the leader of the terrorists as he waved his Uzi around in a threatening fashion. Rick reacted instantly and dived at the man's legs using a classic rugby tackle to bring him down. Then he pulled out his Fairbairn-Sykes fighting knife and stabbed him in the side of the neck, severing his external carotid artery. Bright red arterial blood gushed onto the pavement as passers-by fled in terror. Some of them were already trying to contact the police on their mobile phones.

Rick removed the Uzi from the dying terrorist's grip, aimed it at the nearest bad guy and squeezed off a three-round burst at the man's chest. The 9 mm rounds struck home and punctured the man's heart. The battle had only been going for less than a minute but Rick had already eliminated half his opponents.

'For Christ's sake, get the fucker before he kills us all!' said one of the two remaining terrorists. 'If we can't abduct him, we'll have to kill him.'

But Rick was already moving fast, heading towards the cover of some parked cars. He knew that if he held off his assailants for a few minutes more, a police armed response unit would surely arrive as the whole of London was on terror alert. As 9 mm rounds whizzed past his ear, Rick dived behind the front wing of a parked red Ford Mondeo. The thin metal bodywork of the car would offer no protection from bullets but Rick intended to have the engine block between himself and his assailants, giving him makeshift armour protection.

Now the terrorists were crouched behind a blue Skoda Octavia saloon. One behind the front wing and the other next to the front passenger door. Rick could just see the top of his head through both front windows.

Rick steadied the stock of the Uzi against his right shoulder, took careful aim and squeezed the trigger. Four 9 mm rounds punctured the Skoda's driver's door, went right through the other side and killed the terrorist instantly. He slumped to the ground, dead.

'First lesson in urban combat,' shouted Rick. 'Car bodies offer no protection from bullets because the metal is paper thin. Someone should tell Bruce Willis. Now, are you going to surrender or am I going to have to kill you as well?'

There was no response from the last terrorist. Rick considered his options. The gunman was protected from bullets by the car engine block, so his best plan would be to race down the pavement on the same side of the road, keeping as low as possible, cross the street quickly and then shoot him. It was risky, but probably the only chance he had of eliminating the man before the police arrived.

Rick checked the number of rounds left in his magazine and shifted his position. As he was just about to make his sprint, he felt an intense blow on the back of his head and the pavement rose up to hit him in the face. Rick rolled over as blood spilled on the concrete. A heavily built man stood over him. He was wearing a stocking mask and clutching an Uzi.

'That's right, Mr Fernscale. We sent two teams to grab you since we know your capabilities. And now you're coming with us on a journey to meet someone who wants to talk to you.'

Rick felt his jacket being ripped off by two strong pairs of hands. Then his left sleeve was rolled up, a tight tourniquet was put around his upper arm and something was injected into a vein at the front of his elbow. He was aware of a police siren in the distance, then everything went grey.

*

Laura stands in front of me in her white wedding dress. 'We'll meet again one day, my darling. You know I will always love you more than anyone I have ever met. I know what you are doing right now is to avenge what happened to me. But remember that two wrongs don't make a right and your actions may eventually destroy you.'

A small wisp of smoke drifted upwards from the hem of Laura's wedding dress. Then orange flames appeared, spreading upwards until the whole outfit was ablaze. Laura's alabaster skin turned red and blistered as her hair frizzled. Her face turned black as the 1000 degree centigrade, petrol-fuelled blaze scorched off all the skin. Her nose burnt away and then her eyelids as she screamed, 'Help me, Rick, help me!'

Rick's eyes snapped open. Where was he? He was sitting in a comfortable leather seat. To his left was a large oval Perspex porthole. Bright sunlight shone off an aluminium wing. Underneath it was a single podded jet engine. The sky was bright blue and a couple of miles below was an endless sheet of cloud which looked exactly like cotton wool. He was in an airliner but it had been converted to executive specification. There were few seats and all the tables and bulkheads were made of highly polished walnut.

The interior of the aircraft smelled of wax polish and flowers. Sitting across the aisle from him was a well-built man of Middle Eastern appearance. He had obviously suffered serious injuries in the past as the scarred right side of his face drooped and had an artificial eye. His right hand was a prosthesis which had an inbuilt electric motor to move the fingers, as evidenced by an occasional whirring sound. Two men clad in black shirts and trousers sat in nearby seats and kept their Ruger pistols trained on Rick.

'You're probably wondering what happened to you in the last few hours, Mr Fernscale,' said the big man, in a Middle Eastern accent. 'Yes, that's right, I know your name. We have our sources. My name is Khalid and I am the executive director of *The Seven*. What the Americans call the 'Head Honcho'. By the way, the name *The Seven* describes only the founding members like myself. We also have thousands of ordinary foot soldiers. I decided that Merlaux was probably compromised after L'Arconne was tortured to death. I take it that it was you who carried out that despicable deed?'

'It was indeed,' said Rick. 'You've probably noticed that I like my terrorists well done.'

Khalid did not react and continued his monologue. 'Let me tell you about this aircraft. It is a Boeing 737 which was in regular airline service until 2020. Because of the coronavirus pandemic, some airlines went bust. Others grounded their older aircraft. I bought this 737 for a low price and had it converted into an executive jet.

'We're on our way to our main base, in the Indian Ocean, north of Madagascar. A small island a few miles across which doesn't even appear on some maps. The Americans built an airfield there in 1943. It has an 8,000 foot concrete runway which can easily handle a 737. Once there, I have some matters which I want to discuss with you. In the meantime, perhaps you would like to enjoy the flight. A doctor has already attended to your wounds and as a gesture of good faith I will have your handcuffs removed. You will of course have two armed guards nearby at all times to make sure you don't try anything. We have a flight attendant on board who will serve you drinks and meals. And we will be making a couple of refuelling stops on the way.'

Rick relaxed. He had expected to be taken somewhere grim to be tortured to death but this wasn't too bad. He had experienced far worse during SAS selection when he had been deprived of food, water and sleep and made to stand with arms outstretched against a wall in a classic 'stress' position. This was luxury by comparison. A flight attendant arrived with a meal. Turkish kebabs with spicy rice and a side dish of houmous and flatbreads. All washed down with Lebanese white wine.

To follow there was strong black coffee accompanied by fresh figs and Turkish delight. A lot better than the spam, eggs and chips he used to eat in the mess at Hereford. After this delicious meal Rick felt drowsy, closed his eyes and had a couple of hours of much-needed sleep.

He was woken by an announcement on the aircraft's PA system. The Captain said the aircraft was about to land at Luqa airport, Malta, for a refuelling stop, and that passengers were to fasten their seat belts. Five minutes later the aircraft descended through a thin cloud layer and landed on the main runway. Rick peered out his porthole and noticed that all the buildings were a honey colour. The landscape looked arid and sun-scorched. After coming to a standstill, the pilot powered down the engines as the Luqa groundcrew pushed a set of steps towards the airliner and the flight attendant opened the front passenger door.

A black Mercedes limousine approached the 737 and halted just a few yards from the steps. Then a middle-aged man wearing a beige summer suit got out of the limousine, ascended the steps and entered the passenger cabin. He looked directly at Rick, who thought he seemed familiar.

'Good afternoon, Mr Fernscale. My name is David Marshall. I am the British Defence Secretary!'

CHAPTER 28

TRAITOR

14 September 2022, 10:57 hours

David Marshall sat opposite Rick and accepted a glass of iced mineral water from the flight attendant. Two tall, well-built, short-haired men wearing dark suits and sunglasses entered the passenger cabin. They were obviously part of Marshall's personal protection team as they both had earpieces and a slight bulge under their left armpits which indicated a shoulder holster. Rick had already noticed two other similarly dressed men wearing dark glasses standing on the tarmac near the steps carrying MP5s.

Marshall spoke: 'You don't seem very surprised to see me, Mr Fernscale. One of the UK's most important politicians sharing an airliner with a man who has been on the FBI' s most-wanted list for many years.'

Rick sipped the last of his black coffee and then answered: 'No I'm not surprised at all. There's a lot about *The Seven's* activities that doesn't add up. That failed drone attack for example. It went ahead even after the army set up missile batteries in Hyde Park. A professional terrorist organisation would have switched to a different plan. And that attempt on the Prime Minister's life. Highly risky. I reckon both attacks were meant to fail...The question is, why?'

'Go on,' said Marshall. 'I'm interested to hear your analysis.'

'My guess is that they were designed to cause fear in the general population, and also increase support for the government and the Prime Minister. You've been promulgating fear ever since the virus pandemic and one way to keep it going is with a terrorist campaign that can be used to justify further draconian measures.'

'Quite correct. And the Prime Minister wasn't even in Downing Street on the day of the drone attack. We made sure he was secretly moved to Chequers the day before. There was little chance of him being assassinated by Rashid either. That wasn't the Prime Minister in the car, it was a double. And our agents had already tampered with the bomb so it wouldn't go off. The surgeon thought he was implanting plastic explosive in Rashid's belly but it was actually Marzipan. It looks and smells much the same. Both smell of almonds, as you will know from your time in the SAS.'

'So is the Prime Minister part of this plan of yours, whatever it is?'

'No he's not. But he will be replaced with someone else who believes in the cause when the time comes. Many politicians across the globe have agreed to our plan to change our world through a Great Economic Reset. Most countries are on board. And those that have declined so far will come under enormous economic pressure to conform. But I am talking too much. I have to leave now to attend an economic summit on Gozo. I will leave these two bodyguards on the plane to provide additional security. That means you will be guarded by four armed men. The armoured cockpit door will be locked for the rest of the journey and there are no parachutes on board so don't even think of escaping.'

'The thought never crossed my mind,' said Rick.

Marshall got up, said a few words in Arabic to Khalid, and left the aircraft. The two bodyguards sat on a couple of vacant seats and took off their sunglasses. They studied Rick intensely.

Forty minutes later, the plane completed refuelling. The Maltese ground crew disconnected the fuel hose from the wing tanks. Then the white BP bowser trundled back to the airport's fuel farm as the main passenger door closed. The port engine started, followed by the starboard, and soon the Boeing was airborne again, heading east. Ahead lay several more hours of flying, including another refuelling stop at Bahrain. Rick reclined his seat, closed his eyes and within a minute was fast asleep. It was a knack he had learned in the SAS.

*

DCI McAllister bit into a McDonald's Egg McMuffin and felt a surge of energy as the high-fat, high-calorie fast food snack elevated his blood sugar level. A few sips from a large paper beaker of hot tea with four sugars followed.

'Magic,' he said. 'Not quite as good as a well-fired Stephens roll with square sausage and a dod of HP sauce but it will keep me going till lunchtime. Oops!'

Salad cream squirted out of the Egg McMuffin and landed on the freshly-printed report which lay on his desk. It was from the anti-terrorist branch at Scotland Yard. They had now taken over further investigation of Rick Fernscale's activities, but were keeping McAllister in the loop as a matter of courtesy. McAllister was fascinated by what had happened. It appeared there was now a connection between Fernscale and the recent downing of an Airbus over London by a terrorist missile. No-one believed that Fernscale was the shooter but he had been spotted on CCTV staking out the hospital where the terrorist suspect had been held while he was receiving medical treatment.

*

McAllister used a napkin to wipe the salad cream off the cover of the report and studied the blown-up prints of the television footage which were inside. A few years ago such photos would have been grainy and hard to interpret but these were in colour and HD.

'He's changed his appearance,' said DS Brown, who had just entered the room. 'Looks like he has dyed his hair blonde and added a moustache and glasses, but our latest body recognition software can identify people by comparing the length of various bones and the size of facial features against a database. Fernscale was put on the database when we caught him on CCTV hijacking a police car after the assassination attempt on the Prime Minister. And take a look at this picture here which has just arrived,' said Brown.

Brown handed McAllister a freshly printed photo which showed an obviously drugged Fernscale being manhandled into the back of a white Transit van by four men.

'Fake number plates as you would expect,' said Brown. 'And there's more. That Transit was found just three blocks away, in an area not covered by CCTV cameras. It was completely burned out and there were no witnesses. It was obviously well-planned. We think Fernscale was transferred to another vehicle but unfortunately we don't know its identity. He could be anywhere by now. He might even have been taken out of the country.'

'It sounds as though we have hit a brick wall, laddie,' said McAllister as he wiped round his mouth with a paper napkin. 'We have no leads and no witnesses. And I've also heard from the anti-terrorist branch that the suspect in Kew Hospital has woken up. He claims he was abducted, drugged and left lying beside the missile launcher. He has no history of involvement with terrorist organisations or radical political groups so he may be telling the truth. It looks as though the whole attack may have been set up just to attract Fernscale and then capture him. Hundreds of deaths just to get one man. They must really want him.'

Mc Allister swallowed his last mouthful of Egg McMuffin, washed it down with hot tea, and then continued:

'Our only lead is Fernscale. We don't know where he is or even if he is dead or alive. But I have a gut feeling that we haven't heard the last of him. Wherever he is right now, he'll be causing trouble.'

*

Rick was woken from a deep sleep by the sound of the 737's undercarriage coming down. The red 'fasten seat belt' sign was on and he could see the flight attendant speaking into a microphone, asking everyone to return to their seats and fasten their seat belts. The Boeing dropped through a thick cloud layer. Then it broke into clear sky as it descended towards the ocean. Rick craned his neck to see better but all he could see was turquoise-blue sea in all directions. Surely they weren't going to land in the water?

Then a patch of sandy, sun-scorched ground appeared underneath the port wing as the pilot throttled back the engines further and lowered the flaps. There were no houses to be seen, just palm trees, rocks and sand. The aircraft got lower still and Rick caught a glimpse of an airfield perimeter fence and a narrow tarmac road with a yellow Land Rover on it. A whirling red-and-white radar scanner sat atop a concrete blockhouse to his left. The end of the runway appeared. Grey concrete marked with white stripes. The Boeing got lower still. There was a loud thump as the pilot made a perfect three-point landing. Immediately the engines screamed as the pilot engaged reverse thrust and slowed the 737 rapidly to taxiing speed.

As the Boeing taxied to the small terminal building, Rick craned his neck to see out of the porthole. There were jagged mountains in the distance and lots of palm trees. But just one tarmac road that Rick could see, no hotels and no houses. Dotted around the airfield were a few olive green military trucks with chunky tyres. Just beyond the perimeter were four batteries of Franco-German Roland surface-to-air missiles. Rick was reminded of the British-owned Ascension Island which was off the west coast of Africa, close to the Equator. Rick had never been there but his father had stopped there briefly on his way to the Falkland Islands in 1982 and had shown Rick a few 35 mm snaps.

The flight attendant opened the door as a yellow truck arrived with a set of steps mounted on the back. Then a blue Mercedes limousine drew up at the foot of the steps and a chauffeur got out.

'This where you get out, Mr Fernscale. Two bodyguards will walk in front of you and two behind so there is no chance of you escaping.'

Rick descended the steps in the scorching sunshine. Even the handrail of the steps was hot to the touch. He took a look around and noticed a huge matt green eight-wheeled vehicle with enormous chunky tyres. It looked like the massive TEL (Transporter Erector Launcher) vehicles used by the Iraqis to launch Scud missiles in the first Gulf War. The SAS had made considerable efforts to destroy these vehicles and their deadly cargo during the war, including the famous 'Bravo Two Zero' mission which had been recounted in a best-selling book and TV movie. But this vehicle was carrying a missile which was larger than a Scud. What was *The Seven* up to?

Khalid spoke:

'I see you've noticed our missile. We call it the Vengeance and it can carry a 2,000-pound payload over 7,000 miles. That means we can hit London if we have to! It is all part of *Operation Armageddon*. And you know what Armageddon means. The end of the world as we know it.'

CHAPTER 29

THE VILLAIN'S LAIR

Sweat rolled down Rick's forehead as he entered the limousine's passenger cabin. He guessed the outside air temperature must be forty degrees centigrade, with high humidity. Fortunately, the inside of the Mercedes was mercifully cool, with copious amounts of refrigerated air issuing from multiple air vents. It smelled strongly of high-quality leather and thick carpets. Rick was directed to the centre rear seat with one bodyguard on either side. Khalid and the third bodyguard sat opposite Rick while the fourth sat in the front passenger seat.

Rick gazed out the tinted windows. He was fascinated by the airfield architecture, which consisted mainly of WW2-vintage American buildings. There were several Quonset huts painted matt olive drab, plus a watch tower ('control tower', in modern parlance) which looked in full working order as two men wearing short-sleeved white shirts and headsets were sitting in the main glasshouse cabin at the top. The only other aircraft on the apron was a white Cessna 172 high-winged light aircraft which had a red stripe along its side.

Beyond the perimeter gates, there was just one main tarmac road which ran around the coast, flanked by palm trees. After a five-minute drive from the airport, the Mercedes took a sharp left turn and travelled along a short stretch of road which led to the biggest mountain on the island. It had the shape of an extinct volcano. The

Mercedes came to a halt at a barrier manned by two soldiers wearing berets and combat fatigues and clutching AK-47s. An officer came out of a white wooden hut next to the barrier, looked inside the limousine, saw Khalid and ordered the squaddies to lift the pole. The Mercedes trundled forward and entered a short length of tunnel which led to a large well-lit car park in a cavern inside the mountain.

Khalid looked at Fernscale with his single functioning eye and motioned with his myo-electric right hand.

'Impressed, Mr Fernscale? I bet you're wondering where we got the money for all this infrastructure. Not all terrorists live in corrugated iron shanty towns, you know.'

The Mercedes halted beside several vehicles which included a couple of M117 jeeps with mounted Browning M2 fifty-calibre machine guns and a yellow Mini Moke. The bodyguards exited the vehicle first and then pulled out Rick. One of them stood behind him and pointed his pistol at the small of his back.

'Towards the lift doors. Now! Don't try anything or I shoot.'

The eight-person lift took Rick, Khalid and the four bodyguards to the second floor. The metal doors swished open. One of the bodyguards pushed Rick forwards.

'This is where you get out!'

Rick expected an interrogation room, or even an old-fashioned torture chamber, but instead he was standing in what looked exactly like the plush carpeted corridor of a four-star hotel. The bodyguards took him to the third door on the left and opened it with a keycard.

'Go inside,' they said. 'We suggest you have a shower and shave. Someone will be along shortly with clean clothes. The door won't open from the inside without a keycard and there's no window. There will be two armed guards outside.'

Rick entered the room, lay on the king-sized bed with a thick blue duvet and Egyptian cotton sheets and stared at the ceiling. This was not what he expected. His SAS training had prepared him for the worst possible treatment. Beatings, waterboarding, electrocution, sleep deprivation, white noise, standing against a wall in the stress position with a hood over his head, that kind of thing. Instead he was being treated extremely well. It was almost like a holiday.

He really needed to escape, get back to the UK and report the existence of this island base to the government. But he had no idea how he was going to do that. So for the moment at least he might as well enjoy the hospitality offered by his captors.

Rick stripped off his shoes and sweat-soaked clothes and left them lying in a neat pile on the floor. Then he walked into the bathroom, washed his face and worked up a lather with the Erasmic soap bowl and brush which lay beside the sink. Then he shaved himself carefully with a Gillette Mach 3 razor and stepped into the shower. A bar of Imperial Leather soap had been provided, plus a bottle of shampoo. Rick spent ten minutes in the shower and then stepped out, dried himself with a huge, thick white bath-towel, sprayed some Brut deodorant under his armpits, brushed his teeth, combed his wet hair and lay on the bed. His muscles had just started to relax and he was about to fall asleep when there was a knock on the door.

A beautiful Filipino maid with shoulder-length dark hair and brown eyes, wearing a dark blue tunic entered. She carried two large canvas bags.

'My name is Maria. I'll be looking after you. I've brought fresh clothes for you, sir. A light beige cotton tropical suit. Short-sleeved white Sea Island cotton shirt. Underpants. Black leather belt and matching Italian moccasins. Grey socks. All your old clothes will be taken away for cleaning and pressing.'

'Thank you.'

'And one other thing, sir. Mr Khalid would like you to join him for dinner at 8 p.m. One of the security staff will come for you at five to eight.'

*

The main dining room in Khalid's lair had been hewn out of solid rock. Only one flat wall had been created with concrete breezeblocks painted white. Four paintings hung on it in ornate gold frames. Rick had no idea who the artists were, but he was sure they were famous. A large crystal chandelier hung from the roof of the artificial cavern and illuminated the long, highly polished mahogany dining room table.

Khalid sat at the head of the table, near Rick. The only other diners were two security men, who sat further down the table and glared at him. The other two bodyguards stood some distance from the table, still wearing their sunglasses as was the norm in such situations. Rick knew this was so he couldn't see where their eyes were looking.

The first course was Beluga caviar served with plenty of Melba toast. *'One could never get enough toast.'* The immaculately dressed waiter poured cooled Chardonnay into Rick's glass with his white-gloved hands.

'Do you like the wine, Mr Fernscale? There will be a different one to go with each course and then cognac with the coffee. I'll be sticking to water and fruit juice but please feel free to imbibe as you wish.'

Rick wolfed down the caviar ravenously. How long had it been since he had eaten food of this quality?

The second course was French *bouillabaisse,* fish soup, made with just a hint of garlic, and warm crusty bread with salt-free Danish butter on a side plate. Then there was a huge T-bone beefsteak for mains, served with creamed potatoes, pickled cabbage and side salad. The wine that was served with each course complimented the food perfectly.

'I don't really approve of the USA, as you will understand,' said Khalid, 'but I must concede they produce the best steaks in the world. The ones you are eating come from Texas. The Argentines claim they make even better steaks but I've never tried them. Have you ever been to Argentina, Mr Fernscale?'

'I haven't but my father nearly made it there in 1982. He was lined up to take part in an SAS attack on the Argentine air base at Tierra Del Fuego. *Operation Mikado* as it was called. It was scrapped at the last moment because many commanders in the SAS thought it would be a suicide mission.'

'Quite so,' said Khalid, his artificial right eye twinkling in the reflected candlelight as he lifted a glass of sparkling mineral water with his whirring myoelectric right hand.

The waiter brought the dessert, which was freshly prepared *Bombe Alaska*. Rick thought it amusing and appropriate that a terrorist leader was giving him a 'bomb' for his pudding.

Rick admired the chef's skill. The outer meringue coating was still slightly warm from the oven while the Italian ice cream inside was sweet, creamy, cold and delicious.

Then it was time for *cafetière* coffee with a cheeseboard, biscuits and a small glass of cognac on the side. Khalid munched a piece of Camembert, sipped a black coffee and turned to face Rick.

'So, let's get down to business. You're probably wondering why I abducted you, transported you to this island and wined and dined you when it would have been so much easier just to have you shot on the streets of London.'

'I was indeed wondering about that,' said Rick.

'Let me give you the big picture,' said Khalid. 'The world as we know it cannot continue in its present form. The main problem is that there are simply too many people on the planet. Almost seven billion. We don't have enough food. And the oil is running out. The air we breathe is polluted. And we are faced with the problems of climate change. With all these problems, the present capitalist system cannot continue.

'You probably believe the world is run by governments but that is only partly true. For some decades, the so-called global elite has been calling the shots. A few hundred billionaires and key politicians who want to run the planet. They want to abolish borders and have a single World Government and World Army. Society as we know it will change forever. There will be no ownership of private property. Everything will be rented or provided by the state. Everyone will be microchipped and subject to constant surveillance. Petrol and diesel cars will be banned. Electric cars will be the norm although even they will be phased out eventually as private car ownership will be banned. People will be encouraged to cycle and walk everywhere, even in cold, damp countries like Britain.

'Small businesses will be bankrupted. People will be forced to live in poor-quality flats and subject to massive state surveillance. Many people will live on a meagre Universal Basic Income. In short, the world will become one massive Communist state. But there is one essential prerequisite of this New World Order. Population reduction. We forecast that the world's population will need to be reduced to just 500 million. And Britain will only have 15 million people.'

Rick was gobsmacked. 'So how do you propose to reduce the population?'

Khalid grinned. He was clearly enjoying this.

'Many methods will be used. The missile you saw at the airport is what we call the Vengeance. It is similar to the Scud used in the 1991 Gulf War but considerably larger and with greater range. After launching from this island, it can easily reach London which is about

5,000 miles away. It carries a biological warhead, a flu-like virus similar to Covid 19, but much more deadly, with a far greater transmissibility and a very high mortality rate. After the missile bursts open over Central London, it will infect everyone within a 25 mile radius. As it is a different serotype from Covid 19, there will be a huge number of deaths. Within days, it will spread to the rest of the planet. Of course we have developed a vaccine which has already been given to members of our organisation and the global elite.

'But the virus alone won't kill enough people for us to reach our target of a world population of just 500 million. So other methods may be needed. Poor medical care and even outright euthanasia. We may even have to set up government-run extermination camps for undesirables. And this is where you come in, Mr Fernscale. You have a talent for killing people and are exactly the sort of man I need in my organisation. If you accept my proposal, you will receive a huge salary which will enable you to live a champagne lifestyle in a sun-kissed paradise. If you want a woman, then one will be provided. As young and beautiful as you desire. And if you have any unusual sexual needs, that can be catered for as well. What about it, Mr Fernscale, do we have a deal?'

'You make it all sound so desirable...and part of me is indeed tempted,' said Rick.

Khalid smiled.

'But unfortunately I have a great sense of natural justice and one of my first tasks would be to hunt down the people who killed my wife and then execute them. Which means you would be top of my hit list.'

Khalid frowned with the uninjured left side of his face.

'I can see I misjudged you, Mr Fernscale. You are nothing but a stupid policeman.'

Khalid snapped the fingers of his left hand. The two security men rose from the table, grabbed Rick by the arms and manhandled him roughly as they dragged him towards the lift.

'Take this man away and see that some harm comes to him. I want him to receive the usual hospitality we give to visitors.'

Rick's muscles tensed as he was bundled into the lift. He was going to be tortured and then killed! The best he could hope for was a quick death!

CHAPTER 30

JAILHOUSE ROCK

The lift doors swished open. Rick was shoved forward. Two guards walked behind him, pistols drawn, while a third strolled in front holding a large bunch of keys. The corridor consisted of unpainted grey concrete breeze blocks and was illuminated with naked light bulbs hanging from the ceiling. There were several cells with gloss-grey metal doors and small barred windows, plus a lounge for the guards, a toilet, and what looked like a torture room.

The leading guard unlocked a cell door on the right and Rick was pushed inside with such force that he almost tripped. The door clanged shut and an unshaven guard with a dark moustache grinned through the small, barred glassless window as he turned the key in the lock. His teeth were yellow and stained and one looked rotten. Even from four feet away Rick could smell his halitosis. Dental hygiene wasn't a priority for the terrorists.

'I'm Miguel. We'll be back in the morning to torture you!'

'But I don't know anything,' said Rick.

'We realise that, but we're going to do it anyway for the thrill of it. Pity you're not a woman or we could have even more fun before we kill you. Ha! Ha! Ha!' The guard pointed to a balding man with a pot belly standing behind him.

'Pedro is a serial rapist so we let him look after all the female prisoners, if you know what I mean. He was sentenced to death in the USA for murder and sex crimes but Khalid sprung him from Death Row and gave him a job. See you in the morning, Fernscale.'

Rick looked around his cell. No bed. No chair. No WC. Just a dented galvanised bucket in the corner, half full of urine and faeces, which smelled a few days old. Flies buzzed around it. The rough concrete floor was covered with dried blood and vomit. Sweat ran down Rick's forehead. The temperature in the cell must be forty-five degrees centigrade. There was no air conditioning, no fan and not even a window. And no water.

Rick went to the door and shouted through the open, barred window:

'You forgot my room service breakfast order. Bacon, sausage, egg, black pudding, hash browns, coffee, brown toast and fresh orange juice. And my trouser press isn't working! Can anyone hear me? Can I at least have some water?'

'Fuck off! Go to sleep, we're busy,' said Pedro.

Judging by the sounds and smells emanating from the next room, Rick guessed the guards were watching porn, masturbating, drinking and smoking skiffs. They weren't the least bit interested in their prisoner's welfare.

Rick found the least dirty part of the floor and lay on it. Falling asleep on a hard concrete floor in a boiling hot room which smelled of stale body fluids while his prospective torturers made a lot of noise would be difficult, but he was sure he could manage it. What would happen tomorrow? Would he withstand the torture? Would he survive? Perhaps the best outcome might be his own death. He had read about people who had died of heart attacks brought on by the stress of 'enhanced interrogation techniques', as the CIA called them.

For hours Rick's busy mind mulled over his likely fate. Then at about 2:00 a.m. he finally drifted off into a fitful sleep.

Laura stands in front of Rick, wearing her white wedding dress. Her hair and make-up are immaculate.

'Do not fret for me, my darling,' she said. 'I am now at peace in a wonderful place. I am not in pain. I am not suffering. Yet I know you are about to face the biggest challenge of your life. You're going to experience great pain but you can handle it. Remember that if you die, you will be reunited with me. You must be strong, Rick, stronger than you've ever been in your life. And whether you come to this world or remain on Earth, I will always be with you. And I will always love you!'

Rick's eyes opened as the cell door flew open with great force. His watch showed the time was 6:03 a.m. Three guards stood inside his cell. They were unshaven and smelled strongly of BO and stale alcohol. All were laughing.

'Wakey! Wakey! Fernscale. It's torture time,' said Pedro. 'No cornflakes and milk for you this morning. Instead we're going to give you some electric shocks, followed by waterboarding. Then we're going to take you outside and burn you to death with petrol. That's right, we're going to have our revenge for what you did to Rashid and L'Arconne.'

Pedro ripped off Rick's stained suit jacket and threw it to the ground. Then the other guards grabbed him and dragged him along the corridor to the torture room. The matt white walls were stained with blood splashes. The only piece of furniture was a large wooden table fitted with a reclining mechanism. To one side was a water-filled galvanised bucket with a large cloth draped over it. In the corner of the room was a large piece of equipment which looked like an electric engine starter. It had a moving coil meter and several coloured lights on the front panel. Thick red and black cables with jumbo crocodile clips on the end issued from the front of the machine.

Miguel pointed his Glock pistol at Rick and spoke:

'Take all your clothes off and lie on your back on the table.

Rick did as he was ordered. Then Miguel and Pedro used adjustable straps to secure him to the table with his feet apart to expose his genitals.

'We're going to start at your feet and then move up your body, gradually increasing the amperage,' said Pedro. 'The pain will be quite excruciating, like nothing you've ever experienced. And just wait till we get to your genitals. Even the most hardened soldiers have been known to scream for their mothers by that point. We won't take things too far though. Too high a current can cause a fatal convulsion or a heart attack and we want to keep you alive for the grand finale, if you know what I mean.'

Rick's muscles tensed up. He closed his eyes. He knew the only way to survive this ordeal was to take his mind somewhere else. Psychologists called it dissociation. He would imagine he was in a tropical paradise with Laura, enjoying a nice picnic while these evil men worked on his body. The picnic scene would become his reality while the torture was just a bad dream happening to someone else. He had read a book on self-hypnosis once and remembered that dissociation in trance was an effective pain control technique.

Pedro touched the two giant crocodile clips to Rick's feet and told Miguel to switch the machine on. Rick's body convulsed and he let out a scream but deep inside his mind he was picnicking with Laura in the sunshine on a tropical beach. She smiled as she passed him a smoked salmon sandwich and poured him a glass of cool white wine. The pain in his feet was there but it was as though it was happening to someone else. His body was in a separate compartment to his mind.

For a full half-hour, Pedro prodded Rick with the crocodile clips, ending up at his genitals. Rick screamed and his body shook every time an electric shock coursed through his body.

'We'll have to stop there,' said Miguel. 'At the amperage and voltage we're using, there is a serious risk of a fatal heart attack or a cardiac arrest. I recommend we stop now unless you want to kill him.'

'You're right,' said Pedro. 'We want him to experience the horror of waterboarding, Bring the bucket over. Put the cloth on his face and recline the table so his head is below his feet.'

Miguel did as Pedro asked and then poured half a bucket of cold water over the cloth.

Rick felt he was drowning as he couldn't get any air through his nostrils or mouth. Every cell in his body was crying out for oxygen. But he had to stay calm. He remembered what he had learned during his attachment to the Special Boat Service. Just as he had done some months earlier, when he fell into the Thames, he had filled his lungs with air before the cloth had been applied to his face. And he had taken his mind to another place. He imagined he was scuba diving with Laura in the Bahamas. The water was crystal-clear and shoals of brightly coloured fish swam past. Laura wore a white bikini which showed off her toned body. It was like one of the underwater scenes in the James Bond film *Thunderball.*

After fifteen minutes of waterboarding, Rick was motionless.

'Is he dead?' asked Miguel.

Pedro checked Rick's radial artery pulse. He couldn't feel anything. But he had a good external carotid artery pulse in his neck and his chest was moving with each breath.

'He's still alive, but possibly unconscious,' said Pedro. 'Let's put him back in his cell and then we can have breakfast. After we've eaten, we can take him outside and burn him to death.'

Pedro and the third guard, who was called Heinrich, dragged the semi-conscious, naked Rick along the corridor by his arms and shoved him into his cell. Rick fell onto the floor. Then Pedro returned with a green plastic petrol can and a box of matches. Rick looked at him through half-closed eyes.

'See what we've got here, Fernscale! We're going to have breakfast and then we're going to have a barbecue. You'll be the meat!'

Pedro exited the cell and locked the door, cackling as he did so.

Ten minutes later, Rick heard the sound of a trolley coming along the corridor. He peered through the tiny window and caught sight of Maria, who had brought him some clothes the day before. The three men were having a full cooked breakfast served by her. Crispy bacon and fried eggs, pancakes, coffee and orange juice. Rick felt his stomach rumbling.

Twenty minutes later, the guards had finished their breakfast and were burping and farting. Pedro picked his nose while the others lit up cigarettes. Maria cleared all the plates and cups from the sitting room and stacked them on the trolley. Rick's eyes nearly popped out his head when he saw what happened next. Maria stood in the corridor and unbuttoned her blouse to her waist. She was wearing a black bra and had a sensational cleavage. Then she lifted the hem of her skirt to reveal stockings and suspenders.

'Like the view boys? Who would like to go first? You can do anything you like but just one at a time. I don't do threesomes.'

Maria showed the three guards a hip flask she had brought.

'It contains rum which I know you all like, plus a rhino horn supplement which will make you harder and give you a better orgasm. I want you all to drink some before you have me.'

Pedro stood up, a bulge visible in his trousers.

'I'm the senior guard so I'll go first,' he said, taking a swig from the flask. 'We'll use cell three, because three and four are the only ones with beds.'

Pedro and Maria entered cell three. The door shut behind them. A few minutes later Rick heard Pedro speaking:

'I'll be the best lover you ever had, Maria. I'm going to enter you now.'

Two minutes later Rick heard Pedro letting out a gasp as he ejaculated. A few more minutes passed and then Rick heard the sound of the senior guard snoring. A little while later Maria emerged from the cell completely naked and invited Miguel to join her in cell four.

Rick moved away from the window and lay on the floor. He knew he would soon die but still felt dead tired. He closed his eyes and fell asleep. He had only dozed for fifteen minutes when he was awoken by the sound of a key turning in the lock. It was Maria, this time dressed in combat fatigues and boots, with her hair tied back. She was carrying a pile of clothes consisting of an olive green combat shirt and trousers, a military belt, underpants, socks and boots.

'Put these on,' she said. 'I don't have much time to explain. Khalid forced me to become a comfort woman for his men. There are ten of us. We were forced into unpaid prostitution under threat of execution. Pedro and Miguel are now dead. I drugged them with rum laced with Rohypnol. It takes about twenty minutes to work. Then I killed them with a potassium chloride injection. It causes instant cardiac arrest. I used to be a nurse so I know how to give intravenous injections. Heinrich is still alive and snoozing in the lounge. You'll have to kill him for me because I could only get two ampoules of potassium chloride from the sick bay.'

Rick dressed quickly, quizzing Maria as he did so.

'So why are you helping me? You must hate Khalid and his organisation.'

'Oh I do. Apart from forcing me to become a comfort woman, he killed my brother. Now he's planning to destroy the world as we know it. I can't stop him on my own. You'll have to help me.'

After Rick had dressed, Maria led him along to the end of the corridor. She opened a set of venetian blinds to reveal a window. Rick gazed in amazement at the scene below. A large part of the interior of the mountain had been hollowed out to create a huge cavern with a flat concrete floor. In the middle of it was the Transporter Erector Launcher (TEL) vehicle he had seen at the airport. A gigantic yellow crane was lifting the white Vengeance missile from the vehicle and transferring it to a launch pad complete with red gantry.

'It's the same missile you would have seen at the airport yesterday,' said Maria. 'What you're looking at is effectively a missile silo. Directly above the missile is a pair of semi-circular steel doors which are camouflaged on top. It will enable the missile to be totally concealed until the moment of firing.'

'So when is the missile going to be fired?'

'In just forty-eight hours from now.'

'Forty-eight hours?'

'Yes, Rick. In just forty-eight hours London is going to hit by a missile with a biological warhead. Millions will die and in a matter of days every country in the world will be infected. We are looking at Armageddon!'

CHAPTER 31

MESSAGE IN A BOTTLE

15 September 2022

Rick turned pale as the implications of Maria's words sunk in.

'Khalid mentioned a missile at dinner last night. But I had no idea we had so little time left. We've got to inform the British Government.'

'The missile is being fired in forty-eight hours,' said Maria. 'Is there enough time to get troops and warplanes here?'

'I don't know, Maria but we've got to try. But first of all I have to eliminate Heinrich.'

Rick entered the torture room and picked up the large wet cloth which had been used to water-board him. Then he went into the guard's rest lounge, got behind the seated Heinrich and pressed the cloth tightly over his mouth and nose. The guard awoke from his drugged sleep and flailed his arms around. Maria twisted his arms around the back of the chair and held them there while Rick maintained the pressure and checked the wall clock. Three minutes without air should be enough to kill him, but he would make it five to be certain. After three minutes, Heinrich stopped moving. Rick kept the cloth in place for another two minutes and then released it. He checked Heinrich's radial and carotid pulses. Nothing. Then he pulled his eyelids open one at a time. Fixed dilated pupils. He was dead. Job done.

Now he had to send a message to the British Government to warn them of the missile attack. But how? All the guards had walkie-talkies but no mobiles or satellite phones. There *was* an internal phone system in the base but – according to Maria – there was no way of getting an outside line.

But there was a laptop in the lounge. That was what the guards had used to view porn. He could send an email to the UK. But to whom? MI6, the British Government, GCHQ, the SAS, the Ministry of Defence? He had no idea, and in any case he didn't have their email addresses. And his message might not be believed. It might even end up in a spam filter and be disregarded.

After a couple of moments thinking over the problem, Rick came up with a solution. He could get a message to his friend Norm, who had hired the boat out to him. The vessel that he had used in the abduction of L'Arconne. He was ex-SBS and still had contacts at the Ministry of Defence and the Admiralty. He had won medals and kept his nose clean. So he would probably be believed. Would it work? He had no idea but he had to try.

Rick selected Microsoft Edge on the laptop and found Norm's Boat Hire website. Then he selected the 'Contact Us' tab and composed a brief email which outlined the situation. He mentioned the estimated location of the terrorist island base. How a missile armed with a deadly virus warhead was going to hit London in forty-eight hours. He suggested the Ministry of Defence ask the Americans to take satellite photos of the island to confirm his story. Then the British Government must despatch strong forces. He gave details of a joint SBS and SAS operation which the two of them had taken part in some years ago. This was classified information, so Norm would know that the message must have come from Rick. He also mentioned that his favourite meal was Chinese roast duck with pineapple and egg fried rice, washed down with Tsing Tao beer. He hoped that was enough to convince both Norm and the MoD that the email really was coming from him and that the information was genuine.

Rick clicked on 'send' and then deleted the computer's internet search history to cover his tracks. Then he slammed the laptop cover shut and turned to Maria.

'I hope that does the trick. It might work, it might not. It's a bit like sending a message in a bottle. I just hope Norm checks his emails regularly.'

'What do we now?' asked Maria.

'First, I have to get some grub down my neck. I haven't eaten since yesterday evening. Then we have to find some weapons, plus some food and water, and get the hell out of here. We'll have to hide somewhere on the island until the cavalry arrives.'

There was still food left on the trolley, plus some orange juice and coffee. Rick wolfed down pancakes, bacon and fried eggs, drank the remaining orange juice from the jug and had a cup of black coffee. Then, with Maria's help, he searched the lounge for any items that might aid their escape.

Eventually they found three Kalashnikov AK-47 7.62 mm assault rifles in an unlocked metal locker, and six spare magazines. Plus three Glock 17 pistols with four spare magazines and Rick's treasured Fairbairn-Sykes combat knife which had been taken off him when he was captured. Their next priority was food. In a cupboard in the lounge they located four packets of biscuits, two bars of chocolate, four cans of spam and three large plastic bottles of still mineral water. Rick also found a small shovel with a short handle under the sink which he knew would come in handy.

'We'll take two AK-47s and a couple of the pistols, plus all the spare ammunition, the knife and the shovel. And all the food and water. Do you have a bag?'

'I've got two large canvas holdalls which I used to carry all the clothes I brought you.'

'OK, that's fine. I would have preferred a Bergen but that will have to do. The AKs have carrying straps and we can stuff the spare mags into the pockets of our combat fatigues. Everything else can go in the bags. Now show me the quickest way out of here.'

Maria shouldered her AK-47, and Rick did likewise. Then Maria led the way down the corridor as Rick carried the heavy bags. Near the end of the passageway was a PVC-framed window. Maria took a key out of her pocket, unlocked the window and swung it open.

Rick looked out. It was a hot, sunny cloudless day. The whole island appeared to be made of volcanic rock. About eight hundred yards away was a second, smaller mountain which had a lot of trees and vegetation growing near the top. Rick looked down. There was a drop of ten feet to the ground. During parachute training he had learned to jump off a twelve-foot wall and land without injury. He gave Maria a quick tutorial on the dos and don'ts of making a jump. The last thing he wanted was for her to break or twist an ankle.

'You go first, remembering everything I said. Then I'll throw the bags, aiming well to one side of you. Then I'll jump!'

Three minutes later, the two of them were on the ground, heading for the other mountain as fast as their limbs could carry them. Rick knew that at any moment other guards could arrive and the three bodies would be discovered. It wouldn't take their enemies long to work out what had happened and get after them. At this range they could be gunned down by a couple of rifle shots from the open window. They had to move as fast as possible.

After another ten minutes effort, they reached the base of the adjacent mountain and scrambled up the slope. They would go quicker if they dumped the rifles and the bags but they needed them. Thirty minutes later they reached the tree line. Rick relaxed as he knew they couldn't be spotted now.

'Let's take a breather now,' said Rick. 'Stay behind a tree.'

Rick took a swig of water and then passed the bottle to Maria.

'We'll rest for a couple of minutes then resume our climb to the top.'

Rick sat under the shade of a palm tree and enjoyed the view. The sun rose high in the sky and it looked as though it was going to be another spectacular day. Tropical birds were singing and there was a gentle, warm breeze. This would be the ideal location for a sunshine break if it wasn't for the fact that there was a large group of criminal psychopaths on the island who seemed determined to destroy civilization!

'Right, let's go now,' said Rick, shouldering his rifle. 'It should only take us another half-an-hour to the top.'

'What are you going to do once we get there?' asked Maria.

'I'm going to build us a hide so no–one can spot us. That's why I brought the shovel. You'll see. By the time this escapade is over, you'll have learned a few SAS survival secrets.'

*

The three guards who comprised the 10:00 a.m. to 6:00 p.m. shift opened the door to the main corridor of the jailhouse section of the mountain base.

'Hello. Anyone there?' asked the senior guard for that shift, whose name was Alphonse. There was no response but that was no surprise. The lazy bastards were probably all sleeping after a night of porn, drugs and canned beer. Still he had better check on Fernscale, if he was still alive that is. If he wasn't in his cell, his incinerated corpse would be somewhere outside and would require burial.

Alphonse looked in Fernscale's cell. The door was open and he was gone. Then he systematically checked every cell and room. All three guards were dead, two of them in cells and one in the lounge. What had happened? How was he going to explain this to Khalid? Alphonse pressed a large red alarm button on the wall of the corridor and klaxons sounded throughout the complex. Then he picked up the phone in the guard's lounge and spoke to the control room.

'Fernscale's escaped. Search the entire complex. Red alert.'

On the adjacent mountain Rick heard the klaxons sound as he completed the digging of the hide. He had done this many times on operations, sometimes in very inclement conditions. A hide was just a large oblong hole in the ground covered with branches and whatever vegetation was available. A pair of SAS troopers could remain there for days without being spotted. The usual purpose of a hide was to permit observation of enemy positions without being detected. Rick's hide would allow him and Maria to avoid capture until British forces arrived...assuming that Norm had read his message.

*

Khalid shook with anger as his deputy, Le Blanc, gave him the bad news. Fernscale had somehow overpowered three of the guards and escaped. No trace of him had been found in the base and two AK-47s and a pair of pistols had been stolen from the guard's lounge. And Maria was also missing.

'This is sheer incompetence,' said Khalid. 'Fernscale was outnumbered three-to-one and unarmed, yet he gave our men the slip.'

'I know,' said Leblanc. 'But we believe Maria helped him. She has gone too and two vials of potassium chloride and a packet of Rohypnol have been reported stolen from the sick bay.'

'You'd better get after them,' said Khalid. 'Send a search party.'

'We'll do what we can,' answered Le Blanc. 'But it's a big island and we only have a limited number of men. Our priorities are defending this base and the airport. And we don't have a helicopter or tracker dogs.'

'Send what men you can spare but make sure they are back within six hours. Nothing must delay the firing of the missile. That is of paramount importance.'

*

Norman Arnott turned the key in his front door lock and entered his house – an 18th century property which overlooked the harbour. He yawned profusely. He really needed breakfast and a shower but be felt too tired to bother. He had been up all night fixing a problem with a Perkins marine diesel engine. It was needed for a wedding party boat hire at 3:00 p.m. so it was a priority. He really should check his emails but that could wait also. He wanted a few hours sleep first so he could think straight. Norm got into his bed and was asleep within five minutes. He was so tired he thought he might sleep for eight hours, or maybe even nine. Only then would he check his messages.

CHAPTER 32

HIDE AND SEEK

15 September 2022, 13:14 hours

After two hours of back-breaking work, Rick finished the hide. He had created a large oblong hole seven feet long, by four feet wide and four feet deep, and lined the bottom with palm leaves. The hole was covered with loose branches and vegetation that Maria had found. Rick stood a few feet back and admired his work. His SAS instructors back at Hereford would have been proud of him as the hide blended in perfectly with the surrounding landscape. Provided that any search party didn't walk directly over the hide and fall in, or bring sniffer dogs, they should be safe.

Rick and Maria rested on the bed of palm leaves for a moment. Then Rick spoke:

'We may as well have our lunch now and then we can take turns to sleep. I've left a little peephole just large enough to see out of. All we have to do is survive until British Forces arrive... *if* they arrive, that is.'

Rick opened a can of spam and shared the contents using his combat knife. It tasted delicious. One of the one-litre bottles of still mineral water was only partly full so Rick drank half the water and then offered the bottle to Maria. After she had finished, she passed the empty bottle to Rick who unfastened his trousers and pulled down his underpants.

'I'm going to have to pee into this empty bottle. When we used hides on operations we used to pee into jerrycans and crap into plastic bags to help us avoid detection by sniffer dogs. We brought all our piss and shit back with us.'

Rick managed to get all his urine into the bottle without spilling a drop and sealed the cap. Maria lay beside him. She smelled gorgeous. Even a little healthy sweat didn't lessen her allure.

'Don't pull your trousers up just yet Rick. You're a big boy, aren't you? Since you've gone to all the trouble of getting your penis out, maybe you'd like to use it for something else?'

Rick looked into Maria's eyes and sensed her desire. Then his mouth came down on hers...

*

Norm opened his eyes and looked at the bedside clock. It was four minutes past two. He had enjoyed six hours of deep, refreshing sleep and felt much better. Now it was time to do his chores. His assistant Alex would take care of the wedding party booking at 3:00 p.m. but he still had a lot of paperwork to catch up with. Norm filled the kettle with water, switched it on and put two slices of bread in the toaster. As everything was heating up, he checked his emails on his PC.

As usual, there were twenty unsolicited sales and marketing emails to delete. There was also a boat hire enquiry which must have come via his website.

'Holy Moses,' said Norm. 'It's from Rick.' He couldn't believe what he was reading. Was this a wind-up? According to the email, Rick had been abducted by *The Seven*, the terrorists responsible for the recent atrocities in London, but had escaped. He was now on a small island 300 miles north of Madagascar, which was being used by the gang. He requested urgent satellite reconnaissance and the despatch of a strong military force to take the island before a missile with a biological warhead could be launched at London on 17 September.

Rick then mentioned details of a classified mission they had both taken part in, plus his favourite food. And there was also a note about Defence Minister David Marshall. He was working for *The Seven* and should be arrested immediately.

Norm's mouth opened in awe as he slumped back in his computer chair. He had to warn the British Government. He still had a friend who worked at the Admiralty. If he phoned him immediately and then forwarded Rick's email, they would put things in motion. But was there enough time? The missile was to be launched in just forty-two hours. Could British forces get there fast enough to stop the terrorists? Bloggs reached for his Rolodex, found his friend's phone number, picked up his landline phone and punched in the number. After a few rings a robotic voice answered. There was an automatic call handling system. They were receiving an unexpected number of calls and he was eleventh in the queue…

*

Maria lay against Rick's chest and enjoyed a few minutes of blissful sleep. It was cool in the hide as it was sheltered from the blazing sun. Rick was wide awake. Though he desperately wanted to sleep, he knew he had to remain alert to stay alive. He had already got used to the usual noises of a tropical island. Birds singing. Monkeys screaming. And that ever-present sound of insects, which he found strangely soothing.

But there was another noise. Something new. Men shouting to one another. Rick looked through the peephole and saw a gang of men wearing tropical fatigues and bush hats, all carrying AK-47s as they slowly climbed up the mountain. They were well-spaced out. Rick counted twelve men. Not a large force but probably all Khalid could spare at this crucial time.

'Maria, get your rifle ready. Take off the safety catch but put your right finger in front of the trigger guard to prevent an accidental discharge.'

'Are we going to open fire, Rick?'

'No, we're in a good position and could probably take most of them down, but the shots will be heard back at the base. Once they've established our exact location, they could send a stronger force and attack from two directions. That's what I would do. Stay as quiet as possible and only fire if we are discovered. We must not be taken alive. The best we can hope for is a quick death. They'll probably gang rape you before they kill you.'

'I know, Rick. I would rather die than let that happen.'

'If capture looks imminent, I will shoot you in the head myself and then blow my own brains out.'

Rick and Maria lay motionless as the search party approached. Rick held his breath as they passed on either side of the hide without noticing it and continued towards the peak.

'We're OK for now,' said Rick. 'All we have to do is stay alive and undetected until help arrives. But we're not out of the woods yet.'

15 September 2022, 19:07 hours

COBRA meeting, Whitehall

The Prime Minister looked uncharacteristically grim as he opened the folder which was lying in front of him on the wooden conference table. A lot had happened in the last four hours. There was credible evidence that the terrorist group known as *The Seven* was planning a missile strike on London using a long-range rocket which had a virus warhead. The projectile would be launched about thirty-eight hours from now from a base on a small island north of Madagascar which had been used by the USAAF and US Navy in World War Two. An airfield had been built on the island by US Navy engineers, the 'Seabees,' but had been abandoned in the 1950s.

'Satellite photos taken in the last hour by the Americans have confirmed all Fernscale's claims,' said the Prime Minister. 'The dossier you all have in front of you contains several high-resolution photos. They show that the airfield is operational. The runway has been resurfaced and extended and the apron has two aircraft on it, a Boeing 737 and a Cessna 172, according to the photo interpreters. The terrorists also have four mobile surface-to-air missile batteries mounted on tracked chassis beyond the airfield perimeter. Our photo interpreters think they are the Franco- German Roland SAM. As you may know, an early version of this system was deployed at Port Stanley airport during the Falklands War and shot down a Sea Harrier.'

Defence Minister David Marshall, who had just returned from a conference in Gozo, looked uncomfortable as he studied the dossier.

'Can you excuse me, Prime Minister. I need to visit the bathroom. I think I'm going to be sick. Probably something I ate on the plane back from Malta.'

Marshall fumbled in his inside pocket for his smartphone as he left the room. He had to get in touch with Khalid urgently and warn him that British forces were on the way. As he walked into the corridor outside the briefing room, he was confronted by two burly plain clothes police officers. The older of the two held up his warrant card.

'David Marshall, my name is DCI Hallam from Scotland Yard, anti-terrorist branch, and I am placing you under immediate arrest. You are charged with treason. You do not have to say anything but it may harm your defence if you do not mention, when questioned, something which you later rely on in court. Anything you do say may be given in evidence. And I'll have your phone right now, thank you very much. You can make one phone call from a landline to your solicitor when we get you to the station.'

DS Ellis pulled out a pair of handcuffs and secured Marshall's hands behind his back. Then he frogmarched him along the corridor and down the stairs. A police car was waiting outside.

The Prime Minister watched Marshall disappear and closed the door.

'Another thing. David Marshall has just resigned…well, sort of. That means you've been promoted, Peter. You're the new Defence Secretary. You're ex-Royal Navy so you're the ideal person for the job.'

West beamed as the Prime Minister returned to his seat.

'Thank you, Prime Minister. I will carry out the job to the best of my ability. Now can you tell us how the UK is going to respond?'

The Prime Minister sat down, took a sip from a glass of water and then spoke:

'The terrorist island base is 5,000 miles from the UK. That's not as bad as the Falklands which were 8,000 miles away but it's still quite a distance. We do have some naval forces, including the aircraft carrier HMS *Queen Elizabeth*, in the Persian Gulf at the moment and they could arrive at the island in two to three days. That would still be too late, so the only way we can intervene in time is by sending troops by air. Twenty men from the 22 SAS Sabre Squadron regiment left RAF Brize Norton an hour ago. They are travelling in the new RAF Airbus A400 Atlas tactical transport. It can cruise at 487 miles per hour. By using an RAF Voyager air refuelling tanker flying from Akrotiri in Cyprus, we can have the first boots on the ground within ten hours.'

'What about the Rolands?' said the new Defence Secretary, Peter West. 'Could they not take down the A-400?'

'The Admiralty have thought of that,' said the Prime Minister. 'Although HMS *Queen Elizabeth* will not arrive in time for the initial strike, it can still launch F-35Bs on its way south. Carrying long-range tanks and flying at their maximum range, two F-35Bs will launch the new Spear 3 missiles at the Roland batteries and then continue to Nairobi to refuel and re-arm. After refuelling, they will be available for tactical air support for the SAS. As you know, the Spear 3 has not finished all its service trials but as HMS *Queen Elizabeth* had a dozen on board we thought this was an ideal time to try it out. The same thing happened during the Falklands War in 1982 when we used the new Sea Skua helicopter-launched anti-ship missile even though it had not completed its service trials.

'We are also sending a thousand paratroopers south in a second wave of A400Ms. They are due to leave Brize Norton within an hour. Half will drop on the missile base and the others will secure the airfield. Once the airbase has been taken, we will fly in in further reinforcements via Nairobi. This third wave will land at the airfield and will discharge further troops and vehicles, including some trucks and light armour. Eventually the naval force will arrive and will engage in mopping-up operations. Any terrorists who are not killed will be taken back to Britain and interned.

'Priority, though, will be given to neutralising the missile so the initial SAS assault is crucial. The SAS commanders at Hereford have suggested the best tactic will be to blast through the silo doors at the top of the mountain, abseil down ropes and then place small plastic explosive charges on the side of the missile control vanes. That should damage the missile enough to prevent launch without causing a huge explosion.'

'It sounds like quite an impressive plan,' said West. 'The only snag is that military operations rarely go to plan. As Von Moltke once said,

'No plan ever survives contact with the enemy.'

'I know,' said the Prime Minister. 'And if the terrorists fire their missile ahead of schedule, we will be completely screwed.'

CHAPTER 33

AIR LIFT

15 September 2022, 19:27 hours

Twenty men of Air Troop, Sabre Squadron, 22 SAS sprawled in the cavernous belly of the RAF A400M Atlas four engine transport as it thundered southeast at 35,000 feet above France on its way to the Mediterranean. The A400M was a major advance on the old Lockheed C-130 Hercules which it had replaced. Equipped with four powerful Europrop TP400-D6 turboprop engines, each delivering 11,000 horsepower, and fitted with contra-rotating sabre blade propellors and swept-back wings, it cruised at nearly 500 mph and was considerably quieter and roomier than its predecessor.

All the troopers faced Captain Andy Harrington, who had set up a large flatscreen TV monitor connected to his laptop.

'Listen up, men. I'm going to show you our latest intelligence.'

Harrington displayed a series of satellite photos which had been provided by the CIA at Langley.

'We don't know how strong the enemy forces are, but they are probably concentrated in two locations.' Harrington used his laser pointer. 'Here at the airfield and the rest at this missile base which has been built inside an extinct volcano.'

'The inside of the mountain has been hollowed out to create a launch pad and missile silo. There are two semi-circular metal doors at the base of the old volcano crater which have been painted to match the surrounding terrain. We can assume they will open just prior to missile launch. We'll use our standard HALO, High Altitude Low Opening, parachute technique. We'll jump from 18,000 feet using oxygen masks and open our parachutes at low altitude. If all goes to plan, we won't be seen from the ground. Our drop zone is flat ground to the west of the mountain.'

'What about radar, boss? And air defences?' asked Trooper Hargreaves.

'There's a basic surveillance radar at the airport. Plus another on a nearby mountain. And four tracked Roland SAM units beyond the perimeter. But we've got them covered. Thirty minutes before our drop, two F-35Bs flying from HMS *Queen Elizabeth* will launch twelve of the new Spear 3 mini cruise missiles at the radars and SAM units. That's an allocation of two missiles per target in case any of the munitions are duds. So we should have a clear run. There are no indications of radar or SAMs around the mountain itself. There's also no sign of anti-aircraft artillery either, anywhere on the island.'

Trooper Hargreaves nodded. Then Sergeant McKinnon spoke:

'Will our force be sufficient sir? We could be seriously outnumbered. Including you, we will have just twenty-one men. What is the plan once we hit the ground?'

'That' s a good question, Jim. In the past the SAS has achieved great results with small numbers of troops. Some of Paddy Mayne's airfield raids in North Africa were carried out with just four men. Our sole aim for the first part of the operation is to prevent the firing of the missile. Nothing else. We are authorised to destroy it if necessary. But the scientists back home would prefer us to capture it intact so it can be examined. In this respect the raid is going to be like *Operation Biting*, the Bruneval Raid in February 1942 when the paras captured a German radar station on the French coast and shipped the important bits back to Britain by boat. You may have read about it in the history books. It was the first ever operation by British parachute troops.

'However, we won't be on our own for very long. Within two hours a thousand men of the Parachute Regiment will drop on the island. Half will land near the airfield and capture it, the other five hundred will drop around the missile base. Two hundred and fifty of these will land near us, the rest will assault the main entrance.

'Once the airfield is captured, further A400Ms and C-17 Globemasters will land with further troops and heavy equipment, including vehicles and light armour. After a further two days a Royal Navy task force will arrive, including the carrier HMS *Queen Elizabeth*, a Type 45 air-defence destroyer, two Type 23 frigates and several Royal Fleet auxiliaries. There may be a couple of landing ships as well but we're still awaiting confirmation from the Admiralty.'

'It sounds like a well-planned operation,' said Sergeant McKinnon. 'But how do we get into the missile silo and disable the rocket?'

'We're not going in the front door, Jim. It's too well defended, with machine gun posts on either side. So that will be left to the paras. What we're planning to do is ascend the mountain, go down into the crater and blow open the semi-circular launch doors with plastic explosives. Then we will drop ropes into the silo and abseil down. Our plan is to disable the missile, not destroy it, so we will damage the control vanes at the base of the rocket using small explosive charges. These shouldn't be powerful enough to explode it, but will damage it enough to make it incapable of launch. We do have a back-up plan though. If it looks as though we are going to fail, a single F-35B will bomb the silo. The only snag is that the blast may wipe us all out. But the MoD thinks it will be a price worth paying!'

*

Rick opened the second tin of spam while Maria ripped open the biscuits. They had spent just one day in their hide and had already used up more than half their rations. Rick reckoned they had enough provisions to last just one more day. After that they would have to leave the hide to find more food and water if they wanted to survive. Rick put a spam-covered biscuit in his mouth and looked through the peephole. The sun was now setting in the west and the whole island was bathed in a golden glow. In these latitudes, darkness came quickly.

Even though the light was poor, Rick was sure he could see movement on the slope below the hide. He looked again and saw two shadowy shapes ascending the slope and heading straight for them. They were both wearing military fatigues but were unarmed...and they were holding hands. What on earth was going on? Was it a terrorist and one of the 'comfort women?'

As the two figures got closer, Rick realised they were both male. Then, when they were above the tree line, Rick saw them kiss and mumble something to one another. They walked even closer to the hide and then one stopped, took down his trousers and underpants and lay face down on the hide. Seconds later, he crashed through the thin carapace of branches and leaves and landed on top of Rick and Maria. Rick acted immediately, his reflexes honed from years of training.

He grabbed the man's head, yanked it back and slit his throat from one side to the other with his Fairbairn-Sykes combat knife, severing both external carotid arteries. The man would bleed to death in less than a minute but Rick knew he had to deal with the other terrorist before he could raise the alarm.

The other man looked about twenty, with dark greasy hair and a visible bulge in his crotch. Rick burst out the hide as the man screamed, turned, and started to run down the hill. He had only got a few yards when Rick brought him crashing down with a classic rugby tackle. Rick put his left hand over the terrorist's mouth and stabbed him in the heart with his razor-sharp knife. Blood spurted everywhere. A couple of minutes later, the young terrorist's eyes closed and he died.

'Did you really need to kill them both?' said Maria.

'Yes, I did,' said Rick. 'They had discovered our hide. If I had let them live, they would have reported our position to Khalid. Now you're going to have to help me bury them. Then we will repair our hide and stay there until our troops arrive.'

'How long will that be?' said Maria.

'I don't know,' said Rick. 'But I wish they would get a bloody move on!'

RAF Brize Norton

15 September 2022, 20.35 hrs

The airbase was a hive of activity. Every A400M and C-17 Globemaster transport aircraft that the RAF could spare was sprawled on the floodlit apron, rear loading doors open. Jackal armoured vehicles and DAF four-ton trucks reversed up aircraft ramps as hundreds of paratroopers disembarked from vehicles and boarded the planes. Forklift trucks made their way to the aircraft carrying wooden crates of food and ammunition. It was the biggest British airborne raid since *Operation Musketeer*, the invasion of Suez in October 1956, which had been a military success but a political disaster.

The paras were taking enough food and ammunition to last a week. After that they would be resupplied by the Royal Navy task force which was already steaming south from the Persian Gulf.

Dozens of reporters stood outside the perimeter fence wondering what was going on, but the MoD had issued a press statement saying it was all an exercise and was unconnected to the recent spate of terrorist attacks. Privately, ministers had agreed there would be a news blackout until the operation was over, in case there was mass panic in Britain. The Scientific Advisory Group for Emergencies (SAGE) had not been informed.

The first fully-loaded A400M taxied to the end of the runway, applied brakes, revved up its four whistling turboprops and then took off, leaving four faint trails of exhaust smoke. It had been agreed that, to save time, every aircraft would take off independently as soon as it was fully loaded and passed pre-flight checks. All the aircraft would be refuelled in mid-air over the Eastern Mediterranean. After making their drop over the island, they would fly to Nairobi where they would be refuelled again. As soon as the airfield was secured, the rest of the force would land there and discharge their troops and equipment. It was the greatest movement of RAF air transport for decades. But would this force be sufficient to save Britain and the rest of the world from disaster?

*

'Two of our men are missing,' said the guard Captain to Khalid. 'Sanchez and Villeneuve. They didn't return from their break.'

'It's dark now so there's no point in searching,' said Khalid. 'If they have not returned by the morning, we will look for them. But firing the missile is our priority. I want it ready for launch by dawn. Have the liquid oxygen tanks topped up overnight. In view of recent developments, we may have to fire it ahead of schedule. It could be just twenty-four hours to doomsday.'

CHAPTER 34

DEATH FROM THE AIR

16 September 2022, 07:05 hours

Ramos rested his AK-47 assault rifle against a railing and sipped a tin mug of strong, black sweetened coffee as he looked out to sea. It was a perfect morning. The sun rose behind him with just a little haze on the horizon. The only sound, apart from the waves and the chatter of monkeys and tropical birds, was the diesel engine of the tracked Roland unit just twenty feet to his left. It was ticking over at low revs, just enough to provide electrical power. Khalid had given orders that the mobile SAM batteries were to be manned around the clock, with their radar units switched on. Ramos finished his coffee, lifted up a pair of Zeiss binoculars and scanned the horizon. Nothing. The odd porpoise and dolphin but no sign of naval activity. No destroyers or frigates. No aircraft carriers. No submarines. No landing craft. Not even a patrol boat. Well, that was good. With any luck the British and Americans didn't even know about this place. It didn't even appear on some maps.

His reverie was rudely interrupted by twelve grey dots just above the horizon. They were flying at low level in a loose formation and coming straight for him at tremendous speed. What on earth were they? They were too small to be aircraft – could they be some kind of missile?

As they got closer, they split up and appeared to go in different directions. Ramos twigged that two were heading directly for the Roland unit to his left. As they neared, he realised they were cylindrical unmanned aircraft, like flying torpedoes but with tiny wings. *They were small cruise missiles.* Ramos raced for the safety of a sandbagged slit trench which had been dug to provide shelter in the event of an air attack, but didn't make it. Seconds later, the first Spear 3 cruise missile smashed into the Roland unit and exploded, followed by a second, equally devastating, munition. Bits of sharp metal flew in every direction, decapitating Ramos and amputating his left arm at the shoulder joint. The tracked chassis was overturned by the force of the blasts and caught fire. Within seconds, more Spear 3 missiles hit the three remaining Roland units, turning them into burning hulks. Then a pair of missiles struck the rotating radar scanner on top of a nearby mountain, while a single projectile struck the radar at the airport. The last missile didn't hit anything and landed in a field before exploding.

A few miles away, Rick and Maria heard the explosions and came out of their hide, but remained hidden in the trees. Six separate plumes of black smoke were visible against the blue sky. The sound of distant klaxons warned of an air raid. Then all went quiet. Exactly thirty minutes later, Rick spotted four faint vapour trails high in the azure blue sky. A few minutes passed and then he caught sight of a large number of tiny dots speeding to earth.

'Why don't they open their chutes, Rick? They will get killed,' said Maria who was standing behind him.

'They will in a minute, Maria. It's what we call a HALO drop. High Altitude, Low Opening.' A moment later – when the men were about five hundred feet from the ground – all the rectangular, steerable chutes bloomed open and the soldiers of Air Troop, Sabre

Squadron, 22 SAS landed on the flat ground between the two mountains.

Maria knew nothing about parachuting but was impressed with the obvious skill of the men who had all landed so close to one another. With well-practised movements, the soldiers ripped off their oxygen masks, goggles and white bone dome helmets and discarded their thick, insulated flying suits to reveal lightweight tropical uniforms in desert camo. Most of the soldiers were armed with 5.56 mm M16 rifles, some of which had underslung M203 40 mm grenade launchers.

'Time to break cover,' said Rick. 'Carry your AK-47 on your back using its sling but raise both hands above your head as though you want to surrender.'

Trooper Collins raised the alarm. 'Two X-rays descending the slope. Shall I take them out?'

Captain Andy Harrington looked through his binoculars at the two rather dishevelled figures who were coming down the mountain. A fit man of about forty with blonde hair and a bushy moustache and a rather tasty brunette with an enviable figure, who was clad in combat fatigues. The man was wearing a bloodstained battle dress shirt and military trousers. The face looked familiar.

'Don't shoot, Dean. I have no idea who the woman is but the man is one of our own. Rick Fernscale, no less.'

Captain Harrington called out. 'Rick it's me. Captain Andy Harrington. We were briefed to expect you. What on earth have you done to your hair...and that moustache? You look like the repair guy in one of these 'I've come to fix your refrigerator' porn videos!'

Rick laughed. 'I wouldn't know since I don't watch porn. But it's good to see you again, and this time we're definitely on the same side. This is Maria by the way. She helped me escape. So what's the plan?'

'The paras are on their way by air. A thousand men with orders to capture this base plus the airport. Once that is taken, further reinforcements will be flown in, including vehicles and light armour. Our immediate task, though, is to stop the missile launch. We're going to climb up that mountain behind us, descend into the crater and blow open the silo doors with explosives. Then we'll drop ropes alongside the missile and abseil down to the bottom of the silo. Our technical experts have advised us to blow holes in the control fins next to the rocket engine. That will not destroy the missile but will render it incapable of launching. At that point we will have completed our immediate goal and can wait for para reinforcements to arrive before we capture the entire missile base. But I need to ask you some questions. Are there any sentries guarding the crater area and do they have any defences such as machine guns or landmines?'

'I haven't seen any,' said Rick. 'But when we escaped, the base wasn't on red alert. Now that the missiles have struck, I expect they'll have ramped up the alert level!'

*

Deep inside the mountain base, Khalid viewed the multiple TV monitors which showed the surrounding terrain. A seated technician worked a computer mouse to zoom in on the group of soldiers which had gathered in the flat ground between the two mountains.

'Our radars have been destroyed by the missile attack. But we still have our TV cameras and other sensors. What are your orders, sir?'

'Man all defensive guns. These soldiers are probably from the British SAS. I see they have been joined by Fernscale and that treacherous bitch, Maria. As soon as they come within range of the guns, open fire. Kill them all!'

Khalid turned to his chief scientist who was standing next to him wearing a white coat and carrying a clipboard.

'How soon can we launch the missile?'

'As you ordered previously, we topped up the liquid oxygen tanks overnight and have already carried out all pre-launch checks. We can fire the missile fifteen minutes from now.'

'Good, make it so! I expect the SAS attack to fail because of our defensive firepower, but stronger forces may be on their way. We must launch as soon as possible.'

Khalid took a key from his pocket using his good left hand and put it into a lock next to a large red button on a control panel. Then he turned it ninety degrees to the left. An orange indicator light came on. All he had to do was press the large red button and the missile would launch.'

'Good,' said Khalid. 'We launch in fifteen minutes. Now we must deal with the SAS force.'

*

Five SAS troopers carrying backpacks lead the attacking force as it scrambled up the slope in the morning sunshine. There was little vegetation, just large boulders made of volcanic rock. Rick, Maria and Captain Harrington followed close behind while the other troopers were well spread out, alert for any possible threat. They were all moving as fast as possible as every minute counted. Even Rick felt out of breath. His heart thumped in his chest.

Rick estimated they would reach the rim of the crater in just ten minutes. But what was that object twenty yards in front of him? From a distance it looked like a volcanic boulder, but even at this range it looked fake, like the plaster rocks he had seen in the original *Star Trek* series when he was a kid. As Rick watched, the boulder rolled backwards pushed by an opening metal trapdoor. A familiar weapon rose up. It was a machine gun, but with multiple barrels like a vintage Gatling gun. Several wires and cables were attached to it. On top of the weapon was a small TV camera connected to a thick armoured cable. Rick knew what they were facing and shouted a warning:

'Minigun! Take cover everybody!'

Rick and Maria dived behind a boulder while Harrington and his sergeant took cover behind an adjacent rock. The Minigun opened fire with a blinding yellow muzzle flash and a familiar noise which some had compared to ripping canvas and others thought was like a buzzsaw. Rick had great respect for this weapon. Based on the 19th century Gatling gun and powered by an electric motor, the General Electric M134 Minigun could spew out 3,000 x 7.62 mm rounds per minute which meant that any person that got in its way would end up as mince.

Seven of the SAS troopers didn't get behind cover fast enough and were cut to pieces in seconds. The slopes of the extinct volcano were strewn with dismembered bodies. Blood ran down the slope and dried quickly in the hot morning sun. The assault on the crater hadn't even started and already the attacking force had taken thirty-three percent casualties.

Further Miniguns were popping up at different points near the top of the extinct volcano. Rick reckoned there were eight guns surrounding the crater to deter attack from any direction. He yelled at Harrington:

'Throw me your binoculars, Andy.'

Harrington complied and Rick peeked round the side of the boulder to take a look at their tormentor through powerful lenses. He shouted out his observations so the others could hear:

'It's a General Electric 7.62 mm Minigun on an electrically powered mount. I guess it's remotely controlled from a bunker inside the mountain. I can see a small TV camera on top of the gun. There are bits of armour plate around the gun and a piece of armoured glass in front of the TV camera. Tell your men to fire at the gun and concentrate on the TV camera.'

'Open fire,' said Harrington.

A volley of 5.56 mm bullets struck the Minigun emplacement and bounced off the armour plate without effect. Rick contributed to the attack by firing off a few well-aimed single shots with his AK-47. The Minigun fired back with a series of one-second bursts, causing the soldiers to crouch down behind the rocks. Rick saw that it had a limited traverse of forty-five degrees to either side, controlled by electric motors.

'We need something heavier,' shouted Rick. 'Andy. Have you brought any 66 mm LAW rockets with you?'

'Dean's got one in his Bergen but he's some distance from you.'

'OK, I've got an idea. Have you got a flare pistol?'

'Yes,' answered Harrington.

'OK, I'm going to count from one to three. When I reach three, I want you to fire a flare to the north to distract the Minigun operator. It will give Dean enough time to get the 66 to me. Remember I'm a marksman and a great shot with the 66. If anyone can hit that gun emplacement, it's me.'

'OK, I've got the flare pistol ready.'

'One... two... three... shoot!'

Harrington fired the flare pistol. A brilliant ball of red light flew upwards in an arc and landed on the ground a hundred yards away. Deep inside the mountain, the Minigun operator was puzzled. What were the British doing? But the deception worked and he moved the joystick which controlled the gun. The camera atop the gun tracked the glowing ball. The crosshairs on the TV screen were now centred on the flare. The operator had no idea if this was just a flare or some other weapon. He knew that some guided missiles had flares on their tail to assist aiming. Better to be safe than sorry. He pressed the fire button on top of the joystick and unleashed a hail of lead at the target.

Trooper Dean Collins saw his chance. While the Minigun operator was distracted by the harmless flare, he raced towards Rick and gave him the LAW rocket launcher. Rick loved this weapon. His father had once told him about he had blown the tail off a parked Argentine Pucara aircraft with one of these single-use bazookas. Rick removed the end caps and pulled the telescopic firing tube out to full length. The foresight and rear sight popped up. After checking that no-one was standing behind him, he aimed carefully, pushed the safety catch off and pressed the fire button. A small rocket shot out the front end of the weapon and scored a direct hit on the square of armoured glass in front of the TV camera. The hollow-charge warhead worked exactly as advertised and punctured the glass with a jet of white-hot metal. The kinetic energy of the impact also knocked over the Minigun.

'Now we need to blind the other weapons,' shouted Rick. 'Fire smoke grenades in front of them. It will neutralise the TV cameras for a minute or two. Enough time for us to get past them.'

All the troopers with M203 launchers loaded smoke grenades and fired them at the remaining Miniguns that were on their side of the mountain. Then all the surviving soldiers emerged from cover and charged towards the lip of the crater. As they descended towards the two camouflaged semi-circular doors at the top of the silo, there was a loud electrical whirring sound as the two launch doors flipped open. The ground shook with an ear-splitting roar and then the nose cone of a huge white rocket emerged vertically from the silo.

'The missile is launching,' said Rick. 'Get back over the lip of the crater and take cover. The rocket engine's blast could kill you.'

All the SAS men, plus Maria and Rick, raced back over the lip of the crater just as the rocket fully emerged from the silo. A huge flame as bright as burning magnesium spewed from its tail. White smoke was everywhere. All the soldiers coughed and struggled to breathe. Three of them were not adequately sheltered from the blast and burned alive.

Rick looked up and saw the missile accelerating skywards with a glowing tailflame. It was on its way to London. Nothing could stop it.

CHAPTER 35

THE END OF THE WORLD?

16 September 2022

Four RAF F-35B fighter-bombers flew over the smoking crater as the terrorist missile climbed higher in the cloudless azure blue sky. Rick felt a pain in his gut. Despite the best efforts of the SAS team, Khalid had foiled their plan by firing the missile a day early. The four F-35Bs circled the mountain at low altitude as though awaiting instructions. Two of them carried a pair of Paveway laser-guided 500 pound bombs each, while the others had air-to-air missiles on their underwing pylons. All four aircraft had underwing long-range tanks and had flown off HMS *Queen Elizabeth*. If they had arrived a few minutes earlier they could have bombed the missile silo. The SAS assault force would probably have all died but the world would have been saved.

Captain Harrington pulled out his satellite phone and selected MI6 on speed dial.

'Greyhound to Trap One. The bird has flown. Repeat. The bird has flown.'

Harrington turned to Rick.

'What do you suggest we do now, Rick?'

'I think we should abseil down that silo and take the control room. Perhaps we can divert the missile or explode it. Let's go!'

Harrington selected two of the troopers for a very important task.

'Gordon and John, I want you to knock out the remaining Miniguns with grenades. As long as you attack them from behind, you should be safe as they have limited traverse. It's a very important job because the paras will be landing soon and we don't want them wiped out. Once you have completed this task, I want you to follow the rest of us into the silo.'

The remaining eight SAS troopers took nylon ropes from their backpacks and donned thick leather gloves. Then they hammered pitons into the rock around the opened blast doors, attached one end of the ropes to them and then threw them into the silo.

'I'm coming with you,' said Rick. 'Maria you stay here. This is going to be dangerous.'

'No Rick, I've a score to settle with Khalid,' said Maria as she slung her AK-47 around her neck. 'I know how to abseil, or *rappelle* as the Americans call it. I attended university in Colorado and was in the mountaineering club.'

'OK you win, but just stay behind me,' said Rick as he grabbed a rope and started to climb down the shaft.

10 Downing Street, London

'I have bad news,' said the Prime Minister. 'Our mission failed. The terrorist missile was launched early and will strike London in forty minutes. Is there any way we can shoot it down?'

'The Sky Sabre battery in Hyde Park might stand a chance,' said Junior Defence Minister Tony West. 'Let me phone them immediately.'

West lifted up his mobile and dialled a number. There was palpable tension in the room as the number rang. The caller answered and West explained the situation. A moment later his face drained of colour. 'I see,' he said. 'And how long will it take?'

West put down the phone. The British Cabinet looked at him intensely.

'Bad news. The Giraffe Radar, which forms a crucial part of Sky Sabre, is down at the moment. Technicians are fitting a new mother board. It will be another hour at least before it is working!'

*

Rick, Maria, Captain Harrington and eight SAS troopers stood at the bottom of the silo in front of a locked door which gave access to the inside of the missile complex.

'We don't have a Remington 870 with us so we'll need some plastic,' said Harrington. 'Simon, would you like to do the honours?'

Trooper Simon Henderson took a small lump of plastic explosive out his backpack, stuck it against the door lock and attached a detonator. Then he connected a long cable to it and took shelter with the others on the far side of the shaft. Henderson attached the wires to the terminal of a mini-plunger, pulled it up to charge it and then pressed it down with great force. The plastic charge exploded, blowing a football-sized hole around the lock and making the door swing open. Without waiting for the smoke to dissipate, Rick and Harrington raced down the corridor which led to the control room. The others followed, clutching their rifles.

10 Downing Street, London

The Prime Minister was in despair. His elbows were on the conference table, his hands gripping both his cheeks and his mouth downturned. *How had he got it so wrong?* He had been confident that the SAS could stop the missile firing and, even if they failed, there was a good chance that the F-35Bs could blow the silo to kingdom come with their laser-guided bombs. Now everything had unravelled.

If only he had asked for assistance from the Americans. They had satellite-guided JDAM bunker-busting bombs that could be launched by stealth bombers and were one hundred percent accurate. If only he had ordered the evacuation of London…if only he had told SAGE… if only… if only. Now it looked as though three-quarters of the population of Britain was going to die. And then the virus would spread to the rest of the world. *And it was all his fault!*

'Excuse me, Prime Minister, but I have an idea!'

The Prime Minister looked up at his Defence Secretary.

'What?'

'Back in June, I suggested we move a Type 45 Daring class air defence destroyer to the Thames Estuary. It has Sampson 3D radar and the new Sea Viper missile system which is one of the most advanced SAMs in the world. I believe it could intercept the terrorist missile provided it gets a head-on shot rather than a hit from the side.'

'Has this ever been done?'

'No, but it is theoretically possible. The Type 45 with its Sea Viper system has been considered for anti-ballistic missile defence. But to get a better angle on the target, the ship will have to move at least fifteen nautical miles further west.'

'Contact the ship now! Order them to shoot down the terrorist missile!' said the Prime Minister.

West picked up his phone.

'Put me through to the Captain of HMS *Danae*. Urgent!'

*

Rick, Andy and Maria raced along the corridor, followed by several SAS troopers. A second locked wooden door barred their progress. This one was a relatively flimsy affair and Rick shot out the lock with three rounds from his AK-47 and then flung open the door.

Khalid stood in the middle of the control room. Around him were computers, monitor screens and seated technicians wearing white coats and headsets. Multiple coloured lights blinked on and off.

'You're too late, Fernscale. In just thirty minutes the missile will discharge its lethal cargo over Central London. Most of the population of the UK, and then the world, will die. It will be Armageddon, followed by a New World Order. There is nothing you can do!'

'The missile must have a self-destruct system. Or maybe you can divert it?'

'I can't do either of these things. You've been watching too many James Bond movies. The missile is entirely autonomous. Once it is fired, there is nothing anyone can do to stop it.'

Rick pointed his AK-47 at Khalid.

'You're lying. If you don't stop the missile, I will shoot you.'

'Go ahead! Make my day, as your capitalist hero Dirty Harry might have said. Dying for my cause will be an honour.'

Rick lowered his weapon. Then Khalid's skull exploded as two 7.62 mm rounds hit his head at close range. The terrorist leader fell to the floor, blood, brains and cerebrospinal fluid splattering everywhere.

Maria stood motionless, holding her AK-47. White smoke drifted from its muzzle. Two empty brass cartridge cases lay on the floor.

'To use another Dirty Harry quote, I think he's shit out of luck,' she said. 'But what are we going to do now, Rick?'

'Nothing. The paras will be here soon, but, as for the fate of the world, it is now out of our hands.'

The Thames Estuary, near London

The 8,500 tonne Type 45 air-defence destroyer HMS *Danae* steamed west towards London at her maximum speed of 32 knots. Captain Robertson spoke to the engine room on the internal phone system:

'Give me every ounce of power you can generate. We've got to get at least fifteen nautical miles further west as fast as possible.'

'Aye, aye sir.'

Robertson turned to his Air Warfare Officer.

'What's the latest update on the missile's position?'

'It's hasn't been picked up on our S1850M air surveillance radar yet. Too far away and too high at present. But American satellites are tracking it and feeding the information to our own fire-control computers by datalink.'

'Good. We'd better move to the Operations Room. As soon as we're in a better launch position, we'll calculate a firing solution.'

10 Downing Street, London

The Prime Minister studied the huge widescreen television which took up much of the wall of the conference room. It was now showing a live feed from a camera inside the Operations Room of HMS *Danae*.

'How long till *Danae* gets within range?' he asked.

'Another ten minutes,' said West. 'It won't be an ideal firing solution. That won't be possible for another twenty minutes...the time we expect the missile to reach Central London. This is going to be touch and go!'

The Prime Minister covered his face with his hands. He had never felt so anxious in his entire life.

HMS *Danae*, the Thames Estuary

'I think I can get a firing solution now,' said the Air Warfare Officer. 'We've got a good lock with our Type 1045 air tracking radar. The target is now descending towards Central London at supersonic speed.'

'Open fire,' said the Captain.

There was a loud bang and then a single Astor 50 missile shot out its vertical launch silo on the foredeck, trailing white smoke behind it. In the Operations Room of HMS *Danae*, the crew looked anxiously at the main radar screen. It showed a large orange blip representing the terrorist missile as it hurtled down through the stratosphere. A smaller point of light on the screen showed the Astor missile as it moved closer to the target. When the two dots connected, the enemy missile would be destroyed.

The Astor had only half-an-inch to travel on the radar screen when it veered off course.

'We've lost radar lock,' said the Air Warfare Officer. 'What are your orders?'

'Fire another missile,' said the Captain.

A second Astor shot out its silo towards the target. Again, the SAM veered off course before it hit the target.

'What are we going to do now?' said the Air Warfare Officer.

'We're going to wait a few minutes and then try again. The range will be less and we should get a better lock-on.'

'The enemy missile is going to hit London in six minutes. What are your orders?'

'We'll fire with three minutes to go.'

10 Downing Street, London

The Prime Minister was beside himself with anxiety. The tension was unbearable. He needed a drink. And maybe half-a-dozen tranquillisers as well.

'Why doesn't the Captain fire another missile?' he asked.

'The Captain knows what he's doing. He's very experienced in Air Warfare,' said West. 'He once commanded a Type 42, the immediate predecessor of the Type 45.'

HMS *Danae*, the Thames Estuary

'Three and a half minutes till the terrorist missile hits,' said the AWO.

'Prepare to fire!'

'Three minutes and ten seconds till missile hits.'

Robertson looked at the wall clock.

'Fire now!' he barked.

The third Astor missile streaked out of its launcher. A moment later the crew saw a dot on the radar screen approaching the larger blob of light which represented the enemy rocket. The two dots merged and a 'bloom' appeared on the radar screen, signifying a hit. Up on the bridge of the *Danae* one of the crew looked out a window and saw a bright flash above the clouds. The world had been saved!

The Captain turned towards the TV camera in the Operations Room and spoke:

'One terrorist missile splashed with Sea Viper. I think that calls for a free bottle of rum for every crew member, Mr Prime Minister.'

In 10 Downing Street the Cabinet cheered loudly. Many of them slapped the Prime Minister's back. The Royal Navy had saved the world. Everyone was jubilant... except for the Prime Minister, who was crying like a baby.

CHAPTER 36

JUBILATION

16 September 2022

The news broke at 5:37 p.m. Twenty-three minutes later there was a live Press Conference from Downing Street, chaired by the Prime Minister, which explained what had happened in the last few days. The security services had learned of a terrorist plot to hit London with a missile tipped with a virus warhead which would kill two-thirds of the population and then spread to the rest of the world.

The government had taken decisive action to counter the plot. A strong force of SAS troopers and paras had flown 5,000 miles to capture the terrorists' island base. After fierce fighting, the base and the island's airport had been captured with minimal casualties. Most of the dead and wounded were in the SAS component of the force. Although the soldiers arrived too late to prevent the missile launch, the rocket was subsequently shot down over the Thames Estuary by a Royal Navy Type 45 destroyer. The whole operation had been triggered by intelligence supplied by an ex-SAS man who had been held captive by the guerrillas. The Prime Minister said that the terrorist group known as *The Seven* had been behind the scheme but most of its members had now been killed or captured. Security services around the world were now hunting down any remaining cell members.

The following day the British newspapers went berserk. *The Sun* ran a huge headline *Gotcha!* (for the third time in its history) above a picture of HMS *Danae*. Below the photo was another caption *Navy Saves Britain!* Early editions also carried the headline *The Paper that Supports our Boys* (again a repeat of what they had said in 1982), though in later issues this was changed to *The Paper that Supports our Armed Forces* in recognition of the fact that many women now served in the British military.

The *Daily Mail* ran a seventeen-page special on the operation, which included a detailed article about the Type 45 destroyer which was titled *Type 45 – The Supership that Saved Britain*. There were cutaway drawings of the vessel and details of its amazing Sea Viper system. There were also features on the SAS, the paras and all the aircraft that had taken part in the operation including the Voyager air refuelling tanker, the F-35B Lightning and the A400M and C-17 transport aircraft, plus a timeline explaining how events had unfolded.

Most of the papers approved of the government's handling of the crisis, and praised the decision to have a news blackout until the military operation had concluded. A snap poll by You Gov showed that ninety-seven percent of the population supported the military action.

Some backbench Tory MPs offered their congratulations to the Prime Minister but pointed out that the Royal Navy only had six Type 45s instead of the original twelve that were planned. The Leader of the Opposition said he was pleased with the outcome of the raid but disappointed that the government had not kept him in the loop until the operation was over.

In a lengthy article in *The Telegraph,* a leading historian said that the raid, which the MoD now referred to as *Operation Thunderbird,* had restored Britain's prestige on the world's stage. The UK could now flex its military muscles anywhere in the world thanks to the new *Queen Elizabeth* class aircraft carriers and their air wings. He also noted with some satisfaction that the operation had been carried out without any assistance from the US military. The positive outcome of the raid, he said, had helped to heal the massive trauma caused by the coronavirus pandemic.

Meanwhile, three different authors said they intended to write a non-fiction book about the operation. Some Hollywood producers said they would be very interested in making a movie about this amazing military operation but might make a few changes to ensure the film's success at the US box office. For example, they might cast an American action star in the lead role of the mystery SAS man who had saved the world. Brad Pitt and Tom Cruise were two names that were being bandied about. In addition, they thought the film would have greater box office potential if American (rather than British) forces were the protagonists.

10 Downing Street, London

17 September 2022, 08:00 hours

The Prime Minister finished his toast, coffee and boiled egg and faced his Cabinet. He had only had four hours sleep the previous night but felt elated and energised.

'Thank you for joining me for this working breakfast. I think we can all congratulate ourselves on a job well done. I've just had a report from the Porton Down scientists. The virus warhead was completely incinerated by the explosion and there appears to have been no contamination of the estuary. We can assume that this new variant of coronavirus has been completely eliminated. SAGE are pressing for a precautionary six-month lockdown of the entire UK but on this occasion I'm not going to accept their recommendations.'

The Cabinet laughed.

'What's going to happen to Fernscale?' said the Junior Defence Minister, Tony West. 'In theory he could face prosecution for the murder of two terrorists on British soil.'

'I know,' said the Prime Minister. 'But I've already phoned the Director of Public Prosecutions and suggested that that course of action would not be in the public interest. He agreed. I'm sure there would be a public outcry if we brought a criminal case against him. In fact, I'm considering a medal for him. He's no longer in the army so he can't receive any of the usual military decorations. But I suggest we give him the George Medal plus a large cash payment, say £5 m, so he can start a new life abroad. He's going to have to keep his head down for the rest of his life as there will still be people who are angry at what happened and want him dead.'

The Cabinet nodded in approval.

SAS Headquarters, Stirling Lines, Hereford

30 September 2022

Rick rested in a comfortable armchair next to the fireplace. Next to him sat Maria who looked at him with love in her eyes as she showed off her triple-diamond engagement ring. Captain Andy Harrington entered the room carrying a tray with three mugs of steaming hot coffee and a plate of biscuits. Rick always felt at home in the Officers' mess at Hereford. He never tired of looking at photos of his father or the pristine Stinger missile launcher which was mounted above the fireplace.

'We don't usually allow civilians into our base,' said Harrington. 'But we'll make an exception in your case. And I've got some news. The government has announced there will be a victory parade through London next month. All the forces which took part in *Operation Thunderbird*, as it is now called, will be present. There will be a flypast by F-35Bs, A400Ms and C-17s followed by some AH-64 Apache helicopter gunships which were based on HMS *Queen Elizabeth*. Then there will be a march through London by the paras and the SAS. All the SAS soldiers will be wearing helmets and dark glasses to protect their identities. We wondered if you might like to participate as a kind of parting shot?'

'I'd be delighted...as long as I can't be identified.'

'We suggest you travel in the front passenger seat of a Land Rover. As you know, the Landy is being phased out of British Army service as production stopped years ago. But our mechanics have restored an old Series 2 long-wheelbase version and repainted it in 1960s gloss dark green. We use it for ceremonial duties only. You can see it in the car park. Take a look out the window.'

Rick turned round and spotted a gleaming vehicle in the car park. Its dark green paint glistened in the sunlight. It had obviously been machine polished with car wax and its tyres painted with high-gloss tyre paint. All the wheel nuts had been painted red and small pennants had been mounted on each front wing. But why did it have such a long aerial fitted on the front offside wing?

'It will be an honour,' said Rick. 'I'll also put on a false beard as well, just to be on the safe side.'

'By the way, the Landy also has some interesting mods under the bonnet. It's got...'

Harrington had been interrupted by Corporal Harris, who had raced into the mess.

'Sorry to intrude, Andy, but there's a call for you. MI5. They say it's urgent.'

Central London, 14 October 2022

Hundreds of thousands of people had crowded into Central London to witness the Victory Parade. Tube trains and buses were packed. Fortunately, the weather was kind. A warm autumn sun shone down from a clear blue sky and people dressed in shorts and T-shirts. Press and TV reporters from all around the world had gathered in the capital to witness this historic event. A Fox News reporter said that the Brits were the best in the world at staging this kind of military pageantry.

The parade was preceded by a flypast at 12 noon. This was even more spectacular than originally planned. Leading the aircraft were two Hurricanes and five Spitfires of the Battle of Britain Memorial Flight, followed by the Flight's sole Avro Lancaster PA474. Then there was a last minute addition: an airworthy De Havilland Mosquito twin engine fighter-bomber which had been flown all the way from the USA (via Newfoundland, Greenland and Iceland) by its American owner as a way of expressing solidarity with the British. Then a Douglas C-47 Dakota of the Battle of Britain Memorial Flight swept low over The Mall, signifying that the British armed forces had a long history of paratrooper operations.

Next came two Fairey Swordfish torpedo bombers of the Navy Wings, The Royal Navy Historic Flight. It was hard to believe that these apparently flimsy, slow biplanes had inflicted so much damage on the enemy during WW2.

Then came the modern aircraft. Four F-35B fighters zoomed over the crowds followed by three Royal Navy Wildcat helicopters and a trio of Apache attack helicopters which had flown off HMS *Queen Elizabeth* to provide tactical air support during the operation. Last came four A400M transports and two C-17 Globemasters which had proved crucial in getting troops south as fast as possible.

After the flypast came the parade. Travelling north-east up The Mall, it was led by a single vintage Series 2 Land Rover with highly polished green paintwork. Following close behind were an assortment of sand-coloured army vehicles which had been landed on the terrorist island. Then came the soldiers. Thirty men of the SAS, all wearing black kit, helmets and respirators to protect their identities. They were closely followed by a thousand men of the Parachute Regiment who all wore sand-coloured desert camo battledress and red berets. The crowds went wild and waved Union Jacks. Others carried placards with slogans such as *We Love Our Armed Forces* and *Britain Number One Again! Thank you, Mr Prime Minister!*

The biggest cheers from the crowd were prompted by the last military element in the parade. Two hundred Royal Navy sailors who walked in front of a slow-moving, dark blue DAF four- tonner with RN markings which was towing a flatbed trailer carrying a seventy-five foot-long model of a Type 45 destroyer.

The procession passed through Admiralty Arch and then turned right down Whitehall. The parade was now moving south past the MoD buildings which were on the east side of the road. Then Whitehall became Parliament Street and the throng of vehicles and soldiers continued towards Westminster Bridge.

In a high building on the east side of Parliament Street, Serbi Kokorov, a sleeper agent with *The Seven,* was hunched over his Barratt fifty-calibre sniper rifle. He hated everything American but had to concede that the Barratt was the best weapon of its kind in the world. The example he was using had been captured in Afghanistan and then sold on the black market.

Kokorov looked through the telescopic sight and kept the crosshairs on his target – the front passenger window of the pristine Land Rover which was leading the SAS contingent. He had received intelligence that Rick Fernscale, the man most responsible for the failure of *Operation Armageddon*, would be sitting in the front passenger seat. He had also been told that his target would be wearing a helmet, dark sunglasses and a false beard. Through his sight, Kokorov could see that his target matched this description. It was Fernscale all right. No doubt about it. In a few seconds he would be dead.

Kokorov put the crosshairs of his telescopic sight on Fernscale's head. He aimed just below the lip of the helmet. At this close range a fifty-calibre round would burst the skull. He squeezed the trigger gently and felt the powerful recoil of the Barratt against his right shoulder. The Triplex toughened glass passenger window of the Land Rover shattered and broke into hundreds of tiny cubes. Blood sprayed everywhere inside the driving compartment of the Rover and dribbled down the outside of the door. The inside of the windscreen was also coated with blood and what looked like brains. Job done.

Kokorov smiled with satisfaction as he packed the Barratt into its carrying case. Now he would have to move fast before the police caught him.

As Kokorov was packing away his weapon, the front door of his apartment was blown open by a powerful plastic explosive frame charge. Two SAS troopers in black kit, respirators and Kevlar helmets burst into the flat, followed by two more, all clutching MP5s.

Kokorov tried to speak but was instantly cut down at close range by a burst of fire from two MP5 submachine guns. The four troopers ripped off their respirators. One of them was Captain Andy Harrington.

'We arrived too late,' said trooper Dean Collins. 'If we had got here three minutes earlier, we could have saved Rick.'

Harrington said nothing and looked out the window.

*

Maria knew something was wrong. She had heard a shot. Rick's Land Rover had stopped. Then there had been the sound of police and ambulance sirens. Maria forced her way through the crowds and vaulted over one of the metal barriers. An ambulance and a police car were already on the scene. A policeman stood by the Land Rover talking into his personal radio. The vehicle's front passenger window was smashed. Blood was everywhere.

Maria ran up to the Land Rover and pulled the front passenger door open. A headless blood-spattered body fell out and landed on the road.

Maria screamed. 'No, this isn't fair! After all we've been through, how could this happen! We had so much to live for. How can there be a God if he lets things like this happen?' Tears streamed down her cheeks. A policeman offered her a tissue.

'I wouldn't cry so much, my love. You'll ruin your mascara.'

A tall bearded man sporting Ray Ban sunglasses stood beside her. He turned towards Captain Harrington, who was still carrying his MP5. Andy's respirator was dangling round his neck.

'She's marrying me in six weeks in Cyprus and she doesn't even recognise me with a false beard. I think she's needing her eyes tested.'

'You're alive! But how?' said Maria, as she put her arms around Rick and hugged him.

'Take a look at that body on the ground.'

Maria studied the 'corpse' more closely. The neck was made of plastic.

'It's a mannequin, a tailor's dummy. We filled the head with stage blood, Kensington Gore as it is known, plus a little offal and a dod of plastic explosive, a detonator and a trembler switch to make sure it exploded when it was hit.'

'But the driver could have been killed! You still took a risk!'

'Not at all. The driver is a dummy as well. You see the vehicle is radio-controlled. MI5 set up the whole thing to catch *The Seven's* last sleeper agent in Britain. As a result we have also nabbed another corrupt politician who was leaking secrets to *The Seven*. You'll read about it in the papers tomorrow.'

'So that concludes the whole affair then, Rick,' said Harrington. 'Any chance you would consider coming back to the SAS as an instructor? We have new recruits who could learn from your experience?'

'It's a tempting proposal, Andy. But I've got another reason for living now. In six weeks I will be marrying Maria in Cyprus. And then we'll have a new life together running our own diving school in Paphos. Third time lucky, that's what I say.'

'So will you *never* join the SAS again, Rick?' said Maria as she clasped his right hand.

'I don't think so, but I guess I should never say never again,' said Rick.

THE END

ABOUT THE AUTHOR

Colin Barron was born in Greenock, Scotland in 1956 and was educated at Greenock Academy (1961-74) and Glasgow University (1974-79) where he graduated in Medicine (M.B. Ch.B.) in July 1979. He worked for the next five years in hospital medicine, eventually becoming a Registrar in Ophthalmology at Gartnavel General Hospital and Glasgow Eye Infirmary.

In December 1984, he left the National Health Service to set up Ashlea Nursing Home in Callander, which he established with his first wife and ran until 1999. He was the chairman of the Scottish branch of the British Federation of Care Home Proprietors (BFCHP) from 1985 to 1991 and then a founding member and chairman of the Scottish Association of Care Home Owners (SACHO) from 1991 to 1999.

Colin has always had a special interest in writing – his first non-fiction book, *Running Your Own Private Residential and Nursing Home*, was published by Jessica Kingsley Publishers in 1990. When he was at

Glasgow University, he was editor of SURGO (Glasgow University Medical Journal) between 1977 and 1979. SURGO subsequently won an award from *The Glasgow Herald* for best student magazine in 1979. In late 1978, Colin was asked to write an article *How to Improve a Student Medical Journal* which appeared in the *British Medical Journal* in March 1979 and has been reprinted and revised in three separate editions of the BMA's *How To Do It* book.

Colin was also the Art Editor and Motoring Correspondent of *Glasgow Medicine* between 1984 and 1986. He is a former cartoonist, having contributed to *Glasgow University Guardian, Ygorra, Glasgow Medicine, Scottish Medicine* and *BMA News Review*. In February 1977, the Greenock Arts Guild held an exhibition of his work along with that of two other local cartoonists.

He has also written about 150 articles for various publications including *This Caring Business, The Glasgow Herald, Caring Times, Care Weekly, The British Medical Journal, The Hypnotherapist, The Thought Field* and many others. He was a regular columnist for *This Caring Business* between 1991 and 1999 and the editor of SACHO *Newsline* between 1991 and 1999.

Colin has always had a special interest in hypnosis and alternative medicine. In 1999, he completed a one-year diploma course in hypnotherapy and neuro-linguistic programming with the British Society of Clinical and Medical Ericksonian Hypnosis (BSCMEH), an organisation created by Stephen Brooks who was the first person in the UK to teach Ericksonian hypnosis. He has also trained with the British Society of Medical and Dental Hypnosis (BSMDH) and with Valerie Austin, who is a top Harley Street hypnotherapist. Colin has also been a licensed NLP practitioner. In 1992, he was made a Fellow of the Royal Society of Health (FRSH)). He is a former member of various societies including the British Society of Medical and Dental

Hypnosis – Scotland (BSMDH), the British Thought Field Therapy Association (BTFTA), the Association for Thought Field Therapy (ATFT), the British Complementary Medicine Association (BCMA) and the Hypnotherapy Association.

Colin has been using TFT since early in 2000, and in November 2001 he became the first British person to qualify as a Voice Technology TFT practitioner. He used to work from home in Dunblane and at the Glasgow Nuffield Hospital.

Colin has also had 40 years of experience in public speaking and did some training with the John May School of Public Speaking in London in January 1990.

In May 2011, his wife Vivien, then 55, collapsed at home due to a massive stroke. Colin then became his wife's carer but continued to see a few hypnotherapy and TFT clients. In late July 2015, Colin suffered a very severe heart attack and was rushed to hospital. Investigation showed that he had suffered a rare and very serious complication of myocardial infarction known as a ventricular septal defect (VSD), effectively a large hole between the two main pumping chambers of the heart.

Colin had open heart surgery to repair the defect in August 2015 but this first operation was unsuccessful and a second procedure had to be carried out three months later. On 30 November, he was finally discharged home after spending four months in hospital. Unfortunately, he also developed epilepsy while in hospital which meant he had to give up driving for a year.

As a result of his wife's care needs, and his own health problems, Colin closed down his hypnotherapy and TFT business in April 2016 to concentrate on writing books and looking after his wife. His second book, *The Craft of Public Speaking*, was published by Extremis Publishing on 30 June 2016 and was followed by *Planes on Film* (2016), *Die Harder:*

Action Movies of the 80s (2017), *A Life By Misadventure* (2017), *Battles on Screen: WW2 Action Movies* (2017), *Practical Hypnotherapy* (2018), *Operation Archer* (2018), *Victories at Sea: On Films and TV* (2018), *Travels in Time* (2019) and *Codename Enigma* (2019).

His interests include walking, cycling, military history, aviation, plastic modelling and reading. Colin can be contacted via his writing website www.colinbarron.co.uk

Printed in Great Britain
by Amazon

62640928R00163